EYES OF CHINA BLUE

A haunted house reveals its disturbing
secrets to a troubled author

E W Grant

Copyright © 2022 E W Grant

All rights reserved

The characters and events portrayed in this book are fictitious. Any similarity to real persons, living or dead, is coincidental and not intended by the author.

No part of this book may be reproduced, or stored in a retrieval system, or transmitted in any form or by any means, electronic, mechanical, photocopying, recording, or otherwise, without express written permission of the publisher.

ISBN: 9798367598032

Dedicated to my son, Kyle.

CONTENTS

Title Page

Copyright

Dedication

Chapter One	1
Chapter Two	7
Chapter Three	13
Chapter Four	19
Chapter Five	24
Chapter Six	30
Chapter Seven	36
Chapter Eight	43
Chapter Nine	49
Chapter Ten	58
Chapter Eleven	67
Chapter Twelve	72
Chapter Thirteen	77
Chapter Fourteen	86
Chapter Fifteen	96
Chapter Sixteen	103
Chapter Seventeen	111
Chapter Eighteen	117

Chapter Nineteen	123
Chapter Twenty	129
Chapter Twenty-One	135
Chapter Twenty-Two	142
Chapter Twenty-Three	150
Chapter Twenty-Four	156
Chapter Twenty-Five	164
Chapter Twenty-Six	172
Chapter Twenty-Seven	179
Chapter Twenty-Eight	185
Chapter Twenty-Nine	192
Chapter Thirty	200
Chapter Thirty-One	206
Chapter Thirty-Two	213
Chapter Thirty-Three	220
Chapter Thirty-Four	227
Chapter Thirty-Five	233
Chapter Thirty-Six	239
Chapter Thirty-Seven	245
Chapter Thirty-Eight	250
Chapter Thirty-Nine	257
Chapter Forty	264
Chapter Forty-One	270
Chapter Forty-Two	277
Chapter Forty-Three	283
Chapter Forty-Four	290
Chapter Forty-Five	296
Chapter Forty-Six	302

Chapter Forty-Seven	309
Chapter Forty-Eight	314
Acknowledgement	317
About The Author	319
Books By This Author	321

CHAPTER ONE

Moving In Day, November 2012

The house had been charming and full of light on that bright summer's day when I viewed it with the estate agent. I had left dizzy with excitement, imagining how cosy and homely it would be once it was mine.

By the time the sale was completed, it was November. My disappointment was gut-wrenching and I choked back bitter tears as I followed the removal men into the dismal living room. The magnolia tree in the front garden, viewed from the living room window, had looked so beautiful with bright green leaves in the summer months. Its winter form was stark and twisted, its black branches contrasted against an iron grey sky. I tugged the long, plum-coloured, velvet curtains and a cloud of dust hung for a moment in the dank air. I imagined how grand and lavish they once would have been. Over the years curtain rings had been lost or broken so they drooped haphazardly and were bleached and puckered at the edges, like a long discarded ballgown. The whole room was dilapidated, from the wallpaper which curled and peeled in damp places to the ornate cornices, draped with dusty cobwebs. The carpet beneath my feet was sticky, matted and mouldy, producing an awful smell that made me nauseous.

I shuffled across to the window overlooking the back garden, my head pounding. I hoped to find something to justify my purchase of this old Victorian pile. A paved patio extended from the house and disappeared under a tangle of brambles and creepers. A greenhouse stood to one side, its panes broken and cracked. Trestle tables buckled under pots of brown, wilted plants. A solitary lounger chair stood in the middle of the patio, its soft upholstery rotting away to reveal a rusty, metal skeleton. Evidence perhaps that the previous owner had not expected any company to come knocking.

My hands trembled as I peered between my fingers. I noticed an old sideboard, heavy and dark against the wall.

"What's that ugly old thing doing here?" I said aloud.

Egyptian sphinxes and hieroglyphs were carved out of chocolate-coloured wood. The surface was ruined where hot cups had been thoughtlessly placed, leaving white rings. I opened a drawer full of stuff, including old black and white photographs, champagne corks and playing cards. I retrieved a grey, material ball lodged in the back and teased it into shape. Although it was stained and dusty it had been an elegant lady's glove with intricate lace at the cuff. It was dainty, fit for a ladylike, delicate hand and not a large hand like mine.

The removal men were banging about upstairs as I plodded up the wide staircase to see what they were up to. The house had three storeys, plus a basement. What had particularly attracted me was a hexagonal, domed attic room at the top of the building, looking out over the River Thames and Hampton Court Bridge. I hoped by inhabiting this beautiful space I would overcome the writer's block that had plagued me for the past two years.

"It's going to be bloody difficult to get this big old desk up those narrow stairs, love," said a burly removal man, towering over me. He smelled of perspiration and booze, the booze most likely from the night before, and I felt the familiar longing.

"I think it comes apart if you take the desktop off," I replied, pushing past him.

The attic resembled a lighthouse and the 360-degree windows gave the impression of a room floating in the air. The ceiling resembled an enormous inverted eggcup, crisscrossed with dusty cobwebs.

I closed the heavy door to muffle the sounds of the men downstairs. A large mirror was attached to the back of the door and I unexpectedly caught sight of my 40-year-old, dishevelled appearance – old jeans, a shapeless top and dark, curly hair escaping from the hurried ponytail I'd tied earlier.

The sun peeked out of a blanket of clouds and I was momentarily blinded and groped to close one of the wooden, slatted shutters. The sun's rays exaggerated the angles of the room, distorting the perspective and I felt disorientated.

I would position my desk with the mirror behind me so I wouldn't get disappointing glimpses of myself. I couldn't wait for the removal men to leave so that I could clean the place. When I was busy, my longing and despair could be kept at bay for a while and hopefully I would fall exhausted into bed and enjoy natural sleep.

As I opened the door, the removal man shouted up at me from the bottom of the short staircase. "'Scuse me, love. We've taken the desk apart and we're ready to put it in the room. Also, we've got the children's bunk beds off the wagon. What room do you want them in?"

The small mattresses leant against the wall as another man, his feral eyes scanning me, awaited my instructions.

"That room, please," I pointed to a large room overlooking the garden. The twins would adore this room; it was big enough to accommodate all their toys and books. I felt a lump in my throat. I wondered when I would see them again.

By six o'clock the furniture was in and the removals men, thankfully, had gone. The house felt very quiet after the chatter and general mayhem the men had brought with them.

The silence was shattered by the doorbell ringing and I attempted to tidy my unruly hair with grubby hands as I rushed to the door.

Charlie, my sister, closed her umbrella as she stepped

into the hallway.

"You're in, then?" she said, kissing me and patting my arm. "At least it's easy to park here, not like Holland Park. I spent a fortune on parking when I visited you there."

"You didn't need to come so soon. The place is a mess," I said, watching her remove her wet coat.

"I just wanted to make sure the move went well and that you— well, that you are okay?" she said.

"I am, so you don't need to worry," I sighed. "Why don't you go home?"

"Well, I'm here now."

She ran her finger along dirty surfaces, grimacing as I gave her a tour of the place, although she claimed the attic room was 'delightful'. We finished up in the kitchen, where I made tea.

"Why isn't Freddie here to help?" she asked, blowing on her tea.

"He's on location at the moment," I answered.

"Convenient," she said, frowning.

"He's got to work," I shrugged.

"Is he contributing?" she asked, narrowing her eyes.

"It's something we need to work out when he moves in," I sighed.

"Oh, so he is moving in this time, rather than turning up when it suits him?" she said.

"You just don't understand."

"No, you're right, I don't understand," she planted her elbows on the table. "You left a perfectly decent husband and lost custody of your twins because of Freddie. He comes and goes as he pleases. He's a terrible influence on you and, worst of all, doesn't seem to give a flying fig about you."

"It's not quite like that," I said shakily as I grabbed the cups and took them over to the sink.

I gripped the worktop, adding, "You're happy with your executive husband and suburban semi, but I needed something more. I needed passion and adventure."

"And where's it got you, Moira? You can't write, you've lost your lovely home in Holland Park, and you've lost your children."

"Temporarily," I interrupted.

"You're a long way from taking care of them again. You can't even take care of yourself!"

I looked out of the window at the dark garden. I thought I saw Charlie hovering near my shoulder in the reflection. When I spun around she was still sitting at the table.

"This house is a new start for me," I said, rubbing my temples. "No one knows me here and Freddie and I can make a proper home together."

"And the writing?" she asked.

"I've been writing since we were kids so it'll come back to me," I said, with more confidence than I felt. "I'll get up early every day and the clouds floating past my garret will inspire me."

I returned to the table, forcing a smile.

Charlie held my hands. "I dearly hope so. I've been so worried about you and so has Cliff."

"Really?" I uttered, snatching my hands away. "He's so busy with Miss Perky Boobs and turning my children against me."

"Don't be so unkind," she scolded. "He's done so much more than you'd expect of an ex-husband and Debbie's nice once you get to know her."

"Traitor," I hissed.

"She's doing a great job of looking after the twins, and for that, you should be grateful."

Charlie eventually left and I got on with the massive job of cleaning the place. By nine o'clock I was shattered but not sleepy. I slumped in my garret, drumming my fingers on the desk.

The streetlights twinkled as the bare tree limbs shook in

the stiff breeze. It was so unlike my Holland Park house, where traffic rumbled past all day and all night.

I switched my computer on, scrolling down the usual list of fan emails. Anxious messages reminded me that I hadn't published anything for years and begged me to start writing again. If only I had such a plan. There was also a message from my former agent, wishing me well in the new house. That was nice of her, considering how often I'd let her down. I sat back from the large screen, humming a tune that I didn't recognise.

I'd intentionally given all my bottles of booze away and promised myself a 'dry' house. The intention lasted until about 9.30 p.m. By then I had a raging headache and knew I couldn't cope. I ventured out into the dark streets and found a small supermarket open. I bought a couple of bottles of cheap wine and scurried back home before anyone could witness my failure.

After the first couple of glasses, I experienced a nice feeling of floating, my body no longer uncomfortable and weighing me down. I was invincible; surely, I would conquer the literary universe once again.

I smiled at my reflection on the computer screen, my dark eyes staring back. To my right I saw a halo— no, wait — it was an elaborate hairstyle. Platinum blonde hair piled high and two eyes, staring at me. Even with the screensaver of my twins I could see the eyes were a bright, china blue. I sat motionless for a while, unable to comprehend what I was seeing. I turned around but saw only my reflection in the old mirror, wine glass in hand and a vacant stare.

CHAPTER TWO

Freddie

In the hazy blur of the next few days, I stupidly believed if I didn't drink before lunchtime, I didn't have a problem. I spent the mornings staring at my computer waiting for inspiration, remembering those pretty blue eyes I'd conjured up in my drunken state. In the afternoon I would give up and set about stripping wallpaper in the twins' bedroom. I was determined to have a proper home for them whenever it was I would be allowed to see them again.

It was lonely rattling around the house. But Charlie was a midwife and was working nights for the next few days, so I knew I wouldn't see her again for a while. And Freddie? I hadn't heard from him and I had enough pride left not to call him.

"Moira. What the hell have you been doing? You look like shit!" Freddie leaned against the doorframe as I answered the door.

"Thanks," I said, pulling the door wide open and glimpsing myself in the hall mirror. I hadn't slept properly for days. I had purplish marks under my eyes and I looked older than forty years. "Where have you been?" I asked as he strode into the living room.

"Wow, this is quite a project, babe," he said, looking around, his emerald green eyes taking everything in. "Are you sure you haven't bitten off more than you can chew?"

"I was banking on getting some help," I replied.

"Don't break my balls," he grinned.

"I had to downsize or be declared bankrupt," I reminded

him. "I haven't earned any serious money for two years. I needed a place I could afford, which was also big enough for the twins. And it's got a basement that would make a great photographic studio."

"Slow down, darling. I wouldn't want to mess things up for you. I won't stand in the way of your children coming home," he said, kissing my forehead and holding me close as I snuggled into the warmth of his body. I had just begun to feel comfortable in his arms when he pushed me away and headed towards the adjoining dining room.

"Jesus, what's this old antique doing here? I don't remember it at Holland Park?" he said, running his hand along the old sideboard.

"It was here when I arrived," I said, coming up behind him. "It's full of loads of old stuff. I thought I'd have a look through it before I got rid of it. Find out what kind of people lived here."

He opened a drawer and pulled out some old black and white photos.

"Hey, these are old prints. Like, really old." He shuffled through them and then stashed them back into the drawer. "Let's go to the pub."

The Marquess of Granby was very near the little supermarket I often frequented. It was crowded for three o'clock on a Thursday afternoon. Everyone seemed to know each other and eyed us suspiciously. All of that changed when I put my credit card behind the bar and generously bought the whole pub a drink.

"I'm a famous author, you know," I said to a middle-aged woman wearing a very short skirt and cowboy boots.

"Darling, I know you are; you've told me at least ten times! Come on, let's have another drink," she beamed.

She strode towards the bar and I stumbled after her. A tall, dark man caught me by the elbow as I nearly tumbled.

"There you go, take it easy. You're the writer, aren't

you?" he asked.

I squinted up at him. "Oh, you've heard of me, then?"

"No, you were telling us all about it earlier," he jeered, elbowing his companions.

They laughed, their drunken faces ugly in the low light. I pushed past them and slumped against the bar.

Freddie was over on the other side of the room and seemed to be talking earnestly to a young woman in a clingy dress, her long shiny brown hair hanging down her slender back.

The young woman lowered her eyes and moved away as I approached.

Freddie spun around. "There you are, babe. I was just coming to look for you."

I looked daggers at the young woman, who turned away and joined a group of rowdy youngsters at the bar.

"Freddie. She's just a kid," I whined, and immediately hated myself for it.

"She's interested in photography." He shook his head and, as usual, I felt in the wrong. "Come on. Let's settle up the bill and get you back home."

The night sky was illuminated by a full moon, its light reflecting off frosty surfaces.

"Wait there," Freddie said as he went to his car and pulled out a camera. He positioned himself across the road from the house as the silvery moon rose behind the high spire on top of my garret. I heard the camera whirr as he twisted and turned to get the best angle.

I was relieved to get inside the warm house. I hadn't eaten since breakfast and the alcohol felt acidic in my stomach. I slumped on the sofa while Freddie scrolled through the shots he'd taken.

"Who else is in the house?" he asked, frowning.

"No one," I replied.

"Have you put a tailor's dummy up in that room at the

top of the house?"

"Why the bloody hell would I do that?" I asked, making a face.

He left the room, his heavy footsteps vibrating on the stairs to the top of the house. I licked my dry lips, the room was spinning as I closed my eyes. I jumped out of my skin when he returned, bursting through the door.

"What the fuck?" I shouted.

"Look at this," he insisted, his face pale as he thrust the small screen of the camera in front of my eyes.

"It's nice," I said. "The moon backlighting the spire. Very creative."

"No. Look at the window," he said, pointing to the screen.

It took me a few minutes to focus, my brain inert and confused.

"For Christ's sake," he cried, shaking me.

The image showed the moonlight illuminating the attic room, and silhouetted black against the silvery light was a woman wearing a large hat.

"Who the bloody hell is that?" I slurred.

He shrugged holding onto the camera as if his life depended on it.

"It's probably dirt on the lens or something," I suggested.

"No," he shook his head. "It's not that."

I was on the bathroom floor in a puddle of vomit when I woke up the next day. Freddie was nowhere to be seen and I wept, I felt so wretched. I took two painkillers, washed the sick off as best I could and went to bed.

I slept all day. When I eventually emerged from my duvet, the room was dark and cold. I clutched the bannister as I went downstairs. My handbag lay on the floor, its contents spilling out. I picked up my phone. Shit, Cliff had called about ten times. I hit the call-back button, biting my bottom lip.

"Moira?"

"Yes, it's me." I tried to sound normal but my voice croaked.

"You've done it again." He sounded annoyed.

"What have I done?" I asked, cringing and wracking my addled brain for the answer.

"You were coming to see the children after school today. They wanted to show you their projects," he said.

Shit.

"Oh, yes. Sorry about that. I had a meeting in London that overran," I lied.

"Don't give me that, Moira. You probably got pissed last night and were too hungover to do anything useful today. I don't know why you lie," he lectured.

It felt like he'd knifed me in the guts and I held my belly, gasping for breath.

"Moira?" he said.

A small sob escaped. "I'm so sorry," I mumbled, trying not to completely lose it.

"You've disappointed Jacks and Rosie once again," he pointed out.

"Their fucking names are Jackson and Rosanna. Please don't let your snotty wife make up fucking names for my children," I said, the effort of snarling spitefully depleting me of the small reserve of energy I had left.

"There's no need to be like that. You should be grateful Debs looks after our kids," he reasoned.

"Grateful. Fucking grateful," I spat the words out. "You take my kids away from me and I'm supposed to be grateful?"

I heard a deep sigh. "I'm not having this conversation again. You haven't been a fit mother since you ran off with the photographer and you know it."

The phone went dead and I threw it across the room. I stamped up the stairs to my safe space, my garret, my cupola in the clouds. I flopped at my desk, sobbing loudly. How dare he? How fucking dare he tell the truth so articulately?

I drenched the front of my t-shirt, sobbing loudly. I sensed that she'd be there. The lovely face, the pale hair and those bright, blue eyes reflected on the dull computer screen. I wiped my eyes with the back of my hand. Was I hallucinating? I stared back at the blue eyes for what seemed like ages until a chill settled in the base of my spine. I spun around, but I was alone in the room. I shook with fear; the options were not good. Either I was hallucinating or something inexplicable and unbelievable resided in this room.

CHAPTER THREE

Melted-Face Man

Three long weeks passed before Cliff allowed me to see the children again. I had to beg him on the phone and then he only agreed to a few hours on the following Sunday. I managed to limit myself to just one bottle of wine the evening before and had gone to bed early.

Cliff herded the children through the door, frowning over their heads at me.

"You've got them until five o'clock," he barked. "Don't leave the house, don't have any of your friends around, and save the drinking until they've gone."

I nodded meekly in agreement as he rushed back to the Volvo where Miss Perky Boobs was impatiently tapping the steering wheel. I closed the door and turned around to see my children glaring unemotionally at me.

"I'm so pleased to see you," I cried, my arms open wide.

They took a step back, summing me up and looking nervous. I dropped my arms to my side, unsure of my next move.

"Come into the kitchen and have a drink," I said, gesturing wildly as they stood immobile. "Then I'll show you your bedroom. It's not finished yet, but I think you'll love it."

They held hands – a habit they'd had since they were toddlers – as they silently followed me.

I showed them all around the house, finishing up in their bedroom. "It's not as nice as our old room in our other house," Jackson remarked.

"It will be, once it's decorated. You can choose the wallpaper," I said.

"We've already got nice wallpaper at Daddy's house," Rosanna added.

"Well, you can have nice wallpaper here, too," I said, trying not to feel annoyed. "How's your new school?"

"It's rubbish," Jackson replied. "There's not even a tennis court!"

My children were used to going to an exclusive, private school that I paid for. I had kept them there as long as I could, getting into serious debt that I was still paying off.

"You go to senior school now you are eleven," I said. "Dad said it was a good school and you were lucky to get in."

"We left all our friends behind in Holland Park," Rosanna said, biting her nails.

"There's no chess club either," Jackson said.

"I know it's a wrench," I reasoned. "Dad and I had to find you a school in this town as we both live here now."

"We know, Mum," Rosanna said, smiling at me. "Debbie explained it to us."

"If Debbie explained it then it must be all right," I whispered as I turned away.

"What did you say?" Jackson asked.

"Oh, nothing," I lied. "You'll both soon make friends and things won't seem so bad."

"Nobody at school likes me," Jackson said. "They call me 'teacher's pet'."

"It's probably because you're bright," I said, patting his shoulder. "Children find that intimidating."

"They don't ask me to join any of the sports teams and I'm good at sports," Jackson said, swallowing hard.

"I'm sorry it's taking you a while to settle. Please just give it more time," I said.

"Rosie and me meet at break time. No one else wants to sit with us," Jackson mumbled.

"That's a shame," I said, shaking my head. "And by the

way, your names are Jackson and Rosanna and not some silly names Miss— erm, Debbie has made up."

"We like our new names," they said in unison, blinking warily.

I didn't want an argument so we went back downstairs and I showed them the garden and the basement. They asked if they could play outside for a while and I agreed. I needed a break from their accusing eyes.

The doorbell rang, I hoped it would be Freddie as I hadn't seen or heard from him. It was Charlie.

"Cliff told me the children were over today so I thought I'd visit," she said, and I pointed her in the direction of the garden.

I watched out of the kitchen window as my children smiled and talked freely to her. I couldn't blame them for not giving me that honour.

I put the kettle on and Charlie joined me, watching as the children laughed and squealed pushing an old wheelbarrow around.

"They're lovely," she said.

"They're lovely to you," I sighed. "They're like strangers to me."

"They need time," she shrugged. "They've had a tough time, leaving friends behind, changing schools, and living with Cliff and Debbie. It's no wonder they're confused."

"Go on, say it," I said, turning to her.

"It's never easy being a mum," she said, squeezing my arm.

"Especially when your mum is terrible, unreliable, and sodden with drink?" I wailed.

"It's not been easy for you," she pointed out. "You had a long and difficult labour and didn't bond with them. You were so traumatised in those early days."

"Maybe I'm not mother material?" I said.

"Nonsense." She wagged her finger at me. "You looked

after the twins while Cliff worked full-time, and in-between feeding and changing you wrote a novel."

"I had to do something," I confessed. "I was going out of my mind just changing dirty nappies all day."

She put her arm around my shoulders. "Maybe it all happened too soon – the big house in Holland Park, publishers in a bidding war for your second novel. The money. The fame?"

"I found it overwhelming and exciting at the same time," I admitted. "I never expected my manic scribblings about fictional historical figures to amount to very much."

"People love your books," she said. "I'm a minor celebrity at work, just because you're my sister."

"I lost my way somewhere in all the fanfare and posh parties," I sighed.

"You were fine until you met Freddie," she said.

"You can't blame him for everything," I conceded. "All that's happened is my fault. Never believe your own publicity. How very true."

"Have you heard from your agent?" she asked.

"Lucy? Yes, she very kindly sent me an email wishing me well in the new house," I replied.

"There, you see?" she smiled. "You haven't entirely burnt your bridges."

I poured boiling water into the coffee cups. "I haven't been able to write anything. I'm so frustrated I feel like throwing my computer out of the window some days!"

"Once you're settled and happy you'll write again. You've written six great books, you can't tell me that's it," she said, warming her hands on the cup.

"I'm flattered you've got such faith in me," I said.

"I've got faith in you," she nodded. "It's Freddie I don't trust. Have you seen him?"

"No," I said, turning away. I hated lying to my sister, but whenever we talked about Freddie it ended in an argument.

I warmed supermarket pizza for the children's dinner and we watched television in their room. It was exhausting

EYES OF CHINA BLUE

trying to think of things to talk about, and they acted indifferently to me whatever I said.

Cliff arrived alone at ten to five and I showed him around the house, while the children stayed in their room.

"There's a lot to do," he said, shaking his head and thumping a wonky bannister back into place.

"I know, but it was affordable," I confided. "I've got plenty of room for the kids, a study for my work, and it's only a mile from your place so we can share the childcare."

"I hope so – one day soon," he said, smiling, his dark blue eyes observing me. "How are you doing?"

"I have good days and bad days," I told him honestly. "I'm still not writing and financially I can only last for six months. After that, I'll need to downsize even more and God knows how that will go. I'll probably end up in a council flat in Tooting."

He looked serious. "I won't let that happen."

Later, alone in my garret, the wind and rain battered the trees and drummed against the windows unmercifully. Once Cliff had left with the kids, I rushed to the kitchen and poured a large glass of wine. It was tough being a mum to two unresponsive, suspicious children. It was almost like they didn't belong to me. Charlie was right: I had struggled after a protracted and complicated birth. And even when I got them home I would burst into tears whenever she visited. I just didn't love them. She reassured me that it took a while for some mums and, as she was a midwife, I believed her.

My phone buzzed. It was Cliff.

"Hi, Cliff. Did the twins leave something here?" I asked, sounding drunk.

"No, that's not why I'm calling," he replied. "Who did you have over there today?"

"Erm, no one apart from Charlie," I said, sitting up straight.

"Come on, Moira. Who's the 'melted-face man'?" he

demanded.

"What the bloody hell are you talking about?" I asked.

"Jackson said they'd both seen the 'melted-face man' in the garden," he said, raising his voice. "Who is he? I'm assuming he's 'melted-face man' because he's drunk?"

I ran my fingers through my hair trying to clear my foggy brain and understand why the children would have made this up.

"I'm waiting for an explanation," he cried. I heard Debbie whisper something in the background. "We trusted you to look after the kids and you introduce them to a drunk. Honestly."

"But, but, but..." I grasped the phone so tightly my knuckles were white.

"It's no good," he said. "You can't be trusted with your own children. Debbie and I've agreed they won't be visiting again until we're sure they're safe with you."

CHAPTER FOUR

Expectations

I asked Freddie to spend the weekend with me. I'd seen so little of him since I moved from Holland Park and I wouldn't be allowed to see my children for a while.

He arrived on a Friday evening astride the Ducati motorbike I'd bought him after my last book reached the bestseller list. I'd gone to the trouble of cooking dinner – just pasta, salad and garlic bread, but it felt like a huge achievement. We sat in the dining room drinking Chianti. His black hair fell in ringlets to his collar and his green eyes were full of mischief.

"Fancy doing a line of coke, babe?" he asked.

"Not really," I sighed. "I'm trying to convince people that I'm a responsible, trustworthy person. I don't think that's going to help much."

He laughed and got a small packet out of his pocket. He expertly made four thin lines of coke on a table mat and offered it to me. "Go on, darling. Sex is ten times better when you're high."

I hesitated as he stroked my face, and then I snorted two lines. I leapt backwards in my chair.

"It's a bit of a shock if you haven't done it for a while," he said, grinning, then snorted the other two lines.

He was right. Sex was great and we were at it for hours. When we were finally satiated he fell asleep immediately and I lay watching him. I had desired him from the moment I saw him at my book launch, three years ago. He'd been hired by my publisher after the usual photographer had been unavailable at the last minute. He was a jobbing photographer then, still doing weddings and estate agency work and only scraping a living. All that changed once he stepped into my world and my bed. Most people I knew – not just my sister – thought him responsible for my downfall.

Freddie had arranged to meet some old friends, Alison and Pete, in Smithfield Market for lunch on Saturday. I hadn't many friends left, but these two were drunks just like me, so we got along fine.

As usual, they were late, so we'd had quite a few drinks when they eventually arrived. Alison gave me a wet kiss. She was an actress and regularly had treatments including botox and more recently lip fillers. Pete was a model, not tall enough for fashion, but he made a good living featuring in advertising campaigns and catalogue work. He was handsome and muscular and spent a lot of time in the gym. Freddie and I had named them Brangelina.

"How was your move to the sticks, Moi?" Alison asked, smiling, showing perfect white teeth between puffy, inflated lips.

"It's only Surrey, not Dartmoor," I replied.

"Is there even a tube out there?" Pete asked.

"South Western Trains, no tube," Freddie replied.

"No tube?" they said in unison, wide-eyed as if they'd heard something shocking.

"Oh, it's such a shame you had to give up that lovely house." Alison empathised as best she could, her face expressionless and paralysed. "You hosted some amazing parties. Do you remember the time your husband came home early and you were fucking Freddie in the marital bed? Do you remember, Pete? We had to keep boring old hubby chatting for ages while you both got dressed."

"I asked him what he did for a living," Pete laughed. "That was a mistake. I didn't have a clue what he was talking about."

"I suppose that's because he has a real job," I said.

They nodded in agreement. "What do you mean?" Alison asked.

They laughed and ordered more drinks, but I felt the shame of that evening engulfing me.

"And how about the time your kids came downstairs unexpectedly and we were all snorting coke and you told them it was icing sugar!" Pete said, throwing his arms in the air.

"You'd chucked your husband out by then, but you were terrified the kids would tell him," Alison remarked.

"Well, I had good cause to worry," I said, taking a big gulp of champagne. "He and his snotty wife got custody of my kids."

"Oh my God, he remarried quickly," Alison pointed out.

"He married his bloody PA," I blurted.

"Oh my God," she repeated, her mascaraed eyes wide open. "What a cliché! You did the right thing, leaving him for Freddie. We all think Freddie's just wonderful."

Her slender manicured hand rested on Freddie's knee.

"Thanks, darling," Freddie winked.

"So are you moving to Surrey?" Pete asked Freddie.

Freddie fidgeted, glancing sideways at me. "We'll see. We're being careful; we don't want to upset her ex."

"Oh, so that's what we're doing," I said, raising my eyebrows.

I lost count of how many bars we visited that afternoon and the taxi home seemed to take hours. Freddie didn't fancy going back to the house so we stopped at the Marquess for a sobering coffee.

"I was under the impression that you were going to move in with me," I slurred, remembering the earlier conversation that seemed like days ago now.

"Babe, I'd love to, you know that. But I don't want to mess things up," he said, breathing coffee breath all over me.

"I dumped my husband and trashed my life," I reminded him. "But I've never really been in a relationship with you, have I?"

"Darling, when the time's right we'll both know," he said, holding my face and kissing me on the lips. "You need another drink. You're getting morose."

I vaguely remember chatting and laughing with random people in the pub. I would suddenly burst out laughing uncontrollably and put my arms around any man who came near me. I even had a snog with a woman called Joy, whom Freddie tried to persuade to return home with us. Joy made it very clear that she only fancied me, which was a bit of a blow to Freddie's ego. I was the life and soul and they would all remember me. What a fool I was!

The next morning I rushed to the bathroom, threw up, cleaned my teeth and went downstairs. Freddie was looking bright and breezy in front of the television.

"Why don't you ever get a hangover?" I asked, holding my pounding head.

"I don't know," he shrugged. "I'm just lucky I suppose."

I sat and put my head on his shoulder. "Would you get me some water?" I mumbled.

He lifted my head and settled me against a cushion and went to the kitchen. He returned with a glass of water but didn't sit again.

"I'd better be going," he said, staring down at me.

"What?" I asked, screwing up my face to focus.

"Look at you," he said. "You'll be comatose all day and I've got work to do."

"But I got a joint from Waitrose," I said feebly. "I was going to do Sunday roast."

"Don't worry about it," he said, putting his gear in a bag.

"Please don't go. I hoped we'd spend the day together," I begged.

"I've got shit to sort out, darling. You understand?" he asked. "Everyone wants a piece of me and I've got shit to sort out."

"No," I cried. "I don't understand. When I had the other house and the parties and the red carpet events, you were always around. I couldn't get rid of you."

"Fucking hell!" he said, stepping away. "I give up my weekend to be with you and this is what I get."

I tried not to sob. "I'm sorry. It's just that I feel terrible and I don't want to be on my own."

"I'm bloody offended now," he said, gathering his things. "Honestly, Moira, I'm trying my best."

"I know. Please forgive me."

"No worries. I'll call you," he said, reaching down and kissing my wet face.

I heard the motorbike growl into action as he drove away.

CHAPTER FIVE

Rising From The Ashes

I was at my desk by nine o'clock every day, but I couldn't write. I would listen to Radio 4 and stare at the blank screen for hours. Most days I managed to last until about three o'clock before my first drink. But on bad days it was more like noon, followed by an afternoon lolling on the sofa watching pointless YouTube videos. I heard nothing from Freddie.

Early December was mild and overcast. Christmas lights adorned pubs and shops, giving the town a false sense of cheeriness. A fine ribbon of mist lay on the Thames and clung to the bare branches of the trees as the blank Word doc on my computer blinked, bright and accusingly. The blue orbs appeared and I spilt my coffee, sitting bolt upright, a tingle running down my spine. This time I was stone cold sober.

The long face had high cheekbones and a pointed chin. She stared and I stared back, my mouth open. How long our gazes were locked I'm not sure; it seemed like ages.

A surge of excitement like an electric shock ran through my body, mostly fear. After two years of gut-wrenching frustration, I suddenly knew exactly what to write.

First Draft

Margaret (I knew this wasn't her name, but it would do for now) was a rare beauty. Everyone knew this apart from Margaret herself. Her angelic appearance would be the cause of much misery for her in the future.

But for now, she lived with her father in Rosebay

House. A grand house by the river Thames, in a small town west of London. It was 1913 and British people still held an unshakeable belief in the power and glory of the British Empire, which would soon be tested beyond all imagination.

Margaret was an unusual woman for those times. Her mother had died a few days after her birth and her father had been too busy and important to manage her upbringing. The people who had cared for her and shown her love were the inconspicuous servants of Rosebay House. People who had more of a stake in the wellbeing of the house and its occupants than the man whose name was on the deeds. Our beauty formed a deep connection with the people who cooked and cleaned in her father's house. Her early education had taken place at the kitchen table in the basement with Annie, the housekeeper, Alfred the coachman and general handyman, and his son, also called Alfred. (Strangely, these names came instinctively to me.) At that table, she learnt that the majority of the population was engaged in a fight for survival, something the upper classes turned a blind eye to, even when ignorance and want were blatantly exhibited in the grim streets of London, or around poor rural communities.

She played childish games with young Alfred and visited the stables to admire her father's smart riding horses and magnificent coach horses.

Finally, when she reached her thirteenth birthday, her father suddenly became aware of how feral she'd become in his absence, sitting astride her pony, her face and hands filthy and showing her long pantaloons beneath a muddy dress. He vowed to take her in hand. Initially, he disallowed her visits to the stables and later engaged a stern spinster to teach her French, art, history and English literature as well as deportment and dancing.

Margaret's happy world shrunk, like being buried alive. Her lively movements of eye and limb, constricted by the strict tutor, to transform the urchin into an elegant Edwardian lady. She became confined to the house unless the weather was fine. Even then she had to wear a silk dress and fussy hat just to walk along the embankment with her tutor.

Not only was she delightful on the eye, her long platinum hair framing high cheekbones and china blue eyes, but she also held a vibrant curiosity about the world. This curiosity gave her cause to question Edwardian society and the state of affairs she witnessed every day. Her father often pointed out that she would never find a husband if she continued to contradict and argue with the young gentlemen he brought home to admire her. That it was unseemly and unwomanly to outwit men and leave them feeling foolish.

Her love for her only surviving parent drove her to indulge many of her father's wishes, even holding grand dinner parties for his friends and colleagues and, with difficulty, endeavouring to hide her superior intelligence when spending a dull evening amongst gentlemen of her class. The spacious dining room, its crystal chandelier creating shards of light on the sumptuous table, was a charming venue for her father to invite young, handsome, successful men, hoping one of them might win her affection.

There was only one problem. The object of her true affection, more often than not, would be sitting below stairs diligently polishing the master's shoes.

Alfred junior, in his twentieth year, was tall and slim with light brown hair that flopped into his blue-grey eyes. The master boasted to anyone who would listen that he had a remarkable way with the horses. He had been employed by Margaret's father since he was fourteen and lived in a local cottage with his mother and father and many sisters. His limited education had taken place at the local school – sponsored by Margaret's father – and he could read and write, which was unusual for children of his class. He was a quietly spoken, hardworking lad and he loved Margaret, although he knew it was in vain.

I wrote five chapters. It just poured out of me as the blue eyes watched without blinking.

By 7.30 p.m. I was flagging. I hadn't eaten all day and I needed a drink. I turned to face the mirror expecting to see my messy hair and puffy, pale face. There she was, blonde hair piled high on her head, her cinched-in waist emphasised by a tight bodice and a flowing, silvery skirt. Although the image was grainy I could make out a huge chandelier glittering in the background, reflecting emerald green walls. She smiled briefly at me as if we knew each other. Then slowly she faded away until only my dismal reflection stared back.

I gasped for breath. I didn't believe in ghosts or the supernatural and nothing like this had ever happened to me before. It felt like she was reaching out to me in 2012, nearly a hundred years later, to write her story and it freaked me out!

I went downstairs to the dining room, leaning against the doorframe, my hand against my forehead. There was a large hook in the ceiling that may have held the chandelier. The former owner had hung a bulb on the end of a long cable and it dangled forlornly, giving weak illumination. I scraped the wallpaper with my thumbnail. Like the children's room, there were layers of old wallpaper but I couldn't tell if any of them had been emerald green.

I stood in the middle of the room imagining what it once looked like and the people who'd laughed and danced there. Once I had some money I would restore it to its former glory.

I smiled at my musings as I rested my hand on the ugly old sideboard. I yanked the top drawer out and took it to the kitchen table, where the light was better. I poured myself a well-deserved glass of wine and sat down to examine the contents of the drawer.

The black and white prints, as Freddie had mentioned, were very old. I held the first one up to the light. An older, stout man in a formal suit with a watch chain hanging from his waistcoat, posed next to a seated young woman. 'Mr and Miss Turner, 1910' was written on the back in spidery handwriting. The image was too small and blurred to be sure it was the woman I'd seen in the mirror. I thumbed through the prints and saw a photograph of a woman holding a parasol and wearing a large hat, her face tilted toward the light, and I knew instantly it was her. I flipped it over and written on the back was 'Miss Lydia Turner, 1910'. My storyteller had a name!

I found more photos all dated 1910, exactly a hundred years ago. Lydia posing against a painted backdrop in an off-the-shoulder dress showing off her long, slender neck and shapely shoulders. A hand-coloured print of her in a blue riding habit, her waist nipped in and a neat, mannish hat pinned to her thick hair. And finally, Lydia wearing a large hat with a crowd of people at what looked like a racecourse.

I couldn't quite believe I was going along with this, but I believed I had found my shadowy companion. The woman I saw in the photographs was the woman I'd seen in the garret. I pondered how I might find out more about Lydia. Then I remembered my brother-in-law, painstakingly analysing the family tree and getting excited about some long-dead ancestor. I grinned. My sister had asked me over to their house hundreds of times and I always made an excuse not to go. I would be killing two birds with one stone.

CHAPTER SIX

Revelations

I arranged to go to my sister's the following Saturday. She and her family lived on a modern estate near Basingstoke. The house was a bland seventies rectangle in a cul-de-sac of other bland seventies rectangles. I received a warm welcome from my brother-in-law, Bill, and Charlie's two grown-up sons. I hadn't visited for a long time and I'd forgotten how comfortable and cosy my sister had made the house. There were dozens of cushions littered about on chairs and sofas, some embroidered and others depicting diaphanous sea creatures. The huge television dominated the room, mounted on the wall over the fireplace.

"You made it, then," she said, taking my coat. "Did you get parked okay?"

"I'm surprised you remembered how to drive," Bill remarked, kissing my cheek.

"Ha ha," I said, with a twisted smile on my lips. "I even remembered the way here."

Bill was of medium height with thinning hair. His work consisted of something to do with procurement. He had explained it to me once, but I still didn't understand what he did. He and Charlie had been childhood sweethearts and had been married for twenty-five years.

"Here, I've brought wine," I said, proudly thrusting two bottles of my finest into his hands.

"Mmm, thanks," he said, disappearing into the kitchen.

"Cup of tea?" my sister offered.

Bill led me into the conservatory which was furnished with bamboo chairs and more cushions.

"What is it you're trying to find out?" he asked, opening his laptop.

"I'm not sure," I said, now wondering why I thought this was a good idea. I'd seen a ghost and here I was trying to link it to a real person. "I found these photographs at my new house." I spread them out on the coffee table. "They intrigued me and I was hoping to find out who the people were. Their names are on the back."

He picked each one up and examined it and then typed something into his computer. He didn't look up or speak for ages so I quietly sipped my tea.

Eventually, he said, "Ah!"

"Did you find anything?" I asked.

"Joseph Abraham Turner," he quoted. "Born 1858, died 1921. He was an important businessman in shipping insurance in Edwardian times. Says here he was a widower and had one child."

"Is there a photograph?" I asked, leaning over to peer at the screen.

"No photos, I'm afraid. Let's have a look at the census for some of those years," he said, chewing his lip. "Here's the 1881 census: Joseph Abraham Turner and his wife Iris, living in Rosebay House. That's your new place, isn't it?" I nodded and he continued: "Then the 1901 census shows Joseph and a daughter Lydia and several servants but no wife. I wonder what happened to her?"

I covered my mouth with my hands. I was dying to tell him, but it would elicit too many questions from him.

"1911 census: still Joseph and Lydia plus servants. That's the latest census; there's a hundred-year delay in sharing the census details far and wide to protect people's privacy." He beamed at me over the laptop.

"Thanks, Bill," I said, smiling back at him. "It's really interesting finding out who lived in my house."

I hoped to find out more but was interrupted by someone arriving in the living room. I vaguely heard Cliff's voice, followed by the twins laughing and joking.

"Oh, my goodness!" I cried, jumping up and rushing over to them.

Rosanna was hugging Charlie and Jackson stood awkwardly in the middle of the room. I attempted to hug him but he was rigid, as if standing to attention. My daughter turned to me and held her doll between us.

"What are you both doing here?" I squealed.

"I arranged it with Cliff," Charlie said. "He's allowed them to stay for dinner so that you can see them."

I nodded, smiling gratefully at my sister.

We sat around the granite island in my sister's new kitchen as she and Bill dished up spaghetti bolognese with garlic bread.

"So how are you both?" I asked the children.

"We're both in the school play," Rosanna said.

"That's great," I said, rubbing her little arm.

"Jack is Joseph and I'm a shepherd," she said, clenching her hands together.

"You must tell me when the play is on," I said. "I'll come and see it."

Rosanna nodded but Jackson didn't look up from his food.

"I've missed you," I said. "I haven't had time to finish your room, but I will do soon."

"Dad says we need a room each now we're nearly twelve," Jackson said, holding a fork full of food in mid-air.

"He's right," I agreed. "There's another bedroom I can get ready for when you come home."

"We live at home already," Rosanna said to Jackson and he nodded in agreement.

"I brought some wine," I said, waving my arms at Charlie as if I was announcing something amazing.

"Maybe we'll have a glass later," Charlie said.

I quickly dropped my hands on my lap.

Jackson was in the conservatory with a very fancy mobile phone after dinner. I knelt beside him and watched as he played a game.

"That's a very fancy phone," I said.

He grunted but didn't take his eyes off the fast-moving images. "Is it Dad's or Debbie's?"

He sighed, putting the phone in his pocket. "It's my phone and Rosie has one too. Dad and Debbie decided we were old enough."

"Oh!" I exclaimed. "Glad I was consulted."

"Would you have stopped us from having phones?" he asked tilting his head.

"I'm not sure. But I'm your mother and I should have a say," I said, patting his hand, which he snatched away. "Tell me what you saw in the garden that freaked your father out the other day."

"It was nothing," he sulked.

"It must have been something," I said. "Your father wasn't very happy about whatever it was you thought you saw."

"We saw him," he leapt up. "We saw melted-face man. He was in your garden. If you don't believe me—"

"I do believe you," I said, reaching for him.

He moved away. "Melted-face man is very sad. Like Rosie and me when you wouldn't speak to Dad anymore."

That was a slap in the face. I slumped against the doorframe as he left the room to join the others.

Charlie arrived with another cup of tea. It was clear the wine was not going to be opened.

"What's wrong? Why aren't you with your children?" she asked.

"They hate me," I replied.

"They don't hate you, love." She stroked my hair. "Be patient. They'll realise what an amazing mother they have."

"I'm a rubbish mum and we both know it," I sulked.

"You were a great mum before all of the… upheavals. And you'll be a great mum again." She tucked my unruly hair behind my ear just like our mum used to.

"I've started writing again," I told her.

"That's great, Moi," she smiled. "I knew you would."

Cliff arrived later and the children ran to him, arms outstretched.

"I've got a bone to pick with you," I said, as the children eyed me suspiciously.

"Can you make it quick? Debbie's waiting in the car," he said, peering out of the window.

"Why didn't you ask me if Jackson and Rosanna should have mobile phones?" I asked.

"It didn't occur to me," he replied, shrugging.

"I am their mother," I cried.

"Then start acting like one," he said.

"Cliff," Charlie warned. "Moira is trying to turn her life around. Please don't have a go at her like that."

"I'm sorry," Cliff said, addressing Charlie. "It's hard to trust her when she lets everyone down so often."

"I've done terrible things that I'll never forgive myself for," I shouted at him as the twins cringed. "But I swear there was no weird-faced man or whatever they're accusing me of."

"Calm down." Charlie took my arm and I shook her off.

"If there are important decisions to be made, I should be included," I ranted. "You and your former PA don't decide things without me."

Just at that moment the front door opened and Debbie stepped in, looking immaculate.

"You've been gone ages, Cliff," she purred. "Everything okay?"

"No, it's not okay." I spat out the words. "You are not

their mother."

I turned to the children, who were clutching their father as if their lives depended on it.

"Let's go," Debbie demanded, herding my children towards the door. "I knew this was a mistake," she said, with a protective arm around each child. "You need to sort yourself out, Moira. You let these children down and Cliff and I pick up the pieces."

They strode off arm-in-arm, Cliff shaking his head as he followed.

I returned home that evening and opened a bottle of wine, taking a large swig. I was irritated that my sister had not allowed me even one glass. Like I would get drunk in front of her and the children.

You have been drunk in front of them many times before though, haven't you?

I pushed the uncomfortable memories away, looking out into the dark garden. I wondered if the children were imagining a weird melted-face man. Perhaps it was something they'd read in a book or seen on their new mobile phones. Or could it be similar to the visions I'd seen of Lydia?

The house creaked and groaned with age but wasn't willing to give up all of its secrets yet.

CHAPTER SEVEN

Lydia and Alfred

When I awoke the next day, my tongue was stuck to the top of my mouth and someone was hammering from the inside of my skull. It was ten o'clock already and I'd planned to be at my desk by nine. I drank a litre of water, took two painkillers, and climbed the stairs to my studio.

First Draft

Lydia was an accomplished horsewoman; even so, her father insisted she was always accompanied and young Alfred was the obvious choice. Richmond Park was one of their favourite hacks. She rode Kelly, a pretty bay who was quiet and dependable until Lydia urged her forward into a gallop across the open parkland. Alfred plodded behind obediently on one of the mighty carriage horses, keeping her in sight but unable to manage more than a lolloping canter.

Under the shivering leaves and in the shelter of an ancient oak they tied up the horses and sat for a while on a large tree stump. Lydia gave Alfred a book that she had enjoyed about an ancient mariner. He would read it later at home by the light of a candle stub in his tiny attic.

"I thought you might find this interesting?" Lydia announced, thrusting a pamphlet into his hands. "It's about the struggle for enfranchisement for women."

"Votes for women?" Alfred read, frowning. "Why

would you give this to me?"

"Read it," she demanded.

"I am," he replied. "I'm not sure of the meaning."

"It's about women having the same rights as men and being equal to men," Lydia explained. "The right to vote, for instance. Even women who own land or pay taxes don't have the vote in this country. It's scandalous."

"I can't see how a woman can be equal to a man. She's not strong like a man for a start," Alfred said. "Most women can't plough a field or shoe a horse."

"It's not just physical strength that matters though. A woman can equal a man intellectually," she said.

"You mean in reading and writing and such like?" he asked.

"Yes, and in ideas and opinions," she replied. "We don't just have to agree with our husbands or fathers. We can have our own opinions and in doing so may disagree with our menfolk."

He thought about this and said, "But what good does it do? A woman will marry and have children and run a home. So why does she have to be learnt and clever?"

"If a mother is educated and smart, then it follows that her children will be. Think of the benefits for us all." She smoothed her blue skirt with a long elegant hand. "After all, you've benefitted from being able to read and write. Just think how it would have helped your sisters if they'd been educated."

"That may be true of your people," he said earnestly, "but my mother and sisters don't need to be clever. They just need to know how to sew and cook. Book reading and such like would be wasted on them."

Lydia sighed and unpinned the small hat as small wisps of hair fell around her face.

"I shan't ever be as clever as you," he said, his mouth turned down.

"Nonsense," she smiled, taking his hand. "You taught me the names of all the birds and the plants. You always know what weather to expect and you handle Father's black moods much better than I do. I make him worse if anything!"

"I believe him to be greatly dispirited at the loss of your mother so young. He has had to raise you and he's at a loss as to what's the right and wrong way to do it." He stroked his chin. "He can make sense of a column of figures or books about the law, but he don't know where to start with you and that is his greatest worry."

"He's constantly putting barriers up and limiting what I can do," she said, narrowing her eyes. "I'm not a child, but I can't go anywhere unless you or a maid comes with me."

"He's just looking out for you," Alfred pointed out. "He's been that good to my family. Taking me on at the stable along with dad when I was a lad. And letting us have the cottage on the cheap."

"I know," she said, pinning her hat back on. "But things are fast changing, especially for women. Father lives in the past."

The china blue eyes appeared and disappeared throughout the day as if checking on my progress. Although it still unnerved me, having some entity present that I couldn't explain, I wrote until it was pitch black outside and the street lamps glowed in the darkness. I switched off the computer and headed down the narrow staircase. The carpet squelched as I stepped on it. I reached down; it was sopping wet. I peered up at the ceiling but that was dry

I went to the kitchen and poured myself a drink. I would only have one this evening. Freddie hadn't returned any of my calls and I was going to drive over to his place and surprise him.

I arrived at Wimbledon Village and even found a parking space. I strode down a narrow mews to Freddie's house. He lived on the top floor and had made one room into a kitchen, and another a small shower room. There was also a living room and a bedroom. The whole of the downstairs was converted into a photographic studio. The living area was compact, but it suited him.

I rang the doorbell and waited for ages before the door opened. The young girl Freddie had spoken to at the Marquess weeks ago opened the door. Her long glossy dark hair hung around her shoulders, and her toned midriff was bare, as she wore a yoga-type top.

"Where the hell is Freddie?" I demanded.

"Freddie," she called, her wide eyes never leaving mine.

He galloped down the stairs, coming to an abrupt halt when he saw me.

"Moira," he said. "How nice to see you. Come in."

I pushed past the girl and followed him up to the living room.

"What the bloody hell is she doing here?" I shouted as she tiptoed in behind me.

"Calm down," Freddie said, holding up his hands. "Zara has been helping me all day with a shoot and I made her a coffee."

I looked from him to her and back again.

"It's a pleasure to meet you," she said, holding out her hand. "Freddie's told me all about you. I love your books."

I sunk to the sofa, my arms wrapped tightly around me, my face feeling hot with embarrassment.

"I'll make your favourite coffee," Freddie mumbled and disappeared into the kitchen.

The expensive Italian coffee machine that I'd bought him gurgled and hissed.

Zara sat opposite, her long, brown legs wrapped around each other.

"Where do you get your ideas for your novels?" she asked.

I'd been asked this many times and had an answer ready. "I'm observant and I listen," I said. "If I'm in a cafe I listen to the conversations around me and imagine what the people's lives are like."

"That's awesome," she said.

"Yeah, I suppose," I said, picking up a magazine.

Freddie returned, putting a coffee cup on the table in front of me.

"What are you hoping to do when you leave uni?" I asked Zara, just to show him I wasn't jealous or suspicious.

"I'm doing graphic design and photography and I hope to be a designer," she said, her almond-shaped, dark eyes looking at me confidently.

"I expect Freddie can teach you a lot about photography. He has such a variety of work," I told her.

"Yes, it's been very useful," she said, exchanging a look with Freddie.

We chatted for a while, although I found her very dull and I lost count of the number of times she exclaimed something quite ordinary 'awesome'. I blathered on about the new book and how excited my agent was.

"She's already talking about an advance once she's seen some early chapters," I said.

"That's brilliant, Moi. I knew you could do it," Freddie claimed, though I couldn't remember any encouragement from him.

"Thanks," I said, forcing a cheery grin but feeling fatigued from writing all day and eating very little. I got up. "I'd better be going." I went towards the door. "I'll just use your loo before I go."

Freddie began to say something as I went into the bathroom, closing the door behind me.

Little pallets of make-up covered every surface. Two toothbrushes stood side-by-side in a glass and, worst of all, tiny black thongs were drying on the shower rail.

Freddie was waiting on the landing when I emerged, his knuckles white as he grasped his hands tightly together.

"You fucking bastard, Freddie! I gave you the deposit for this house," I screamed in his face.

"I can explain," he cried. "She's homeless. I'm just putting her up for a while."

I ran down the stairs. "Don't insult my intelligence, you moron," I snarled through clenched teeth.

I'm not sure how I made it home without crashing the car. I cried all the way, banging the steering wheel at the lights.

"Bastard, bastard, bastard!"

I needed a proper drink.

I sat on a stool at the Marquess's bar with a large G&T. In the mirror behind the optics my red eyes stared back at me accusingly and my hair looked like I'd been dragged through a hedge backwards. What a fool I'd been. Freddie was younger than me at thirty-five, but the girl – she was only nineteen or twenty at the most.

I tilted my head back, draining the glass. "Another, please."

"Mind if I join you?" A man of forty-odd, flabby with thinning, grey hair and crooked teeth, stood next to me, grinning.

"Please yourself," I replied.

"Barman, I'll get that." He held out a ten-pound note.

"There's no need," I said.

"You're the writer, aren't you?" he asked.

"No need to take the piss," I groaned.

"What do you mean?" he said, frowning. "You're Moira Delainey. My wife loves your books."

"She does? That's great," I said, grasping my glass.

"May I have your autograph?" He put a piece of paper and a pen in front of me. "My name's Dave and the missus is Bev."

"I'd be glad to," I said, writing a dedication. "It's nice to meet my readers."

"What a happy coincidence," he said, still grinning. "I'm often up this way on business, although we live in Devon. My wife will be thrilled when I tell her I bumped into you."

All I remember is a fresh drink appearing as soon as I'd finished the old one and laughing uncontrollably at his jokes.

He kindly walked me home and I asked him in for coffee.

"Nice place you've got here," he said as I handed him a cup.

"Thanks," I croaked, hanging on to the mantelpiece as the room spun. "I only moved in a few weeks ago, so it's a bit of a mess."

"It will be lovely once you've renovated it," he said.

"It's haunted," I slurred.

"Of course it is," he sneered.

I thought of Freddie in bed with his young student and blackness descended.

"Why don't we go to bed?" I said, grabbing his sweaty hand.

CHAPTER EIGHT

Love and Other Emotions

Dave squirmed and groaned, pinning me down, his fat belly wet with sweat. I gritted my teeth and shut my eyes, praying for him to finish. Thankfully it didn't last long and he rolled off and fell into a deep sleep. I lay awake all night staring at his pale, hairy back. I'd reached rock bottom.

I encouraged him to leave as soon as possible the next day but he insisted on a shower, breakfast and toast. Finally, he stepped out of the front door, saying, "I enjoyed last night. Perhaps we could do it again next time I'm up here for work?"

"Give me a call," I said, knowing the first thing I intended to do was block his number.

I was shattered, mentally and physically. I'd promised my agent twenty chapters so I had no choice but to make my way to my studio. The stair carpet was still sopping and I vaguely promised to attend to it.

I slumped in front of my computer. I waited desperately for the eyes to appear and fire me up with inspiration. I held my head in my hands as the screen saver showed only my children's bright faces.

I turned to the mirror as music played softly. Lydia appeared, a diamond tiara sparkling in her hair, and a long red dress accentuating her fair colouring. A young man, tall and slim, pulled her close to his breast. The music penetrated like waves as the couple whirled and spun energetically around the emerald dining room. I was spellbound watching the grace of the dancers; it was charming and elevating. Eventually, the music faded, but the couple held each other as if they never wanted to let go.

First Draft
1913, Rosebay House

Lydia's father had purchased a gramophone and there was to be dancing for the young people, while the older folk resided in the comfortable chairs of the drawing room. Alfred senior and junior had removed the large dining table from the emerald room to make space.

Lydia wore a scarlet evening gown with a silky matching scarf and her mother's diamond tiara in her hair. It was nearly time for guests to arrive, so she went around the house checking everything was ready. The new gramophone was in the dining room and she carefully placed a heavy disc on the turntable and wound the handle sticking out of the side. After a few pops and crackles, the music began.

Young Alfred arrived, putting a jug and some glasses on a side table. Lydia crossed the room and closed the door. She took the silky scarf from around her neck and tied it around his. They took hold ballroom style and waltzed gracefully but energetically around the room. When the music ended, neither let go. Lydia kissed him, feeling his soft lips on hers and his strong embrace.

Some hours later, Alfred sat in the basement kitchen listening to the music and laughter from the room above. He had helped the young men with their horses as they arrived in their evening suits. They had taken very little notice of him, flinging their reins in his direction. He realised Mr Turner was presenting Lydia with prospective husbands and his heart filled with dread.

He'd always known this day would come.

EYES OF CHINA BLUE

He was summoned at midnight. The guests were leaving and he was required to bring out the horses. There were carriages lined up for the older couples and with the help of his father they managed to get everyone into their seats. The young men who had ridden waited as their horses were brought out. One fine stallion had not been claimed and Alfred held its bridle patiently.

The big door to the house opened and Lydia emerged in her lovely dress, accompanied by her father and a short, stocky, sandy-haired man in his thirties. They seemed deep in conversation and the horse whinnied, recognising his master. The man held up a hand as if the horse would understand to wait, which it didn't. It pulled back restlessly on its bridle and lifted its large front feet. Alfred spoke softly and the horse immediately calmed down, rubbing his soft nose on Alfred's shoulder.

"We can happily accommodate you if you'd like to stay the night," the master offered.

"I wouldn't dream of imposing," the stocky man replied. "I have rooms booked for the night, not too far away."

"Well, it was very gracious of you to come all this way for our little party," the master said, shaking the other man's hand vigorously.

"It's been my pleasure," the man said, retrieving his hand and taking Lydia's. "I have enjoyed the company immensely."

"It was nice to make your acquaintance." Lydia spoke so softly that Alfred had to strain to hear.

"Charming," the man said as he bowed and kissed her hand. "Would you do me the great honour of taking lunch one day in my London home and meeting my

45

mother?"

"Lydia would love to have lunch with you and your mother. Wouldn't you, dear?" Lydia's father asked.

"It's a long way to travel," she replied.

"Nonsense. I'll send my man with you, you'll be fine." The master gestured towards Alfred.

"I'll look forward to seeing you in Victoria," the gentleman said, releasing her hand.

The gentleman strode over to the horse. "Thank you, my good man," he said, grabbing the reins. He had a round, florid face and copper, bushy eyebrows and Alfred gave him a leg up to mount. He picked up the reins and yanked the horse's head around, nearly trampling Alfred. With a sharp crack of the whip, the horse shot off.

Lydia waited until her father went into the house before she blew Alfred a kiss.

I had completed nineteen chapters. Just one more to go and I could send the whole lot to Lucy, my agent, and hopefully get an advance. I sorely needed the money. I ran a bath and ordered a takeaway. Just as I was opening my second bottle of wine there was someone at the door.

"It's looking much better here," Freddie said, strolling into the living room. "Quite homely with the nice cushions."

"That's my sister's doing," I said. "What do you want?"

"Babe, don't break my heart. I made a mistake. I've come to say I'm sorry," he said, reaching for my hand as I whipped it away.

"Oh, so you didn't mean to get into Zara's teensy, tiny little thongs, then?" I folded my arms in front of me.

"She wouldn't leave me alone. She kept pestering me," he frowned. "I'm only human."

"It looked to me like she'd moved in," I said, picking up my drink.

"I can assure you she hasn't," he said, putting his hand on his heart. "For me, it was just sex and not very good sex at that."

I laughed in his face, the spite rising inside like a sharp sword in my guts as I imagined the two of them writhing together.

"I had great sex last night," I blurted.

"Who with?" Freddie frowned.

"A gorgeous bloke I picked up at the pub." I sounded like a teenager. "And I'm going to see him again."

"Babe, there are no gorgeous blokes in that pub," he said, shaking his head and smiling.

"Well, there was last night and his name's…" I couldn't remember his bloody name.

Freddie leaned on the mantlepiece, assessing me. "I guess that's the end of us," he said softly and went to leave.

I grabbed his jacket. "I only slept with him because of Zara," I cried. "It was horrible. I couldn't wait for him to leave."

He looked away into the distance.

"Please don't go. I love you," I cried.

He took my hands from his jacket and kissed them, pushing my hair back and kissing me full on the lips.

We didn't make it upstairs. We tore at each other's clothes and had frenzied sex on the sofa. Afterwards, I lay close to him breathing heavily, so pathetically grateful that for now, he was here with me.

"I'll call you tomorrow and we'll arrange a proper night out," he said. "To celebrate you writing again."

"Okay," I mumbled.

"We'll go somewhere really special," he said.

"Hang on a moment, why will you call me tomorrow? Won't you still be here?" I asked.

"I can't stay the night," he whispered, stroking my hair. "I've got an early shoot in the morning."

"I need you to stay," I begged.

"Well, maybe for a bit longer," he replied.

Later he left, slamming the door behind him. I spied on him, hiding behind the curtain as he started the car.

He had the speakerphone on and I heard a female voice say, "Hi there."

Just two words but they sounded so intimate and as if the call was expected.

"It's probably his mum," I said, closing the curtain and returning to my wine.

CHAPTER NINE

Suffrage

First Draft

October 1913

Lydia and Alfred were met at Vauxhall Station by Hubert, John Archer, son of John, Cuthbert Archer MP and a carriage drawn by two fine, black mares.

Hubert offered Lydia a well-manicured hand as she stepped up into the sumptuous coach. He waved Alfred away to climb up with the coachman.

Hubert leaned forward, his face pale and blotchy. "I'm so happy you decided to come and meet Mother. She is very much looking forward to your visit. I expect this is your first time in London, being a young lady from a small, relatively unknown town," he said, waving his hand around as if bothered by a flying insect.

"It's my pleasure, Mr Archer," Lydia said. "Indeed, this is not my first foray into our capital city. I have taken tea at Claridge's with my aunt on numerous occasions."

"Ahh, so you know how ghastly the traffic is?" he asked.

"Quite so," she replied, looking out of the window at the horse-drawn carriages and the motorised buses. "Absolutely ghastly."

The coachman stopped the carriage in a street of large red brick mansions. As Hubert led Lydia by the arm towards a door, Alfred followed.

"What are you doing?" Hubert gestured impatiently. "Wait here with Smith."

Alfred stood his ground.

"Alfred, please wait for me," Lydia said, her eyes downcast.

As the couple entered the magnificent building, Hubert pointed out, "You can be too friendly with servants, my dear. They love to take liberties if you're not careful. That chap was being insolent."

"Thank you for being considerate. We have a less formal relationship with our servants, coming from a small, relatively unknown town," she said, glancing at him under her lashes. "I've known Alfred since I was a child."

"Casual, friendly overtures to the lower classes only encourage disobedience," Hubert pointed out, taking her arm. "We must maintain aloof superiority to ensure our British way of life continues. A detached, authoritative attitude is required at all times."

"I'll keep that in mind," Lydia replied.

Mrs Archer was enormous and swathed in brightly coloured silk, including a bandana wrapped around her head. Her beady eyes peered out of wrinkled, flabby folds of flesh.

"It's a pleasure to meet you, my dear," she said without rising. "You are so beautiful, just like Hubert intimated. Please come and sit by me and tell me all about yourself, so that I may get to know you properly. I'm hoping we will be dear friends."

Lydia sat next to her and tried not to wrinkle her nose as the smell of mothballs and cloying perfume radiated from the middle-aged woman.

Mrs Archer pried into Lydia's father's business

concerns and her education. Hubert sullenly picked at the tassels on the sofa, not contributing to the conversation.

"We have the most talked about house in all of England," Mrs Archer boasted. "Tullerton Hall has been in my husband's family for centuries. Hubert, as our only son, will inherit the whole caboodle once his father passes away. That's why it's so important for him to have a cultured, highly-bred wife by his side, to maintain the family's reputation."

"Mother!" Hubert objected.

"Well, it's true, dear," she smiled, showing brown teeth. "The lucky lady who becomes the mistress of Tullerton Hall will be the envy of all London."

"Hubert is very lucky to have such a thoughtful mother," Lydia said.

"Thank you," Mrs Archer said. "It's difficult having only one child to heap all of one's affection on."

"Miss Lydia doesn't need to hear this," Hubert said, getting up and going to the window.

"Of course, we wanted more children." Mrs Archer sniffed into a large handkerchief. "But we weren't blessed in that way."

"I'm so sorry," Lydia said.

"You are getting morbid, Mother," Hubert said, his back turned to them.

"Indeed, I am," Mrs Archer agreed, dabbing at her nose. "We are very blessed to have a fine son."

"So blessed, that when I was a very small child, you sent me away to school," Hubert said.

"We had to ensure a proper education if you were going to eventually be the head of the family," Mrs Archer said, her eyes bulging.

"I didn't get much education during the holidays and at Christmas time, when you saw fit to leave me there," Hubert said.

"Your father was very busy," Mrs Archer said, raising her eyebrows. "We were often abroad."

"I must apologise, Miss Turner," Hubert said, baring his teeth as if attempting a smile. "My mother and I disagree about my upbringing. My boarding school was perfectly adequate and the other chaps treated me well. But being left at school for months on end, not being part of a family, was much to bear at times."

"Nonsense," Mrs Archer snorted through her large nostrils. "It was one of the top schools in the country and I often wrote."

"My best friend, William, always went home for the holidays," Hubert said, arranging his podgy fingers into a steeple. "Occasionally his family took pity on me and asked me to join them. Those were the best times."

He wore a broad smile on his face and a far-away look in his eyes.

"And look what happened to him," Mrs Archer said. "Dead at nineteen. Such a waste of a young man's life."

Hubert nodded, covering his eyes with his hand.

"He hung himself in the family chapel," Mrs Archer confided to Lydia. "They'd spent a fortune on stained glass windows. His mother told me they would never go into that building again."

"It was a terrible time," Hubert said.

"Foolish, selfish boy," Mrs Archer said.

"That's very sad," Lydia said. "Why did he take his own life?"

"There were rumours that he was having an unsuitable love affair," Mrs Archer said. "Nevertheless, no young lady was ever implicated."

Hubert chewed his lip as his mother continued. "You were devastated at the time, weren't you dear?"

"He was my best friend," Hubert murmured.

"This will not do," Mrs Archer brightened and rang a little bell. "I hoped to have a cheerful afternoon, not dwell on unhappy memories." She squeezed Lydia's arm as a maid entered the room.

Hubert escorted Lydia back to the carriage at the end of the visit.

"I hope you won't think I'm incredibly rude if I don't escort you to the station," Hubert said. "Mother likes me to read to her in the afternoon."

"Not at all," Lydia said as he kissed her gloved hand. "I have Alfred to take care of me."

Hubert nodded sternly, glancing at Alfred as he helped her into the carriage.

Alfred sat next to the coachman as he flicked the whip, making the horses walk on. Lydia tapped the roof and peered out of the window, her hat brushing the window frame.

"Would you take us to the Albert Hall?" she asked. "I'm meeting my aunt there."

"Right you are, Miss," the coachman replied.

As the carriage approached Hyde Park a large noisy crowd of women and a few men were gathered. Lydia poked her head out of the window.

"Pull up here, please," she demanded.

Alfred helped her down from the coach.

"We shouldn't stop here," he said, looking around. "There's a mob."

"Thank you," she said to the coachman. "We can manage from here."

The coachman turned the horses around and trotted away.

"Lydia, it's dangerous here," Alfred said.

"It's the reason I came to London and spent three hours with Hubert's awful mother," she said, ignoring him and marching towards the crowd.

Alfred followed, trying his best to protect her as she squeezed through the crowd. A tall, dark-haired woman waved at them.

"Mavis, what on earth are you doing here?" Alfred asked.

Mavis gave him a big smile, "Miss Lydia and I arranged to meet here."

"That's right," Lydia confirmed, taking Mavis's arm. "She's not only my maid, she's also my partner in the struggle for women's rights."

Emmeline Pankhurst mounted the steps to the Albert Hall.

"We women Suffragists have a great mission – the greatest mission the world has ever known," she shouted.

Lydia and Mavis cheered and punched the air.

"We must leave," Alfred said. "Your father would be furious if he knew you were here."

"Just a bit longer," Lydia said.

"I incite this meeting to rebellion," Mrs Pankhurst yelled to huge applause.

"Come on," Alfred insisted, taking Lydia's arm and leading her out of the crowd.

It was great that Lydia was interested in suffrage and women's rights and I wondered how involved she would become. I couldn't wait for her to share more of her story.

Coincidently, I was due to meet my agent in London and on the same day, Cliff had arranged for us to meet on neutral territory for a chat.

Lucy loved the twenty chapters I had sent and promised to negotiate a good advance with a publisher. I could breathe easy for a while. After the meeting, I got a taxi and headed for a favourite Lebanese restaurant Cliff and I used to go to before our divorce.

He was seated at our table when I arrived and I ordered water.

"How are you?" he asked, smiling.

"I'm doing okay," I replied.

He had a glass of beer and I craved a glass of wine, but I wouldn't give him the satisfaction. "I'm writing again which is great."

"That's brilliant," he agreed. "How's everything else?"

"You mean: are you still a drunk?" I said, sipping my water.

"I arranged to meet today so that we could talk in a civilised way about our children," he said. "Debbie was dead against it, but I still came."

"I'm so glad your PA has some say in what we can and can't do," I said, raising my eyebrows.

"Be fair," he said. "She looks after the kids and she doesn't have to."

"What a cliché," I goaded. "Marrying your bloody PA!"

"You had an affair, not me," he pointed out.

"You could have been more imaginative about your choice," I said bitterly.

"And you could have been more committed to our children and marriage," he countered.

I swilled the slice of lemon around in my glass and he tapped his fingers against the table.

"I would like to see my children," I said eventually.

"I want that too," he said running his hand through his fair hair. "But, there have to be agreed rules."

"I expect Miss Perky Boobs has made a list of them," I said, waving at the waiter.

"Please don't call her that," he sighed.

"A large glass of white wine," I ordered from the hovering waiter. I turned back to Cliff. "You have an affair with your PA, you marry her then you give her a boob job. I mean, no one would believe that if I wrote it in a novel."

"I married Debbie eighteen months ago because for at least a year before you were having an affair with the photographer. The photographer you fucked in our bed," he said.

The waiter put the wineglass in front of me and I took a large gulp.

"Furthermore," Cliff continued. "You were drunk every day in front of our children and acted like you couldn't care less about them. How many times did I come home to find you lying face down in a puddle of vomit and random people wandering around the house?"

I closed my eyes, hyperventilating as I remembered my behaviour.

"I'm sorry," I cried. "Somehow I lost control and I haven't been able to get it back. I'm trying to sort myself out. I'm writing every day and I only have a drink in the evening."

"That's a start," he said, shrugging. "You need to stop drinking though."

"I will soon," I mumbled.

"If you want the kids overnight, you must promise not to drink while they are there," he said. "I want you to spend time with them; you're their mum for God's sake. But I need to know they're not in danger."

"I promise," I said, perking up.

"And," he seemed reluctant to say more and I guessed Debbie had a hand in this. "Your sister needs to be present at all times. Including staying over while the children are there. We — I just don't trust you to care for them on your own."

Bloody cheek! But the thought of having my children

cancelled out my objections. I poured the wine into a nearby plant pot.

"I agree," I said.

CHAPTER TEN

Promises

"Hi Freddie," I said, clutching the phone. "I've got some exciting news."

"What?" he said tonelessly.

"There's a writing convention taking place in Lisbon and I've been asked to speak," I said, in a voice several octaves above my natural one. "Why don't you come and we'll make a weekend of it?"

"I'd love to but I'm brassic at the moment. I'm waiting for a big payment to come in," he moaned.

"That's okay; I'll pay."

The publisher had booked us into a posh Lisbon hotel. Freddie looked around appreciatively as we arrived in our cream and gold room. The bathroom was huge with a sunken bath and gold taps. Freddie filled it up to the brim and stripped off, stepping into it, the soap suds clinging to the black hairs on his chest.

"Are you joining me?" he asked, his green eyes twinkling.

"In a minute," I replied, bolting out of the room. Safely in the bedroom, I undressed and wrapped a towel around my forty-year-old, abused body and returned to the bathroom. Freddie was fully submerged, so I took the opportunity to ditch the towel and lower myself into the hot water.

He sat up, rivulets of water cascading down his face and chest and his hair sticking to his scalp like black silk.

"You're so beautiful," he said, lightly stroking my cheek

with his wet fingertips.

I suppose I blushed because he grinned, shaking his head. "You know you're the only woman that I've ever come anywhere near being in love with."

"That's a lukewarm confession," I teased.

"You know it's hard for me. You understand me and that's what I love about you," he said, stroking the inside of my thigh with his hand.

"I love you, Freddie, and I want a life with you," I said.

"When the time's right, darling. It's best not to rush into things. Think of your children." He kissed me and all seemed well in the world.

I did my talk the same day to an auditorium packed with agents and publishers. Freddie circulated, taking photographs. Women looked up and smiled at him as soon as he approached, and he exchanged words with one or two. But, hey, I was the only woman he'd ever come anywhere near being in love with!

We spent the late afternoon wandering the sunlit streets of Lisbon, happily stopping for coffee and patisserie and riding the trams through the ancient streets.

Later we had dinner in an exclusive restaurant and Freddie ordered champagne. After all, he pointed out, we should celebrate my return to success. On the way back to the hotel we happened upon a karaoke club.

"Let's go in," he said, his face flushed.

"I'm an awful singer."

"I know," he agreed. "But it'll be a laugh."

Freddie ordered the most expensive bottle of champagne on the menu as we watched (and, unfortunately, heard) a young woman singing 'Hopelessly Devoted' from Grease. Everyone clapped and cheered generously when she eventually finished. Freddie leapt up and headed for the stage.

"This is for the most wonderful woman in the world," he said into the mic, pointing at me. I squirmed as everyone turned to look at me. To my surprise, he made a good job of belting out Lenny Kravitz's 'Always On The Run'. The crowd got to their feet dancing and clapping as Freddie wiggled his hips to the beat.

We may have drunk three or four bottles of the overpriced champagne, I don't recall. By the second bottle, I was ready to make my karaoke debut. I sang Madonna's 'Like a Virgin'. When I say I can't sing, I'm not being modest! My twins have often commented on my out-of-tune attempts to warble. The audience didn't seem to care though, and I went on to sing many other Madonna numbers and a duet with Freddie: 'The Time of My Life' from *Dirty Dancing*.

I don't remember the taxi ride back to the hotel or getting into the huge double bed. I do remember Freddie ordering Buck's Fizz the next day at breakfast.

We had a wonderful weekend together and I was confident Freddie was committed to having a long-term relationship. I couldn't wait to get home and make plans. But first I needed to sober up.

First Draft

Lydia and Mavis disappeared into Lydia's bedroom for hours on end. This behaviour didn't go unnoticed in a house full of servants. What followed was gossip and jumping to inventive conclusions. Some of these assumptions occasionally reached the ears of Alfred.

"I hear that Miss Lydia and Mavis are busy planning her wedding," Alfred's sister told him as she stirred a big pot on the open range in their cottage. "She'll have all the trimmings, proper wine from France, a lacy wedding dress from London and a train so long it'll take twenty bridesmaids to carry it."

"That's nonsense," Alfred said, shaking his head. "Where'd you hear that?"

"Maud, the laundress told me all about it

yesterday," she replied. "And there's talk of the bridegroom owning a palace somewhere up north with peacocks in the garden and a huge lake, just for the gentleman alone to fish in. Can you imagine? What a perfect life for our Missy."

"It's folk making up silly stories," Alfred said, warming his hands near the fire. "Miss Lydia's head is not turned by riches and big houses."

"You hope," she snorted. "You'll be woebegone the day she does wed."

"What are you talking about?" Alfred frowned, a deep line forming between his eyes.

"The whole town knows you hold a flame for her," she replied. "Since you were both little kids you've been inseparable – plaiting horse's manes and riding the hay wagon back from the fields. We all noticed. The way you look at her, the way she looks at you. The only one that hasn't noticed is her father."

"We were childhood friends because her dad wasn't around and we took care of her. But since she's grown into a fine lady, I respect her, that's all," Alfred said, cupping his chin in his hands as he stared into the flames. "She'll marry a fine gentleman before long. Of that, I have no doubt."

"That fine gentleman she visited in London?" she asked. "The one you said was mean and unpleasant?"

"No," Alfred shook his head. "She can't stand him. She'll never marry him."

"Mmm," his sister murmured, leaning against the fireplace.

"But someday soon she'll surely marry a fine gentleman," he repeated.

One bright morning, Alfred accompanied Lydia

and Mavis along the towpath by the river. The ladies wore warm cloaks and hats, and Alfred was wrapped in a large coat inherited from his father. He walked behind, unable to hear their conversation. The women were about the same height and both slim, but something about the gait and posture of each woman bore witness to her class and upbringing. Fair-haired Lydia glided, her back ramrod straight, whereas brown-haired Mavis swung her hips from side to side.

They stopped at the racecourse that ran alongside the river. A new grandstand had been erected at the far end and Lydia insisted they take a look.

The wooden structure was newly painted white and black and both ladies seemed very interested in it.

"Are you planning on going to the races?" Alfred asked.

"It would be entertaining to see the horses and jockeys and even place a little bet," Lydia said, looking underneath the solid structure.

"There's a big meeting the day after next. Would your father agree for you to go?" he asked.

"You know how Father makes a fuss whenever I want to go anywhere," Lydia replied. "I'd probably have to wait for a day when he can escort me and he's always busy with his work."

"Would he let you go if Alfred went with you?" Mavis asked.

"No," replied Lydia.

"What about your gentleman? He'd go with you if you asked him," Mavis said, her dark eyes twinkling. "A man who owns a castle must have few bob to put on the horses."

"I don't think Hubert would enjoy the races. He

told me once that gambling was a fool's errand," Lydia said, pressing her lips together. "He doesn't own a castle, Mavis, as you well know."

Mavis made a face at Alfred behind Lydia's back.

Alfred was awoken in his narrow bunk by muffled cries later that same day. He dressed quickly and ran outside to see the sky illuminated with orange streaks.

"Something must be on fire," his father cried, running past him and towards the stables.

Fortunately, the stables had no fire, although the horses were jittery. The men ran on towards the racecourse. As they cleared the boundary of mature oaks, they saw the great grandstand consumed with flames and 'Votes for Women' banners pinned to trees and fences. People were filling buckets with water from the river to quench the flames and Alfred ran to help.

The scene was frantic as buckets were passed hand-to-hand along a line of men, women and children towards the fire. Alfred noticed two shadowy figures rushing from the scene. He followed them discreetly, overtaking them when they were out of sight of the racecourse. They wore immense men's coats over their dresses and their hands and faces were streaked with black soot.

"What are you doing here in the middle of the night? Have you both gone mad?" he asked.

"No," Lydia replied, crossing her arms. "We're standing up for our rights!"

"Please don't tell me you started the fire?" he begged.

Lydia and Mavis exchanged a guilty look that answered his question.

"Mavis, how could you risk Miss Lydia's reputation?" he asked.

"I tried to talk her out of it," Mavis replied. "But she was set on doing it and I thought it better for me to go with her than let her get into trouble on her own."

"That's true," Lydia said. "I was determined to do it. But Mavis, I could've managed perfectly well on my own. I know how to make a fire, for goodness' sake. I'm not completely helpless."

"I can't believe you've done this." Alfred ran his hands through his hair. "There'll be serious outcomes."

"We've tried peaceful means of getting our cause heard but no one's listening," Lydia said, dusting the soot off her gloves. "Perhaps now they'll take us seriously."

"That's as maybe, but you've still broken the law," he said, scratching his head. "Come on. We'll creep along the towpath. Hopefully, we won't be seen from the road. Then I'll let you in the house by the tradesman's entrance."

The next day the women insisted on walking to the burnt-down grandstand, despite Alfred's objections. As they neared the site, people – some richly clothed and others dressed plainly – were standing around staring at the black pile of charcoal that had been the grandstand.

Lydia's father was among them and he strode towards them across the cinders that covered the grass, his large cloak streaming behind him.

"It's outrageous," he thundered, raising bushy eyebrows. "Some lunatic women have burnt the grandstand to the ground. The constable said women's rights banners were pinned up near the fire."

"I suppose women are getting frustrated at their voices not being heard," Lydia said. "Perhaps this was the only way to bring their cause to people's attention?"

Joseph Turner turned several shades of purple. "Their voices not being heard?" he growled, spittle at the side of his mouth. "They ought to be busy bringing up children and organising their household! Doing womanly things, not causing all sorts of mayhem."

"But father…"

He marched Lydia away. Alfred and Mavis watched helplessly, as he continually thrust his finger vigorously into Lydia's pale face.

"She'll have to watch herself," Mavis noted. "She'll land herself in a whole heap of trouble, that's for sure."

"She's always been headstrong and her father has never curbed her," Alfred said. "You oughtn't to encourage her though."

"I haven't encouraged her at all," Mavis said. "She caught me with a 'Votes for Women' banner, coming back from a meeting one day. I thought she'd be furious and give me the sack. Once we discussed it, it was clear that she believed in the cause as much as I did. She only agreed to go to London to visit the gentleman so that she could get away and see Mrs Pankhurst."

"That's unbelievable," Alfred said, biting his lip. "I was surprised she'd wanted to visit him as she made it clear she had no liking for him, the honourable whatever his name is. I can't believe she could be so deceitful."

"What's it like loving someone you can never have?" Mavis asked, her head tilted.

"What makes you think I have any feelings for her besides being a faithful servant?" he replied.

"It's the way you look at her," Mavis remarked. "Your eyes give your feelings away. It's no secret. Everyone below stairs knows."

"You're wrong. You're all wrong," he replied, shaking his head.

"You'd be better off longing for a woman you can have." She looked at him under her black lashes. "A woman who would look after you and keep you warm at night. I'd not say no to you."

CHAPTER ELEVEN

Perfidy

I'd finished the chapter just before Cliff dropped the children off. He herded them into the lounge and they stood on either side of him looking terrified.

"Where's Charlie?" Cliff asked.

"She's on the M25 stuck in traffic but she won't be long," I said.

"Are you sure?" he said.

"Phone her if you don't believe me," I challenged.

"I know Charlie wouldn't let the children down," he said, bending to kiss the children goodbye.

"Would you like to see your new bedrooms?" I said once he'd gone, edging up the stairs. "It's all new. The wallpaper, the bedding!"

They reluctantly climbed the stairs behind me.

"I hope you like it?" I said. "You can choose which rooms you want."

"We'll stay in this one," Rosanna replied.

"But I've gone to so much trouble to get you a room each," I cried.

Jackson stepped forward. "The other room faces the garden and we're frightened of melted-face man."

I threw my hands up in the air.

"Tell me about melted-face man," I asked. "Is he a real man?"

Rosanna chewed her hair as they nodded.

"What does he look like?"

E W GRANT

They looked at each other and then at me. "He has a proper face on one side," Jackson said. "And a melted face on the other."

"Does he speak? Does he say anything to you?"

Rosanna removed her wet hair from her mouth. "He just stares up at the window. He can't hear us or see us. He just stares at something."

I rubbed my temples. It was drink time for me, but I wanted to keep my promise to Cliff tonight.

My phone trilled; it was Charlie.

"Sorry, sis. The traffic's at a standstill and I'm only at Hook," she said. "Besides, I've got a terrible migraine coming on. I'm going to have to go home."

I walked onto the landing. "You can't do that. Cliff will come and take the children back," I said, feeling a sympathetic pain developing behind my forehead.

"I'm so sorry, there's just no way I can make it tonight," she groaned. "Phone him and arrange another time. Sorry."

The phone went dead and I peered at the twins sitting on the bed. Jackson was reading aloud.

I was perfectly capable of looking after my children. In addition, I was sure my sister supervising their visit was Miss Perky Boob's idea rather than Cliff's. I would say that Charlie arrived late and left early and the children didn't get to see her. Cliff might check with Charlie but that was a risk I was willing to take.

I'd made the children's favourite supper of fish fingers sandwiches and we sat in the dining room eating in silence.

"This used to be a beautiful room with a sparkling chandelier," I had to say something and this was all I could think of.

"How do you know?" Rosanna asked.

"Oh, I saw it in an old photo," I lied.

"And people danced here," Jackson said.

"Did I tell you about that?" I asked, confused.

"No," he replied. "We knew that." Rosanna nodded in agreement.

"But how did you know?" I asked, feeling a cold tingle up my spine.

"The lady who lives on the stairs told us," Rosanna said.

It was too much. My children were seeing things and I was writing a dead woman's story. I didn't believe in any of this supernatural stuff, yet these things were happening. How could I make sense of the unsettling occurrences in my house? I felt overwhelmed as my mind reeled. In addition, my yearning for a drink was torturing me.

We watched TV for a bit and then they went to bed. I tried hard not to have a drink, but I was twitchy and uncomfortable. I got up and wandered around the room, stopping now and then and questioning what the children had said about the melted-face man.

I would have one glass to settle my nerves. I sat in my favourite chair with my feet tucked underneath me. Just one glass and already I felt ten times better.

Then Freddie called.

"Hi, darling," I said.

"Hi. I just called to see if you had the number of the guy we spoke to at the convention in Lisbon. You know, the one that was interested in my photography for his book launch," he said.

"Yes, I remember. It's on my phone. I'll send it to you."

"Great," he said.

"You remember we spoke in Lisbon about you moving in?" I asked.

"Yeah," he replied.

"Well, you moved a few things into the basement, but I don't see you making any effort to live here," I said, biting my lip.

"We'll talk about it soon. Hang on," he said.

I heard a woman's voice. "Who's that?" I quizzed.

"It's the telly," he replied. "Sorry, I've got to go. Something's burning on the hob."

Freddie had never cooked anything in his life!

I poured a glass of wine and then another and felt a sharp pressure in my chest.

I checked on the twins; they were fast asleep. Rosanna was tucked under the covers and Jackson was lying on top in a sleeping bag. They wouldn't notice if I slipped out. I'd be back before they knew it. I was over the alcohol limit to drive but it wasn't far and I would be careful.

I pulled up near Freddie's house and double parked. I knew how to get around the back and where the spare key was. I let myself in. I could hear moaning and heavy breathing from upstairs. I crept up the stairs and opened the bedroom door.

Zara had her beautiful, naked back to me, astride Freddie. She was bouncing energetically up and down, like she was riding a horse.

"You fucking bastard," I screamed.

Freddie sat bolt upright, pushing the girl aside and revealing his erection. I turned and charged down the stairs.

A car horn blasted in the street, stuck behind my car. I slammed his side window with the palm of my hand, calling him a fucking moron. The young man at the steering wheel looked astonished, his mouth wide open. Then I jumped in my car and sped off.

I had been a complete fool. Freddie had never loved me. He was only interested in furthering his career off the back of my success. The phone rang about twenty times, but I didn't want to hear his excuses.

Cliff was standing by his car, Miss Perky Boobs at the steering wheel and the twins seated in the back as I drew up to my house.

"What's going on?" I said, stumbling over the raised pavement and landing face down, my hands saving me.

"What's going on?" he said. "You went out and left

them."

The twins were crying as I struggled to my feet.

"They phoned us," he said, making an ugly and distorted face. "They said someone was in the house, but it wasn't you and it wasn't Charlie. What the bloody hell do you think you're playing at? Where's Charlie and why are you drunk?"

I swayed, it's true, but I think it was from the enormity of what I'd done.

"I had an emergency," I shrieked.

"Don't give me that rubbish. You went to the pub or you went to see the boyfriend," he surmised, correctly.

Debbie got out of the car. "Leave her, Cliff. All you'll get is a pack of lies."

"Why don't you just fuck off," I shouted.

"You are disgraceful," she said, her perfect bobbed hair shining in the street light. "You're not fit to be a mother."

"Get your own kids and leave mine alone," I screamed at the top of my voice.

"Oh, Moira," Cliff said, his face ashen.

As the car pulled away, my children didn't look back.

CHAPTER TWELVE

I Broke the Law

First Draft

Lydia threw another bundle of kindling through the basement window of the elegant mansion. The grand sash windows reflected orange and citrus streaks from the setting sun.

"I've searched the rooms," Mavis said as she emerged from the grand hallway. "The house is empty apart from the rats."

"I've stacked the basement with dry wood and twigs," Lydia said, wiping her forehead. "A couple of matches should do it."

"It's a pity we rode here and didn't bring a cart," Mavis sighed. "There are some lovely gowns and wraps in the wardrobe."

Lydia smiled. "We're not thieves," she said. "You can choose a gown from my wardrobe when we get back."

Mavis's eyes lit up as she rubbed her hands together.

"Whose house is it?" she asked.

"Malcolm Bridges QC. He lives full-time in London. I met him one evening with my father. He's an odious man. He lectured me on the evils of the Suffragettes. He had the cheek to say he much preferred a fragrant bloom, such as myself, to the unwomanly strumpets currently clamouring for votes. I chose his house to teach him a lesson and because I knew there was no chance of anyone getting hurt," Lydia said. "Let's make haste. Go and pin up the Votes for Women banners."

Mavis scurried away, posting up banners on several trees.

Both women turned at the sound of heavy hooves and a man shouting. Alfred was trotting across a field towards them.

"Quick, set it alight," Mavis said.

Lydia lit a match, reaching toward a newspaper she'd carefully piled under some twigs. The flame jumped into life, devouring the paper and wood. Mavis grabbed a stick from the pile and lit it from the growing conflagration. She tossed it through the ground floor window, shattering the glass. It landed on the plush sofa, starting a new fire. The women stood back, feeling the heat expanding as the flames licked across the ceilings and wooden window frames and doors.

Alfred dismounted, attempting to lead the horse towards them. The horse had other ideas and objected strongly to the leaping orange flames.

"You've really gone and done it now," he warned, the horse prancing and stamping behind him.

"It's properly on fire. We'd better get out of here," Mavis said, taking Lydia by the arm and leading her away.

"It's nearly sunset," Alfred said. "It'll soon look like a bloody beacon. Half the county will be here!"

Alfred followed and helped both women mount their horses.

"I know a shortcut across the fields," he mumbled, mounting his horse. "When you asked me to saddle two horses, I thought you'd be riding out with a gentleman. If I knew you'd be cavorting around the countryside with your maid, setting fire to people's houses, I wouldn't have been so helpful."

"How did you find us?" Lydia asked.

"My father saw you riding across the common towards the farmland, leading Mavis's horse on a rein. I knew you were both up to something. Mavis can't ride and doesn't even like horses," he said, shaking his head. "I followed the hoof prints in the mud."

"You're a crafty bugger," Mavis grinned.

"What were you thinking?" he said, frowning. "You might have got hurt or you could be arrested if you get caught. They throw women like you in prison and I know neither of you would like that."

"We had to do something," Lydia said, staring back at the massive flames leaping into the evening sky from the house. "Don't you see that until women get the vote, their voice is unheard?"

"There's a great many of us who go unheard," Alfred remarked. "But we don't go around burning down people's houses and setting light to grandstands."

"You should join our cause," Mavis suggested. "There are many men who fight side-by-side with the Suffragettes."

"I can understand your reasons for joining the cause," he pointed at Mavis. "But Miss Lydia, you're a lady. Why are you involved in this madcap campaign?"

"I am privileged in many ways," Lydia conceded, riding alongside him, Mavis's horse trailing behind. "But I'm also a prisoner of my class. I have no vote, so I have no independence. My father will marry me off to whomever he chooses. I will never have any money or property, even though by rights, I should have an inheritance from my father. Once I'm married, my husband can take my money, gamble it away or spend it on trinkets for his mistress if he pleases. I will have no say in what happens to my children, where they live or how they are educated. So although I live comfortably and I don't go hungry, I'm completely powerless to make any decisions about my life."

They reined in their horses, camouflaged by a small copse, and watched as silhouetted figures panicked around the burning house. The flames illuminated the darkening sky, engulfing the whole building.

"Let's get you both home before they notice you're missing," he said, taking up his reins and urging his mighty mount into a trot.

The garret had become claustrophobic and so I'd fled and somehow drove to Guildford, a large, well-heeled town in Surrey.

I parked the car and headed for the shops. A musty, warm smell emanating from a pub beckoned me, like a siren. A drink would cheer me up and I would only have one.

I emerged much later into the dull, overcast afternoon, tripping over the step and skinning my hands and knees. People rushed past, their disgusted faces turned away. I managed to get up and stagger to the department store, determined to get my credit card nearer its limit.

The department store was confusing. No matter how I tried to find the technology department, going up escalators and down in lifts, I always ended up in shoes and handbags.

My intention to buy the twins outrageously expensive Christmas presents to gain their love and respect (some hope of that!) was thwarted.

I gave up, discarding my old, battered shoes and forcing my feet into vertiginous, snakeskin high heels. I laughed at my wobbly reflection in the mirror as the shop girls gossiped about me from behind the counter. I staggered over to the designer handbag section, tugging several large leather bags from their gilded shelves and discarding the felt stuffing.

After succeeding to scatter a pile of bags on the floor, I realised I'd lost my handbag and assumed I'd left it at the pub. As I flung open the glass exit doors of the department store, a burly, uniformed fellow stood with his hands on his hips, blocking my way.

"Stand aside," I ordered, in (what sounded to me) my poshest voice.

"Madam," he said. "I believe you've forgotten to pay."

"I don't have my handbag," I challenged. "How can you expect me to pay without my bag?"

"But you are taking one of ours," he noted, pointing to the bag over my arm. "And a pair of our shoes."

I squinted down and was surprised to see a smart tan leather bag dangling from my arm and the snakeskin shoes still crammed uncomfortably on my feet.

The security man hitched his thumbs in his belt, lifting his chin towards the door. For some reason, I found his actions hilarious. I burst out laughing and I continued to laugh, even when I was escorted to the store manager's office.

My brother-in-law, Bill, eventually came to rescue me, as Charlie was working. He explained my drink problem as I sat whimpering, and offered to pay for any damage to the goods I'd handled. My handbag was found on a shelf, replacing one of the expensive handbags I had removed, and I gladly pulled off the torturous shoes.

The store manager was sympathetic and said that this time he wouldn't involve the police. But he would have to insist that I did not visit the store again.

Bill drove me home in silence.

CHAPTER THIRTEEN

Shattered

First Draft

Until 1912, campaigning was largely within the law. Suffragettes chained themselves to railings and generally disturbed the peace. But activism grew to include planting bombs, smashing shop windows and acts of arson.

An average of 21 bombing and arson incidents per month took place in 1913. Suffragettes declaring themselves to be 'terrorists' stood in front of shop windows and government offices in London and simultaneously took hammers and stones from their pockets and smashed the windows.

"I can't believe that you lied to me about visiting London. You said you were seeing Hubert," Joseph said.

"I—" Lydia stuttered.

"Shut up and listen," he said, standing over her. "You've lied. That's bad enough. But you joined a mob of lunatic women and went on the rampage in The City of London! Breaking windows and causing mayhem!"

Lydia fidgeted in the large leather chair in her father's London office, as Alfred stood behind her like a statue. Joseph Turner marched up and down, waving his arms about. Lydia had never seen him so annoyed and wondered what he would do if he knew she and Mavis had set fire to his friend's house a few weeks earlier.

"It was for a worthy cause," she mumbled, still thinking about the house.

"Worthy cause? Are you mad?" he said, leaning over the desk. "You have the opportunity of getting engaged to a gentleman from a distinguished and wealthy family and you put all that at risk by acting like a low-born hooligan."

"I don't want to marry Hubert," she said, biting her lip.

He banged his big fist on the table. "You silly girl. You will do as you're told," he said. "Hubert Archer admires your beauty and poise and hopes his reputation will be greatly enhanced with you as his wife. Our family have no pedigree or ancestry to boast about. It may be that Alfred here has more lineage to be proud of than we do. Your mother would turn in her grave."

Lydia stood up slowly and laid her palms flat on the desk. "My mother would be proud that I stood up for women's rights," she said.

"Sit down," he demanded, jabbing his thick, hairy finger in her face.

Lydia obeyed, wrestling with her lacy handkerchief as he turned his back and looked out of the window onto the busy London street. Alfred nervously shifted his weight.

"The only reason you're not languishing in a prison cell with the other mad women is that the City police know me," her father explained. "They sent a man to find me as soon as they realised whose daughter you were."

"I didn't want to be treated differently from the other women," she said, shaking her head.

"Don't be a little fool," he said, turning to face her.

"I dine with powerful men at my club, including the Home Secretary! I have a reputation to maintain, and whatever your misguided beliefs, you won't be allowed to ruin your life and the prospects of a good marriage."

He chortled. "What kind of life do you think is on offer without a good marriage? It's true; you could remain a spinster and live at Rosebay House for your entire life. But you'd eventually lose your looks and get invited into society less and less every year. You'd shrivel like a plant without water. And once I'm gone, your only amusement would be your needlework and your books. Not an appealing prospect."

"I could work for good causes," Lydia said, adjusting her hat. "I could teach reading and writing and art."

"Good God, girl!" he exploded, making her jump. "How would you pay the servants and keep the horses stabled? You have no idea of the cost of any of these things, you just reap the benefit."

She fidgeted, picking at a silky bag in her lap.

"You need to marry into money," he said, clenching his fist. "Don't you see? It's the only way we will have any kind of genteel existence."

"What do you mean?' she asked. "You are a successful businessman."

"Yes, yes, that may be," he held his palm to his forehead. "But one has to plan for unforeseen disasters."

"Is there anything I should know?" she asked.

He flapped his hand close to her face and turned to Alfred. "Were you involved in this mad escapade?"

Alfred gulped loudly.

"He wasn't," Lydia replied. "I lied to get him to accompany me on the train to London. He knew nothing of my plans."

Alfred exhaled.

"Sir," Alfred said. "I'm very sorry. It is my job to look out for Miss Turner and I tried to talk her out of joining the other ladies. She wouldn't listen to me."

"I know how headstrong she is," Joseph said, shaking his head. "But I won't tolerate this sort of behaviour. Her spirit needs curbing."

"You can't keep me under lock and key," Lydia said.

"That's the last thing I want," Joseph said. "You should be out in London's society so that you may be admired."

He tapped his temples lightly. "Your activities will be curtailed. You will ask for my permission before you go anywhere – and I mean anywhere. You will no longer take the train to London unless it's with me or Hubert." Joseph pointed at Alfred. "My daughter will not meet unsavoury characters back at home. I will hold you and your father responsible if my orders are not followed. Is that clear?"

"Yes, sir," Alfred agreed.

"While we're talking about unsavoury characters," Joseph said. "I will dismiss your lady's maid when she's released from prison. You had better start looking for another."

"No! Please don't dismiss Mavis," begged Lydia. "I made her come today. It was my fault, not hers."

"Nevertheless, she has to go," Joseph said. "Let that be a lesson to the other servants."

Joseph dismissed them with a flick of his hand. Alfred clutched his cap as he opened the door for Lydia.

"You might have stood up for Mavis," Lydia said to Alfred on the train going home.

"You just don't get it," he murmured, his grey-blue eyes sad. "I'm lucky I kept my job. What with my father being employed and our cottage being rented from Mr Turner. My family stood to lose everything and be thrown out on the streets."

"I'm sorry," Lydia said, blushing. "I didn't think of that. It's just not fair that Mavis is cast aside. What will she do?"

"There's no fairness in a servant's life. We are at the mercy of our employers," he said, watching the fields rush past. "All you can do is work hard and keep out of trouble."

Charlie stared out of the window of my garret, her light brown hair styled neatly in a bun. It was a beautiful, chilly December day. The river sparkled, reflecting the bright sunshine.

"Why did you go out and leave the twins?" she asked.

"Freddie," I replied.

"I might have known," she said, pursing her lips.

"I messed up," I moaned.

"You certainly did," she said. "I spoke to Cliff the next day; he was furious. You'll be lucky to see the twins ever again."

I nodded. "I thought as the twins were asleep it would be okay to nip out for an hour."

"Of course not," she said, frowning.

"I know," I sighed. "Very stupidly I let Freddie compromise my relationship with my children—"

"Not for the first time," she interrupted.

"No," I agreed. "But Freddie and I are over."

She laughed.

"I mean it this time," I said, covering my eyes. "I caught him with a girl young enough to be my daughter. I couldn't be more insulted."

"I'm sorry. I know how much that must have hurt," she

said, resting her hand on my shoulder. "It was always going to end with him letting you down in some way. He doesn't care about you and you deserve so much better."

I smiled. "Why do you always believe in me?"

"You've got so much to offer the world," she said.

"Mmm," I said. "I don't think Cliff and Debbie would agree."

"Your parting comment to Debbie the other night, about having kids?" she asked.

"I was annoyed," I replied, shrugging.

"Cliff and Debbie have been trying for a baby for at least a year," she said. "They learned recently that Debbie can't conceive. I know you wouldn't have said it if you knew, but it was badly timed."

"Oh shit!" I said, holding my head in my hands.

"You have bridges to build," she added. "If you've ditched Freddie this time, why don't you think about ditching the drink as well?"

"I can stop drinking anytime I want," I claimed, my chin in the air.

"I say this because I love you," she smiled. "You're an alcoholic. And until you admit it and do something, you'll always struggle."

"I have a drink in the evening," I told her. "I don't drink during the day."

"You're still an alcoholic," she insisted.

There was an awkward silence. She turned again to look out of the window and I chewed my nails.

Eventually, she grabbed my arms. "I've done some research. We could go to an Alcoholics Anonymous meeting together. To see what help they can offer."

"I don't need the AA," I said, making a face.

"Believe me, Moira, you do," she insisted.

First Draft

The basement kitchen of Rosebay House was

warmed by a large metal stove. Alfred hadn't lit the gas lamps, not wanting to draw attention to the figure slumped over the large table.

The kitchen door flew open and Lydia appeared in a long gown, her exquisite hair hanging to her waist in silky tendrils.

"Thank God! You managed to get her here," Lydia whispered.

"I waited outside Holloway when I got word of her release," Alfred murmured. "They had to set her free after she went on a hunger strike. She hasn't eaten in days. She's all skin and bone."

"Hunger strike? Why on earth would she go on a hunger strike?" Lydia exclaimed.

"To continue the struggle, I'm told," Alfred said, shrugging. "Perfectly sane, sensible women behaving like lunatics."

"You are mistaken," Lydia said, her hands on her hips. "Not lunatics, just fed-up with the injustice of it all."

"That's as maybe," Alfred said. "I don't see why Mavis has to pay the price."

"If that is directed at me, may I remind you that I didn't ask Father to get my release from custody," Lydia said, her voice wavering.

"I didn't mean to point the finger. I'm just sorely worried about Mavis." Alfred held his finger to his lips. "If your father catches her here, there'll be hell to pay."

"He's in London for a few days," she said. "That's why I asked you to bring her here. She's safe and I'm going to make sure she gets the attention she needs."

Lydia went to the woman. "Mavis?" she spoke softly. "Let me look at you."

Mavis slowly lifted her head, her dark, dirty hair

hanging over her vacant eyes. A large cold sore encircled one side of her mouth and her lips were blistered and peeling.

"What did they do to you, my dear?" Lydia asked, holding Mavis's chin in her hand.

"They force-feed them in prison," Alfred said.

He filled a cup with water.

"Try and sip," he said, holding the cup close to Mavis's face.

Mavis squinted at him, her dark eyes bloodshot and watery. She sipped cautiously.

"Can I get you something to eat?" Lydia asked, her hand resting lightly on the jutting vertebrae of Mavis's back.

Mavis shook her head, staring into the mug.

"I've heard that it's unwise to feed 'em straight away," Alfred said.

"Where did you hear that?" Lydia asked.

"I spoke to a gentleman outside the prison, waiting for his wife to be released," he replied. "He was very knowledgeable because it was his wife's second imprisonment. If force-feeding doesn't work and the prisoner becomes very poorly, they are released. But only for a short time until they recover."

"You mean she's got to go back to prison?" Lydia asked, eyebrows raised.

"No!" Mavis whispered, peering around the room.

Alfred nodded imperceptibly.

"Listen to me," Lydia said, crouching, her face on the same level as Mavis's. "We'll take care of you, I promise. And we'll think of a way to keep you out of prison."

Mavis began to sob, her shoulders like chicken

wings sticking out of her thin dress.

"You mustn't make promises we can't keep," Alfred said over the top of Mavis's mop of dark hair.

"We have to do something to stop her from going back to prison." Lydia stood up. "She can't take anymore."

"I'll make her a bed down at the stables," Alfred suggested. "I can look after her there. No one will know."

"I'll bring food to help her get better," Lydia said. "We'll help her back on her feet. Maybe I can get her a job under a false name out in the countryside somewhere?"

Alfred held Mavis under the arms to lift her.

"Can you carry her?" Lydia asked.

"She's as light as a feather," Alfred replied.

"Go down the towpath where no one will see you," Lydia suggested.

Mavis hung her arms around Alfred's neck and nuzzled her face into his chest.

CHAPTER FOURTEEN

What Lies Ahead

Angela, my next-door neighbour, drummed her long red, acrylic fingernails on my kitchen table. We'd bumped into each other outside our respective homes several times and I'd mentioned in passing my damp carpet. She'd kindly popped in to loan me a dehumidifier.

Her expensive yoga leggings hugged her athletic figure as her shiny auburn ponytail swung from side to side when she moved her head. Her forehead had a waxy, unlined look that suggested regular Botox.

"Latte, cappuccino?" I offered, starting the coffee machine.

"Black, thanks," she replied, looking around. "My goodness, you have got a lot of work to do here."

"You could say that," I agreed, laughing.

"You'll need a new kitchen and the garden tamed. Have you thought about knocking the kitchen through to that old dining room to make it open-plan?" she asked.

"I love the thought of a proper dining room. I'm thinking of restoring it to its former glory," I said as she examined her bright nails.

"We've gone completely open plan on this floor of our house," she said. "With bifold doors out onto the deck and the hot tub."

"Very..." Tacky, I thought. "...glamorous. It's a shame to lose all the original features of the house."

Her head snapped up and she observed me with cat-like

amber eyes.

"We kept the parquet flooring," she said, tight-lipped. "We entertain on an enormous scale. Our friends love coming to our place. It's always a complete hoot!"

"I'm sure you have a lovely home," I acquiesced, not wanting to offend. "I hope you'll be on hand to advise me when I do the place up?"

She looked at me down her perfect nose.

"My husband and I know plenty of tradespeople," she said. "Don't hesitate to ask."

"Thank you," I said, putting her coffee on the table. "I'll keep that in mind when the time comes."

"So, you're an author?" she changed the subject. "I'm not a big reader, but would I have heard of any of your books?"

"I've had a few bestsellers, but that was years ago," I replied, reeling off a few titles.

"As we're neighbours, I'll make sure I read them," she said.

"I wonder if you know anything about this house?" I asked. "For instance the man who lived here before me?"

"Of course. We've lived here for twenty years," she answered. "The old man, Anthony, was already here before we moved in. He kept himself to himself. We didn't see him very often. He neglected the house and the garden, so we were pleased when you bought the place."

"Not that I've made many improvements yet," I said.

"I'm sure you've got big plans," she said.

I took a large gulp of my coffee.

"Did you know much about him?" I asked.

"He'd inherited the property from a distant relative. It had stood empty for years before that." She bit her lip. "We often saw him staring out of the attic room – your round room at the top. We'd wave, but he'd never wave back. The children used to be upset about that. We'd even ask him over for drinks if we saw him in the town, but he'd always refuse."

"He sounds like a lonely person," I said.

"Yes," she said, nodding. "There was a rumour that a woman stayed with him sometimes, but we never met her."

"Who was she?" I asked.

"We never knew," she replied. "But the children saw her on several occasions in the attic room. Funnily enough, they always claimed she wore a big hat, but they may have imagined that."

"Mmm," I murmured, winding a tendril of hair around my finger as a chill ran up my spine.

"He'd been dead for quite a few days before he was found," she murmured.

"How sad," I said.

"The milkman mentioned that his milk hadn't been taken in for three or four days." She spoke so quietly that I had to lean in. "I knocked on his door and there was no reply. So I called the police. They broke in and found him at the bottom of the stairs to the attic. He'd died of a heart attack."

"I'm sorry, I shouldn't have asked," I said, noticing her eyes blinking rapidly as if she might cry.

"It's fine." She waved her hand. "I hope I'm not unsettling you?"

"No, no, no," I assured her, laughing loudly for far too long.

"He died intestate," she said, once I'd calmed down. "His possessions were sold off and the house put on the market. All the money went to the state, I suppose."

"How sad that he died that way," I said.

"We were very upset, although we didn't know him," she said. "We were the only people who attended his funeral. We had his ashes buried in the churchyard at St. Pauls down by the cricket club. We even commissioned a little plaque in remembrance and I sometimes put flowers on it, when I have the time."

"How thoughtful of you." I smiled. "I'd love to visit his remembrance plaque and put some flowers on it myself."

"You'll find it at the back of the churchyard," she

instructed. "His full name was Anthony Archer."

I felt my jaw drop as I remembered the name from the house purchase. I just hadn't joined the dots since.

"Anyhow, I've got to go." She got up to leave. "I've got a Zumba class in fifteen minutes. Why don't you come one day?"

"Thanks," I said. "Not my thing."

Her laugh faded as she realised I was serious.

"We're having pre-Christmas drinks on Saturday. I'd love for you to come," she said, smiling. "It will be a chance for me to introduce you to everyone. Bring your husband too."

First Draft

Lydia and Hubert sat in the open-topped carriage, as Alfred drove the two smart grey carriage horses around Richmond Park.

"He's an excellent groom and driver," Hubert remarked, pointing his whip at Alfred. "Such lovely posture too."

"He has a knack for horses," Lydia said. "He and his father have worked for us since he was a lad. I don't know what we'd do without them."

"You should never be completely reliant on servants. They take advantage," Hubert said.

"Alfred would never dream of taking advantage," Lydia said.

"I suppose he's married to a pretty milkmaid?" Hubert asked.

"Absolutely not!" Lydia replied.

Hubert leaned over, looking into her face.

"We must change that at once," he said. "He must have a tidy little woman to take care of his needs."

"I doubt Alfred needs our help to find himself a wife, if that's what he wants," she murmured.

"Surely, that's what every man wants?" Hubert

said, his eyes crinkling with laughter.

Lydia removed a glove and held it tightly between her hands.

"You seem agitated?" Hubert said.

"I am just finding the day quite warm," she said, fanning herself with the glove.

Things hadn't been the same between Lydia and her father since that eventful day in London. A bright fire burnt in the hearth of the parlour as father and daughter ate their meal in silence.

"How was your outing with Hubert?" her father asked at last.

"It was puzzling," she replied.

"Indeed. In what way?" he queried.

"He seemed very interested in our servants," she said, tilting her head to one side. "I'm wondering why?"

"It may be, unintentionally, he let the cat out of the bag," her father replied mysteriously.

"Now you, too, are puzzling me, Father." She frowned.

"Hubert, John Archer has asked for your hand in marriage, my dear," he said, rubbing his hand together.

"Oh!" she said, looking down at her own clasped hands.

"And I have happily agreed," he said, his eyes lighting up. "You are to have a Spring wedding."

"Don't I get a say?" she asked.

He looked surprised. "I thought I'd made things abundantly clear after your disgraceful behaviour. It's for your own good. You'll not find a finer man."

"But I don't want to marry him," she said, her hands clasping and unclasping. "I don't love him."

"Your mother and I were not in love when we got

married," he said, swirling his glass of port. "Our parents arranged it all before we even met each other."

"Father, if you have any affection for me, please do not do this. I cannot marry someone I don't love," she insisted.

"You'll learn to love him. It takes time, that's all," he said reasonably. "Your mother, sweet Iris, became my rock and I hers. I thanked God every day for giving me such a capable, devoted woman. When she died I thought my heart would break. She made me promise to take care of you, so I had to find a way to carry on."

"I wonder if she was here if she would want me to marry a man that I can't even tolerate?" Lydia said.

"Your mother would trust the judgement of her husband," he said. "There would be no debate."

"I beg you to at least give me more time," she said. "What is the hurry? I am still a young woman."

"I don't burden you with business worries. Indeed, I don't expect you to have any knowledge of how I provide our excellent standard of living." He shook his head, draining his glass. "There's something you need to know. I was recommended to make several large investments by a close friend at my club. Unfortunately, they haven't worked out the way I planned. You might say our fortune is depleted to the point that we may not make a decent recovery."

Lydia's hand shot to her throat. "What are you saying, Father?"

"I am telling you that marrying Hubert is our only option," he said. "He's agreed to loan me a considerable amount of money to get me out of a hole."

"In return for me?" she asked, tears springing to her eyes.

"I have no choice," he muttered into his glass. "I desperately need the money."

"So you've offered me to him?" she said, twisting a napkin between her fingers. "Like selling your favourite mare?"

"Come come, my dear, it's not that bad," he said, draining his glass and refilling it. "He's not a bad chap. He doesn't gamble or drink too much. You can make a perfectly good life with him and never have to worry about money ever again."

"I would rather live in a broken down cottage with a husband I love than live in a gilded palace with Hubert," she sobbed.

He offered her his handkerchief. "My dear, you don't know what you are talking about."

Lydia arrived at the stable, flapping the rain from her cloak as Alfred fed one of the horses.

"Lydia!" he exclaimed. "What are you doing here? You shouldn't be out on your own."

"I had to come," she said. "Father left for his bridge night and I crept out."

Alfred threw her a clean cloth to wipe the rain from her face, not knowing that the moisture glistening under her eyes had nothing to do with the inclement weather.

"I have something awful and shocking to tell you. I'm to be married to that conceited buffoon, Hubert, whom I could never love or even have any regard for," she said through gritted teeth.

"I thought that would be the case," he said calmly, leaning on the horse's rump.

"Is that all you've got to say?" she asked, looking into his eyes.

"What am I supposed to say?" he replied, taking her hand. "I have always known you would be fixed up with a wealthy gentleman one day. I've known it for the longest time."

She took his face between her hands. "Father is in trouble financially, that's the only reason he wants me to marry. But I'll marry no one but you and I nearly told him so!"

He held her forearms tightly. "I'm not for you. You are a beautiful lady with fine clothes and book learning," he said. "You are bound to marry a gentleman with a castle and footmen. Not a poor stable lad."

"But it's you I love," she said.

He twisted away from her and went to the far end of the stable in the dark. A horse whinnied, feeling the tension between the two people.

"Let us run away tonight," she begged.

He shook his head, turning towards her.

"Run away?" he repeated. "And where are we likely to go? Shall I take you off to some broken down hovel, miles away from here so that no one don't find us?"

He ran a hand through his hair. "How do you think you'd like only having one tatty dress to wear all of the time and going cold and hungry in the winter?"

"I know we would manage," she sobbed. "I could take in needlework and you could look after horses. I know if only we were together, we'd work it out somehow."

"Your father is clearly in some sort of trouble to be asking this of you. And my family," he gulped as he continued. "My parents and my sisters would be thrown out of their cottage and starve or die of cold. All because I ran away with the master's daughter."

"But I can't marry him. I love you, Alfred," she insisted. "Can you honestly say you don't love me?"

"I have to say I don't love you," he said, touching her cheek. "However much it may break my heart and be a terrible lie. I will have to look on while you marry him, knowing, whenever he likes he can hold your hand and kiss your lips. He will have you all to himself."

Lydia sobbed loudly, sinking into his arms. He clung to her, burying his head in her hair. Then he held her at arm's length.

"I'd do anything for you, you know that," he murmured, his face pale and pinched. "But I'd be doing more harm than good if we ran away together. You must go back home and think of me no more, my love."

Alfred closed the stable door, watching Lydia walk away.

Mavis peered out of the hayloft hatch, bits of straw sticking out of her hair.

"So you're letting her go?" she said.

"There's nothing to be done," he said.

He climbed the ladder to the loft and Mavis moved aside, patting the space beside her.

"It's a crying shame," Mavis observed, resting her arm around his shoulders. "Two people who love each other as much as you do should be together. It just don't seem fair to sell Miss Lydia to the highest bidder."

"It's what rich people do," he said. "There's nothing about two folks being in love or even liking each other. It's a bargain between the father and the intended bridegroom and that's the way of the world."

"Perhaps you should run away. There's no saying the master would punish your family for it," Mavis said.

"It wouldn't be proper," he sighed. "Lydia don't

know what it's like to be poor."

"She don't," Mavis agreed. "She's got some spirit though. She's not like other rich women. My friend, who's a maid in a fine house, told me her mistress beats her regularly with a hairbrush. Miss Lydia has never behaved high and mighty. Don't belittle her."

Alfred nodded, resting his head against her shoulder.

"Perhaps we can devise some plan of whisking Lydia far away, without no one landing the suspicion on you," Mavis suggested.

"No," he said. "First and foremost, we need to worry about whisking you away to save you from prison."

"You needn't worry about me," she chortled. "I've taken care of myself since I was thirteen."

I finished writing in the early hours of Saturday morning. I was devastated Lydia's story had taken such a calamitous direction and I dreaded what might come next.

I heard scratching at the door, like a cat trying to get in. I slowly opened it and peered out into pitch blackness. I remembered Anthony Archer dying at the bottom of the stairs and the hairs on the back of my neck stood up. I flicked on the light, stepping out as water soaked into my socks.

CHAPTER FIFTEEN

Destiny

First Draft

Lydia held a finger to her lips as Alfred stepped into her bedroom and closed the door. She listened: the house was silent. The servants had gone home or gone to bed.

"Have you gone completely mad, summoning me to your bed chamber?" Alfred whispered. "I couldn't believe it when Mavis gave me your message."

"Father's gone to Paris with Hubert on business. He won't be back for days," she said, leading him by the arm as he removed his hat.

"Being caught in a lady's bedroom could land me in all manner of trouble," he frowned.

"We won't be caught," she said, reaching up and kissing him on the mouth.

"I haven't seen you since you came to the stable nearly a month ago," he pointed out. "I suppose you've been busy with wedding arranging?"

"Father wouldn't let me leave the house. I asked him to give me more time to get used to the idea of marrying," she sighed. "He argued that I've had my whole life to prepare for the role of wife and mother and there's no point in delaying."

"He's just taking care of you," Alfred said, fiddling with his hat. "Any good father would make sure his daughter was properly provided for."

"It doesn't make it more palatable for me," she said. "My fiancé is still an unbearable, conceited idiot. He told me the other day that his intolerable mother was coming with us on our honeymoon. Can you imagine anything more undesirable?"

She turned and stared out of the window. His face reflected in the glass as he reached his arms around her.

"Do you still think of running away?" he asked, stroking her hair.

"Of course. But we have agreed that we cannot put your family at risk," she replied.

"My family's prospects have suddenly taken a bit of a turn," he smiled. "Two of my sisters are getting married this year and the other one, Elspeth, is taking in laundry and doing surprisingly well. As Dad's health isn't so good, he and Ma are talking about moving down to the coast where her sister lives."

"If you are suggesting we run away before the marriage?" she said, turning to him and resting her hands on his shoulders. "Then I wholeheartedly agree. Any kind of life would be better than being married to Hubert."

"I worry that you'll hate living with poor folk and scratching a living." He held her chin. "It's a hard life. There'll be no big soft bed at night, no nice clothes like you're used to."

"I detest my life," she sighed. "I'd be happy to work and make myself useful rather than sit around drinking tea all day."

He kissed her.

She shrugged off her embroidered gown and it fell to her feet, revealing her naked body. Her glistening hair fell around her shoulders as she removed the pins holding it.

He exhaled noisily. "This is folly!" he said. "I must leave before we are found out."

"You must take what is rightfully yours," she reassured.

"I'd feel better if we were wed first," he said.

"Our love has endured for many years," she said. "Spiritually, we are already man and wife."

"You look like an angel," he said as she led him to the bed.

"Have you been with a woman?" she asked.

"I've loved you all my life, so not much chance of that," he replied.

"Did you ever imagine taking me to bed?"

"I never allowed myself," he replied. "I couldn't bear the heartache."

Lydia unbuttoned his shirt as he lay on his back staring up at the ceiling. He shrugged out of it and turned towards her. He explored every inch of her body with his fingertips and tongue. She stroked his hard muscles, honed from years of manual work. He moved on top of her, his face tense as he eased gently into her. She felt reassuringly engulfed by the weight of his body. His gentle, rhythmic motion excited her in a way she hadn't experienced before. He held onto her, urgently, desperately. His body tensed and then he surrendered to some unknown force and collapsed, breathing heavily.

"I claim you as my wife and nothing will ever change that," he whispered.

"You are my true husband and one day soon we will escape together," she reassured him, stroking his hair. "We'll go far away and they'll never find us."

I'd heard them making love as I tapped away at the keyboard. I didn't peek in the mirror as it seemed voyeuristic. When it quietened I slowly turned. Alfred lay back against a white pillow. His eyes fixed on the bedroom door as if he expected someone to burst in and find him holding his mistress to his breast. His profile was partially hidden in darkness, but I could make out a masculine face, with the gentlest of expressions.

I wished someone would love me with such passion. I tapped a pen against the desk as the image in the mirror faded.

I had no time to dwell. I was invited to a party.

The party was in full swing when I arrived. Angela had not exaggerated: the ground floor of her house was a cavernous, featureless room that opened up onto a perfectly landscaped garden. The bifold doors were partially closed against the December chill, although several guests were already in the hot tub. Steam rose above the bare shoulders and damp heads of the people simmering in the heat.

Angela introduced me to her husband Steve, a tall friendly man with a big beer belly.

"So you're the mysterious, famous author from next door?" he said, taking my hand.

"Not mysterious and not that famous really," I corrected him.

He smiled, holding onto my hand for a second too long.

"Your husband couldn't come, then?" Angela inquired.

"I'm divorced," I answered.

Angela looked shocked as if I'd said I was a paid-up member of the Communist Party.

"We have a few singletons here tonight," Steve condescended. "So you won't feel left out."

"Great!" I said, probably making a hideous face.

"Come with me," he added. "You need a drink."

Lined up neatly on the kitchen island were rows of tall

champagne glasses. I worked my way along each line replacing the empty glass as I went. I chatted with some of the other guests until Steve returned a bit later.

"I love your red frock," he complimented.

"Thank you," I smiled. "It's a vintage fifties dress I picked up some years ago in Kensington Market."

I twirled allowing the full skirt to billow.

"You look like Scarlett O'Hara." He grinned.

I instinctively felt Angela checking us out from the other side of the room.

"Let's get this party started!" I said, dragging him by the sleeve.

An iPod was playing elevator music quietly. I grabbed it and scrolled through until I found what I was looking for.

As I cranked the sound up, 'Stayin' Alive' by the Bee Gees blasted out and I grabbed Steve, dragging him to the middle of the room. I was vaguely aware of people watching.

I whirled, gyrated and danced the 'Funky Chicken'! Steve moved his weight from foot to foot, paralysed with embarrassment. The track finished and a ballad, 'How Deep is Your Love' began. I grabbed Steve, pressing myself against him. He took a deep breath as I pushed my leg between his and felt some stirring and hardening.

I thought it was hilarious. Mr Suburbia was getting an erection, dancing with a poor singleton. I grabbed a handful of his hair and forced his lips onto mine, exploring his mouth with my tongue. He tried to pull away but I held him in a vice-like grip.

The music stopped abruptly. Angela was hovering over the iPod, looking daggers at us, still in a clinch.

"Thanks... for the... dance," Steve stuttered, moving away.

I waved my arms around whooping. Who knew why? Then I lost my balance and fell over a glass-laden coffee table. My dress flew over my head, showing everyone my flesh-coloured, tummy-control knickers as I slammed against the parquet floor.

I must have passed out because the next thing I remember was waking in A&E. I had cut my arms when I fell on the glass and the side of my face stung like hell. My sister sat next to me reading a magazine.

"What the bloody hell am I doing here?" I asked, swinging my legs over the side of the trolley.

"Your neighbours called me," she replied. "You had a nasty fall at their party and they found my number as your 'In Case of Emergency on your phone.'"

"Oh," I exclaimed, remembering the party and my behaviour. "Oh shit!"

"They weren't very nice about you," she said, shaking her head. "They said you were blind drunk when you fell."

"I made a fool of myself," I whispered.

"You snogged someone's husband?" she asked.

"Yep."

"You've been treated for minor cuts," she said. "The nurse was worried about your face, but she's closed the wound with tape and she said it should heal okay."

"That's lucky," I said, touching my face and wincing.

"I suppose I'd better get you home," she sighed. "You'd better stay with us tonight."

Charlie dropped me back at Rosebay House a few days later. I rushed to open the front door, fumbling with the key, not wanting to bump into my neighbours.

"Are you seeing the children over Christmas?" Charlie plonked herself on the sofa.

"I'd like to. Although I haven't heard from Cliff," I replied.

"I can speak to him?" she offered.

"I'd love that," I said, touching the wound on my face which still stung.

"I will speak to him – but only if you agree to come to

an AA meeting with me," she said, her face expressionless, her arms folded.

"There are conditions?" I protested.

"Here's the deal," she said, sitting on the edge of the sofa. "You haven't had a drink for a few days since the party. How do you feel?"

"I feel okay I suppose," I said. "But later I'll feel like shit and alcohol is the only way I'll feel better."

"You've lost your children, made a fool of yourself with your neighbours, and countless other horrible things have happened," she said, not unkindly. "Just because you need a drink?"

She stared, waiting for an answer. I had no answer.

"Please, for your children's sake just give it a try," she begged, tears springing into her eyes. "You know, one day, I'm going to get a call to say you're dead in a ditch somewhere. That's what I dread every time the phone rings."

I felt awful. I had inflicted such pain on her, on my children and myself.

"I will," I said. "I'll come to a meeting with you. I want my children back more than anything in the world."

"Even more than a drink?" she asked.

"Even more," I replied.

CHAPTER SIXTEEN

Ensnared

First Draft

Joseph and Hubert had finalised hasty plans for the wedding when they returned from Paris. The servants at Rosebay House were not included in any of the preparations for the grand affair, held in London. Alfred thought it was probably better that way. He spent the day with the horses, grooming and plaiting manes. Later that night he took his fishing rod and sat by the river, his lantern the only light. He was startled by someone coming up behind him.

"Oh, it's you, Mavis. You frightened me to death," he said as she gathered her skirts and sat beside him. In the dim light, her dark eyes looked huge in her pinched face; she hadn't completely recovered from her incarceration.

"Couldn't sleep, Alfred? Imagining Lydia's wedding night?" she asked.

"The mistress is a married woman now, so I'm not imagining anything of the kind," he muttered miserably.

"Poor Alfred," she said, taking his arm. "You didn't get to run away with Miss Lydia after all?"

"No," he answered, shaking his head. "Her father made sure of it. He returned from Paris and took Lydia off to London to stay with the mother-in-law, while the wedding plans were taking place."

"My poor love," she said, flinging an arm around him.

"Give over," he said, shrugging her off. "What're you doing out so late at night?"

"I've come down in the world," she sighed. "Since I left you and my bed in the stable, I've found it impossible to find work with lodgings. No call for a lady's maid who's a known suffragette and fugitive."

"Lydia offered you money to leave and start somewhere new," he said. "Why didn't you go?"

"I've got a liking for living here," she admitted. "Besides, I can't leave Miss Lydia without knowing her married life will turn out... tolerable."

Alfred snorted and covered his eyes.

"She hates him," he confessed. "He's a prideful, boastful bag of wind. He cares nothing for her, except as a beautiful ornament to dangle on his arm."

"You said yourself, that's the way of rich folk. But I won't leave until I'm sure she's sound," Mavis said. "I'm working at the mill; it's a hard slog. No one knows my real name or cares, and I have a little pallet to sleep on in the corner by the sacks of flour."

"You be careful." Alfred patted her hand. "You can't afford to get into any trouble, especially with the law. And don't you worry, I'll keep a close eye on Miss Lydia."

"Of that, I have no doubt," she laughed.

"You shouldn't be out late at night on the towpath," he said. "There's all manner of undesirables lurking hereabouts."

"I can't live on the little bit of money from the mill," she laughed again.

"You mean you're a lady of the night?" Alfred stared into her face.

"Yeah. Have you got some change in your pockets?" she said, hitching her skirts to show her naked thigh. "Do you fancy it?"

"Don't be daft," he said, pulling her dress down.

"Am I not high and mighty enough for you, Alfred?" she teased.

"You can't get much lower than me tonight," he said.

"Let's sit here together and hope for better times."

The newly married couple returned to Rosebay House for a couple of days to prepare for their journey to Northumberland and Tullerton Hall.

"The church service was very moving," Hubert mentioned to his father-in-law for the tenth time, sitting at lunch in the emerald green dining room. "And the wedding breakfast! Mother must have invited at least three hundred of her closest friends."

"It was a splendid occasion," Joseph said. "The bride was so beautiful. She looked just like her mother."

Lydia did not look up from her food.

"Are you feeling quite all right my dear?" Joseph asked, holding her long fingers.

"I'm fine, Father," she murmured.

"She's overawed," Hubert smirked. "Being the wife of a high-ranking man is daunting when you've only known a sleepy hamlet outside of London."

Joseph raised his eyebrows as Lydia glared at Hubert.

"I have been the daughter of a high-ranking man," she said, her blue eyes staring into the distance.

"Indeed you have," Hubert agreed. "Please don't imagine I meant any slight. I'm only concerned that you don't unduly worry about your new status in life."

"I'm sure Hubert has your best interests at heart," Joseph said. "Your girlhood is over and you're a wife with responsibilities. That's all he was implying."

Hubert nodded furiously. "And soon you'll be a mother," he said, grinning from ear to ear.

Lydia pushed back her chair with a scrape and stared down at her hands. Not for the first time since her betrothal and marriage, a despondent cloud descended upon her slender shoulders. Her life would consist of Hubert's pointless chatter and organising afternoon tea. She wasn't loved in the way she deserved, by either her husband or her father. Her youth and vigour would waste away, leaving an empty husk and a life not lived. She felt the colour drain from her like she was fading into the background.

"Lydia's got a lot to get used to," Joseph boomed, making her jump. "I was overindulgent because her mother died so young."

"Very understandable," Hubert said wiping his thick lips on a napkin. "She's like a young foal in need of breaking to harness."

Joseph lifted a black eyebrow. "I'm not sure that's the analogy I would have chosen."

"Forgive me, Father," Hubert said. "I meant no offence. I should explain that I have long held rigid views on the fairer sex, having been influenced by a paragon among women. I talk of my mother, clearly a woman of breeding and good taste. I believe all women must embrace their feminine nature and endeavour to be obedient, supportive and obliging towards their husband."

Joseph twirled the ends of his moustache, the frown deepening on his face.

"In addition," Hubert continued, belching quietly. "And particularly what attracted me to your splendid daughter. A woman must maintain an excellent refinement in her dress, manners and etiquette."

"You have put a great deal of consideration into how a wife should behave," Joseph remarked. "I wonder if you have expended as much thought on a husband's duties?"

Hubert fidgeted with his red silk waistcoat. "A husband bears the considerable responsibility of providing a safe, comfortable haven for his spouse to thrive and nurture his offspring."

Lydia was unable to speak as bitter bile arose in her throat.

Joseph steepled his fingers, never taking his eyes from his son-in-law. "And what of respect, love and companionship in a marriage?" Joseph asked. "My marriage was arranged. My dear wife and I hardly knew each other on our wedding day. We were blessed I believe," Joseph held a fist to his lips. "We enjoyed a close, loving partnership that greatly enhanced as the years went by."

Lydia moved closer to her father and he smiled and patted her hand.

"I'm sure Lydia and I aspire to emulate your fine example of matrimony," Hubert said, his eyes downcast as he slathered butter on a bread roll, stuffing half of it into his mouth.

Joseph squeezed Lydia's hand as she managed a weak smile. Hubert made small grunting noises devouring the roll and she cringed.

"I have a fancy to go riding this afternoon, my dear," Hubert said, addressing Lydia as he continued chewing.

"As you are aware, we have a couple of splendid mounts in the stable," Joseph said, brightening up. "I'll get someone to go over and ask for them to be readied."

"Don't worry, Father," Hubert smirked. "I'll take pleasure in going myself."

Hubert excused himself with an exaggerated bow and left the room.

"I believe, in time, Hubert will make a very satisfactory husband," Joseph shrugged, still holding Lydia's hand.

"The deed is done. You wanted me to marry him and I have obeyed," Lydia said. "It cannot be undone."

"If there were any another way, you know I would have—." He stuttered, pursing his lips.

"Don't fret," she assured. "I would not be responsible for bringing us down in the world, that would be unforgivable. I know you have my best interests at heart."

"Your mother was taken from us so quickly," he whispered. "I've always worried that something would happen to me and you'd be left destitute and alone in the world."

"It's too late for regrets," Lydia murmured. "I am Mrs Archer. Wife to a rich man who may one day become a Member of Parliament or even a Lord. I'll want for nothing. I'll have the finest clothes and my children will be educated with England's nobility."

"I wanted you to have an affectionate, loving marriage," he frowned, a deep line between his eyes. "I fear I have ensnared you with a man who is a thoughtless, puffed-up popinjay."

Lydia shrugged. "He's my husband, 'til death do us

part. You needn't fear. I will make some kind of a life for myself, despite Hubert."

"You'll never want for money, that much is certain," he nodded, patting her hand.

Alfred hammered a stake into the ground as Hubert strolled into the yard.

He straightened up, feeling a droplet of sweat coursing down his bare chest.

"That must be hard work," Hubert said, licking his lips.

"It's just my job," Alfred replied, hastily pulling his shirt over his head.

"Why have you not been to see my new wife?" Hubert remarked.

"My duties don't take me up to the house," Alfred mumbled, walking away.

"I know you'd love to see her," Hubert grinned. "And congratulate her on our marriage."

Alfred stopped and turned. "I wish you and Mrs Archer all the best," he said, and went into the stables.

Hubert came up close behind him. "I hope very much that you'll stay on as our coachman. I know how good you are with the horses and Mrs Archer would like that too."

"That's very kind of you, sir," Alfred said, forking hay.

"I have very much enjoyed sitting behind you in the carriage, watching you drive the horses on our outings to the park," Hubert said. "I anticipate there will be journeys in the future that I may need to make, without my wife by my side. Times when you and I will take trips on our own. I very much look forward to getting to know you better."

Hubert moved closer. Alfred stopped what he was doing but didn't look up from his task.

"On our wedding night, you were very much in my mind," he hissed close to Alfred's ear. "Despite my wife's obvious beauty, somehow my thoughts wandered back to you."

Alfred turned, staring at his master's flushed face and bright eyes.

"A man of my rank needs sons, you see," Hubert explained. "Lydia will fulfil that need, but I have other needs."

Alfred took a step back.

"Remember, the stables and the house will one day be mine. Lydia? She's already mine. You could have a good life here and admire Lydia from afar, but nothing comes for free." Hubert smiled, turned on his heel and whistled as he went.

CHAPTER SEVENTEEN

The Reckoning

Charlie and I arrived at a modern, chic office block on a busy high street. It was nothing like what I thought an Alcoholics Anonymous meeting would be. I imagined it held in a run-down, draughty church hall or community centre with down and outs lingering about outside.

The chairperson opened the session, explaining the format and what to do if the fire alarm sounded. I already had alarm bells going off in my head, but Charlie was beside me, calm and reassuring. The chairperson asked if anyone would like to speak and a young woman of nineteen or twenty stood up. She wore a shapeless cardigan that hung off her thin frame, her hair lank around a gaunt face.

"I'm Sandra and I think I'm an alcoholic," she began, pulling at a thread on her cardie. "I used to think I was fun and outgoing. But I realise that I'm only like that when I've had a drink. I need a nip of brandy in my coffee, to get me going in the morning and several glasses of wine at lunchtime and again in the evening."

Everyone in the room hung on her every word; you could have heard a pin drop.

"I recently got fired for being drunk," she continued, her bottom lip quivering. "I was an estate agent and I loved my job. The problem is, without a drink I can't face people, or imagine they will like me." She smiled at an older woman sitting next to her. "I came here today because I don't want to live like this. I realise something's got to change." She dabbed her eyes with a tissue as she sat back down.

A man stood and scanned the room. His face was strong and angular with high cheekbones and slightly slanted, deep-set eyes. I had seen him somewhere before but couldn't think where.

"I'm sure I'm an alcoholic," he said with a natural, engaging smile. "I'm Mark. I've drunk all my adult life and destroyed everything good or worthwhile. I may look familiar and that's because I used to be a famous TV presenter."

I recalled where I'd seen him. He had been a good-looking, entertaining young man on morning television, several years ago.

"Most of the time, I was drunk, live on air," he admitted. "They tried to straighten me out, but in the end, I was just an embarrassment."

He looked much older, his features dominated by a haunted look.

"At one point I lived in my car under an underpass," he said, running his hand through thick, dark hair. "I'm lucky. My brother routinely fishes me out of any shit-hole I've landed in. He dragged me along to this meeting today. I've attempted sobriety many times before and failed. This time I can't afford to fail. I've reached rock bottom and the only way is up."

Many people stood and spoke that day. Their stories all had one thing in common: losing control to alcoholism.

Charlie smiled as the meeting wrapped up. "Well done!"

"I haven't done anything," I moaned. "I'm not ready to wash my dirty laundry in front of a room of strangers."

"You came and that's a big step," she insisted.

We crowded around an ancient coffee machine and I carelessly elbowed someone, turning to apologise.

"What are you, a shot putter?" Mark complained, rubbing his arm.

"I'm so sorry," I said.

"No matter," he said. "I didn't see either of you ladies

spilling the beans."

"Not ready to spill yet," I joked. "Hi. I'm Moira and this is my sister, Charlie."

He nodded. "I've never stood up and spoken before today. This time it felt different for me. How about you, Moira?"

"This is my first meeting," I said, wondering how he knew I was the alcoholic. "I have to stop drinking to see my kids again."

"Ahh," he smiled. "That boat has sailed for me. I have a teenage son who'll have nothing to do with me. I don't blame him."

"I'm sorry," I said. "So what's next?"

"They encourage the alcoholic to attend the closed meetings. I've never made it that far." He narrowed his eyes. "But this time I might, if you'll come with me?"

I turned to Charlie, who nodded excitedly. "Do we go on our own?" I asked.

"Sober folk need not attend," he joked.

Charlie and I spent the next day clearing the house of alcohol, as instructed in my AA Starter Pack. Without the booze to sustain me, I felt fidgety, uncomfortable and without focus. In addition, trying to sleep sober was almost impossible. I'd toss and turn, eventually getting up and climbing the soggy stairs to my garret.

A heavy despondency hung over me, like a storm cloud hovering just above my head. I began the next chapter.

First Draft

"Alfred!" Lydia called from the riverbank, watching Alfred carefully negotiate the wobbly, wooden jetty. The water cascaded and swirled around the structure.

He held her hands as he leapt onto the shore. "You made it," he said. "I wasn't sure if the maid would get the note to you without your husband seeing it."

"He's gone to London for the day," she explained. "Thank God. I couldn't wait for him to go."

"Did he hurt you?" Alfred asked.

"He's not a violent man," she replied. "But I despise him, the way he speaks, whenever he touches me. Marriage is not anything like I imagined."

Alfred rubbed her cold hands. "Let's walk," he suggested. "We don't want folk to see us."

They wandered through the woods towards the racecourse.

"I know it unsettles you when I talk about him," Lydia said, sitting on a bench. "But I need to warn you, he's an ungodly man. His tastes are extraordinary."

"He has a strange way about him," Alfred agreed.

"He talks about you all the time. Your fine deportment, your strong but gentle way with the horses," she said, frowning.

"I've heard of men like him," Alfred sighed. "They have no appetite for women."

"You've hit the nail on the head," she exclaimed, throwing her arms wide. "He's utterly indifferent to me. He treats me like a well-bred horse or favourite dog. It's quite demeaning."

"Why don't you talk to your father?" Alfred suggested.

"I tried," she said. "I believe Father regrets arranging the marriage so quickly, now he knows Hubert a little better. He had good intentions, but he can see how unhappy I am. He stays at his club, unable to face the truth."

"I thought you'd live in London or at your husband's northern family home," Alfred said.

"He insists on living here," she shrugged. "I'm not sure what draws him to such a provincial little town."

Alfred kicked a stone with his foot.

"Has he been to see you about your position?" she asked.

Alfred nodded, pushing gravel around with the toe of his boot.

"You will stay on?" she said, grabbing his arm.

"I will watch over you," he said. "And if the man causes you any harm, God help him."

As I chewed my nails slumped in the garret, the next instalment of the novel seemed out of reach, like trying to recall a vivid dream when waking. I stared for hours at the screen, devoid of inspiration. Every part of my body hurt. I wasn't sure if it was exhaustion or the worrying turn of events for Lydia.

The builder had been to inspect the damp, rolling back the carpet to reveal wooden steps.

As I clip-clopped down, sobbing came from the room. I returned and closed the door to reveal the mirror. Lydia was sitting on the floor, her slender, white hands hiding her beautiful face. I reached out and touched the mirror, but the image faded and disappeared.

When I got downstairs, Charlie had left shopping for me. My Starter Pack also suggested regular, healthy eating and I was very proud, as I switched the oven on, to have made macaroni cheese from scratch.

A thud emanated from the dining room. When I investigated, I found the door of the old sideboard wide open, assisted, no doubt, by an invisible hand. I looked around the dim room, biting my lip and scratching my head.

"There's something here I need to see," I said, to no one in particular.

Inside the cupboard were a few old newspaper cuttings.

One showed a photo of the Edwardian wooden jetty (these days replaced by a modern metal version), poking out into the deep channel of the river for the pleasure boats to moor. Three men had been seen behaving in an inebriated manner at the end of the jetty after a night out. All three had fallen into the water and perished. Their bodies had washed up, miles downstream, entwined around each other.

Another was the announcement of Mr Hubert, John Archer and Miss Lydia Turner's marriage. There was also Lydia's small Bible, her name neatly written on the fly paper and a card announcing the christening of Hubert, John Archer in April 1915.

CHAPTER EIGHTEEN

Christmas Time

I met Mark the following week outside the same brightly lit, modern office building for our first 'closed' AA meeting. As he strolled towards me, it was hard to believe a well-built, healthy chap like him was an alcoholic. On closer inspection, his restless eyes and the way he nervously scratched his arms as he spoke, revealed his addiction.

If the first meeting had been a mixture of people, the 'closed' meeting was even more extraordinary. Old and young attended from every walk of life.

Mark stood up and spoke again. This time he elaborated on the pain he'd caused his family and by the time he sat down, his face was wet from crying and so was mine.

Talking to people after the meeting, I realised I wasn't alone. Many other people struggled with this pernicious addiction and the mayhem it brought.

I spent Christmas Day with my sister and her family. She offered to make it a 'dry' Christmas for my sake, but I insisted that they carried on just the same. I wouldn't even risk a glass of bubbly with my Christmas dinner, knowing I wouldn't be capable of stopping there. It wasn't easy, but I was determined to stay sober. Cliff was allowing the children to visit my sister's house on Boxing Day.

I awoke early and excited on Boxing Day. I helped Charlie prepare the meal, making salads and cutting bread. These were ordinary tasks that I hadn't managed for years, having usually been hungover in bed at this time of the morning.

I watched from behind the curtains as the car drew up. The children hugged Debbie before walking towards the house with their father. I felt a twang of jealousy as the children shuffled into the room, their eyes downcast.

"Rosanna, Jackson. Happy Christmas," I said, trying not to be emotional. "Happy Christmas, Cliff."

His eyes lit up. "Happy Christmas, Moira. I'm pleased to see you looking so well."

The children looked at us in turn. They'd probably never heard us say a nice word to each other.

After greeting my sister and her family, Cliff squeezed my arm and left. I was on Cloud Nine. I was sober and trusted to spend time with my beloved children.

I returned home the next day, exhausted but still sober. Not having a drink in my hand, desperate for that rush of excitement to course through my veins, had made me feel incredibly empty and inadequate.

Mark and I had made a pact. If either of us felt we were losing control we would phone the other for moral support. I called him and he picked up the phone at once.

"Oh, thank God," he said.

"I know," I replied. "Being sober at Christmas is bloody stressful."

His laugh was deep and melodic. "I've drank so many fizzy drinks, I'm sure all my teeth will fall out!" he exclaimed.

"I hope not," I said, visualising his warm smile. "Will this feeling pass of being here, but not being here?"

"That's a great description; no wonder you're an author," he replied. "I wish I had an answer. This is all new territory for me too."

"What are your plans for the next few days?" I asked.

"I've got a part-time job," he replied. "In a garden centre near you. I wanted to pay my way with my brother and eventually get my own place. So I thought getting a job was the first step."

"Wow, well done," I said, genuinely pleased for him.

I heard a motorbike outside the house followed by a bang on the door.

"Sorry Mark, I've got to go," I said, rushing to the door.

"Oh, all right then."

My heart sank. He sounded disappointed.

Freddie leant against the wall, a bottle of wine in his hand.

"What do you want?" I demanded.

"Darling, I miss you." He held his hands up, surrendering.

"I thought you had your schoolgirl to keep you company," I sniped.

"Tsk, she's nothing compared to you." He shook his head. "I dumped her."

"So you come running back to me?" I exclaimed.

"She wouldn't leave me alone." His mouth turned down at the corners. "I made a mistake. I should've told her I wasn't interested."

"You didn't look like you were putting up much of a struggle when I last saw you," I said.

"Please," he begged. "Can I come in? I need to talk to you."

"You may come in for a bit, but the bottle needs to stay outside," I replied.

He looked confused.

"You should've brought flowers. I'm on the wagon," I explained.

Freddie followed me through the dining room into the kitchen. The dining room was half papered in a very expensive, shiny emerald green wallpaper I'd found on the internet.

"You're getting on with the old place," he commented.

"I am. And I'm two weeks sober," I smiled.

"That's just great, babe. You should be proud of

yourself," he said.

"I have to get my kids back," I sighed.

"Yeah," he agreed, looking at his phone.

"How's work?" I asked.

"I have to be honest, it's a bit lean at the moment," he replied.

"I wondered why you were visiting," I said.

"How can you say that?" he cried, waving his arms around. "We've been together a few years. Doesn't that mean anything?"

I laughed callously at his hurt expression.

"In those three years you've had other women, gone missing for days without explanation and you've never once said you love me," I crossed my arms.

"I do love you," he pouted.

I couldn't breathe; my heart pounded against my chest. I couldn't stop the smile from spreading across my face as I lifted my eyes to him.

I loved him, that was my problem.

My sensible, rational brain didn't get it. But my heart longed for him, whatever he did.

"It would have to be different this time," I heard myself saying.

"Whatever you say," he agreed, wrapping his arms around me.

It felt farm animal-like and slightly disgusting, making love sober. Afterwards, I laid my head against his chest listening to him breathe, already questioning why I'd decided to sleep with him.

I awoke much later in the darkness as he plonked himself on the bed next to me.

"What's going on?" I asked, rubbing my eyes.

"What the fuck was that?" he whispered.

I sat up, my hair falling into my eyes and switched on the lamp.

He stared wildly around the room, the colour drained from his face.

"What was what?" I asked.

"There's a woman out there," he gasped.

"Out where?" I asked.

"There's a woman on the stairs," he replied, his expression changing from confusion to fear and back again.

"What did she look like?" I asked.

His dark, troubled eyes looked into mine. "Why are you asking me that?"

I ran my hand through my hair. "I know who she is."

I led him up the wet stairs to my studio. I pulled him inside and closed the door.

"I've seen her," I said, pointing at the tarnished mirror. "She appears in the mirror and sometimes she looks over my shoulder and is reflected in the screen."

He tilted his head to one side, scrutinising me.

"You saw her too," I said. "You saw her in the photograph."

"No, it's impossible," he said.

"How can it be impossible?" I argued. "You saw her tonight."

"I saw something," he mumbled, grabbing the edge of the desk.

"What did she look like?" I asked.

"I didn't see her face. She was crouched on the stairs wearing a long gown, hair hanging down her back," he replied.

"What colour was her hair?" I persisted.

"It was dirty, very dirty and wet," he said, scratching his head.

"You may have seen Lydia." I clapped my hands.

"Who the hell is Lydia?" he asked.

"She lived here a long time ago," I said. "I felt her presence the minute I moved in. My novel is kinda being written by her."

He smirked. "You've got a ghostwriter?"

"Don't be a smart-arse," I said.

"Sorry." He held me by the arms. "But you've got to agree, it's all a bit far-fetched. Have you seen this Lydia when you've been sober?"

I wriggled free of him and plonked myself on the sofa.

"It's not some drunken hallucination," I said.

"Then what is it?" he asked, kneeling in front of me.

"It's Lydia," I replied. "She lived in Edwardian times and she wants me to tell her story."

"Ghosts don't exist, darling," he chortled. "And they certainly don't write novels."

"How do you explain what you saw on the stairs?" I said.

"I smoked weed earlier," he admitted.

"And the photo you took of the woman in the big hat?" I asked.

"A trick of the light – you said so yourself," he remembered. "Let's go back to bed."

CHAPTER NINETEEN

Jeopardy

Freddie was appointed as the photographer at a high-brow fashion show on my recommendation. I caught a glimpse of myself as I strode past a mirror in an art gallery near Bond Street, where the event was taking place. I looked fat and middle-aged in the gold, sheath-like dress I had decided at the last minute to wear. I suppose after years of boozing and no exercise that's all I could expect. I berated myself for being too lazy to run up the stairs and check my appearance in the mirror before I left home.

A glass of champagne was swiftly offered to me, by a handsome young waiter in tight black trousers. I declined and headed for a seat at the back.

Freddie postured and pranced, getting his shots of skinny, half-emaciated girls strutting along the runway. He had it down to a fine art: shaking his dark curly hair to catch the light and performing the perfect lunge or squat whilst aiming the camera. I noticed the women in the audience watching him, rather than the models.

The end of the show couldn't come quickly enough for me. The audience gave the designer (a middle-aged woman, dressed appallingly) a standing ovation and we were, thankfully, herded into another room. Freddie was nowhere to be seen, so I hung around pretending to be interested in the ghastly modern art hanging on the white walls. I scanned the chattering crowd. The models had joined the melee and towered over everyone, refusing the finger food they were offered. I waved and smiled at acquaintances, hoping I wouldn't be asked to join them.

A blast of laughter, like a sonic boom, came from a group of young people quite close to me. They were doubled over in fits of laughter, obviously finding hilarity in the ostentatious company they were in. Standing slightly back from the mirth, I noticed a young woman with long brown hair in a tight, black dress that showed off her beautiful young body.

Freddie suddenly appeared beside me. "Okay darling, are you having a good time?"

"Why is your cheap little tart here?" I asked, sucking my middle-aged stomach in.

"I don't know," he answered, scratching his head, looking her up and down. "She must've got an invite from someone."

Zara noticed us staring and had the temerity to give us a cheery wave.

"Why haven't you got a drink?" he said, gulping and turning his back on her.

"Did you invite her?" I asked.

He clenched his hands together, the knuckles white.

"Don't break my balls, babe," he cried. "Would I be stupid enough to invite you and her to the same show?"

"It would be a stupid thing to do," I agreed. "It's just a bit of a coincidence, her being here."

"I might have let slip about the fashion house inviting students to these things," he conceded, knitting his brows tightly together.

"Was that how you got her into bed?" I asked.

"That's uncalled for," he replied, his hands on his hips. "I've apologised. If that's not good enough, I don't know what else to do."

"Perhaps if you hadn't slept with her in the first place?" I said.

"You know what?" he sighed. "If you're going to be on

my case all the time, then maybe we should call it a day?"

His words penetrated like icy glass shards and he turned to go.

"Don't leave me," I whimpered, grabbing his arm. "I'm sorry. I can't help feeling jealous."

He grinned triumphantly and put his arm around my shoulders.

"Now where's that waiter?" He scanned the room.

"There's only booze and although I could do with a drink I'm not going to have one," I gritted my teeth.

"I'll get you some water," he said.

I hadn't realised how utterly tedious these events were, because I'd always turned up pissed. Overdressed, botoxed people jabbering on about which Caribbean island was their favourite and how difficult it was to work out the French taxes on their chateau.

Freddie and I were in a semi-circle group of people when a waiter carrying a tray of champagne approached. Freddie wagged his finger at me. It was the kind of gesture you'd use to discipline a disobedient dog.

I grabbed two glasses, as Freddie continued to chat enjoyably with one of the models. She towered over him, her eyes huge in an emaciated face.

"This is Moira," he announced, waving his hand in my direction. "She's a famous author."

The stick insect offered a long bony hand, which I brushed quickly away with my fingers. I held the first glass up to Freddie's face and flung my head back, swallowing the whole lot. I choked as the bubbles hit my throat. I laughed as the stick insect frowned and moved away.

I held up the second glass, grinning.

"Don't," he murmured as I repeated the procedure, again choking and giggling.

A feeling of well-being washed over me. It made perfect

sense. I didn't have to give up drinking completely. I could drink at social events that didn't include my family and abstain at all other times. I was convinced it would work and felt very pleased with myself.

I paid for an expensive taxi home and threw up on the doorstep and all down my dress. I gave Freddie the door key.

Once inside, I collapsed on the sofa.

"I hope Zara doesn't press charges, for your sake," he told me, hovering at the door.

"Fucking bitch," I bawled, making my head explode.

"She only came over to say hello," he sighed, lighting a joint. "You had no reason to hit her."

"She said I had a lovely dress," I wailed, wiping my soiled dress with a tissue.

"That's nice, isn't it?" he asked.

"I look fucking awful," I screamed. "She was taking the piss!"

He took a deep inhale. "I just don't get you."

I leapt to my feet, screaming in his face. "No, you don't fucking get me."

He threw his hands up in the air and left. I buried my head in the sofa and screamed for a very long time.

I awoke the next day with the most terrible hangover ever. I held my head in my hands as a serrated knife felt like it was being thrust into my head. I even vomited the sips of water I attempted to swallow.

I struggled out of the disgusting dress and threw it in the bin, putting on my comfy dressing gown. My phone showed three missed calls from Mark. I thought I couldn't feel much worse, but knowing I'd let him down made me feel overwhelmingly guilty.

My phone vibrated; it was Mark again.

"Hi," I croaked.

"Moira, sorry to keep ringing, it's just that – are you all right?" he asked.

"Huh?" I replied.

"What's wrong?"

"I'm so stupid."

I recounted the whole sorry story between snotty sobs.

I managed to wash my face and brush my teeth before Mark arrived. If I looked a mess it didn't show on his face.

He hugged me and made some tea, which I sipped, still unsure if my stomach would hold onto its contents.

"I'm so sorry," I said, holding my head.

"Why are you saying sorry to me?" he asked.

"I promised you," I muttered.

"I forgive you," he smiled. "But don't do it again."

"I wish I could promise not to drink again and mean it," I pressed my lips together. "I'm weak. I just caved in."

"You must be prepared to fail," he said, stroking my hair. "I have plenty of times. But the secret is to keep trying and hopefully one day we'll succeed."

"I wish I felt as confident," I said.

"Who is this Freddie character? He doesn't sound like the sort of person you should be hanging around at the moment," he said.

"He's…" I hesitated. "I suppose he's my boyfriend."

"Oh." Mark's eyebrows shot up as he put his tea down. "I thought you said you were single?"

"I was," I mumbled, wiping the back of my hand across my eyes. "He came back and we talked about making a go of it. I'm not so sure now."

"The thing is—" He leaned forward. "If you are involved with someone who is such a bad influence…"

He frowned and appeared to be miles away.

"What of it?" I asked.

"It complicates everything for you and me," he said. "It sounds selfish, but I can't be around you if you are likely to go off and get pissed with this bloke."

"I understand," I nodded. "But, not only was I horribly

pissed, but I also punched Freddie's little tart and sent her flying. I was escorted out of the venue by security. I doubt if I'll hear from him again. He couldn't be more ashamed of me."

CHAPTER TWENTY

Accused

I jumped at the chance of looking after the kids, but I was only granted a couple of hours while Cliff and Debbie went shopping in the London sales.

The dining room was finished and looked splendid. I had bought an expensive chandelier which had taken the builder ages to hang. The emerald green walls shimmered in the refracted light. The twins gawped at the sight.

I had prepared a special lunch of all the things I knew they liked. Sausages on sticks, miniature scotch eggs, cupcakes and trifle.

"Come on," I said. "Special lunch today."

The large new dining room chairs engulfed them.

"Rosanna is vegetarian," Jackson said.

"Since when?" I said.

"Debbie explained that animals are sent to a place called an abba, abba…" Rosanna stuttered.

"Abattoir," I corrected.

"An abattoir," she repeated. "And then men come along and kill them."

"Yes, that's true," I confirmed. "But they've had a nice life if you believe what you see on *Countryfile*."

"I don't want to eat dead things," she said, her bottom lip quivering.

"All right then," I murmured, wondering what vegetable-based food I could offer at such short notice.

After lunch, we played Monopoly for a pleasant few

hours and then the children began painstakingly to put the pieces of a jigsaw together. The large dining room window rattled as the north wind howled and the rain poured. It felt homely and safe in Rosebay House.

My craving for a drink had been growing stronger and stronger all afternoon. I was becoming desperate. So I left the kids and went and sat on the stairs with my phone.

"Moira, it's so nice to hear from you. I thought you had your kids today?" Mark said.

"I do," I whispered. "I'm sober, but I am struggling to keep off the booze and I can't mess up with the kids again."

"Is there any booze in the house?"

"No."

"Do you want me to come over?"

"You'd better not. My ex gets twitchy about me having men friends when the kids are here."

"Think how much you've been looking forward to seeing your kids," he reminded.

"I have," I agreed.

"What do you want, your kids or a drink?"

"I want my kids," I said.

"Sorry I didn't catch that," he said.

"I want my kids," I confirmed.

The children were looking out of the window when I returned to the dining room. The January day hadn't brightened up and the garden was already in darkness.

"Has it stopped raining?" I asked.

"No," Jackson replied with his back to me.

"What's going on out there?" I said, forcing pieces of the blue jigsaw into the incomplete sky.

"It's melted-face man," Rosanna said calmly.

My head snapped up. "You what?"

"It's melted-face man," they spoke in unison as they turned towards me, their eyes open wide.

I looked over their heads as rain pelted down, bouncing

off the paving stones.

"I can't see anyone," I said, ushering them back to the table.

"He's looking for someone," Jackson said.

"Who?" I asked.

"A lady," they chanted.

"Is this something you've imagined or read in a story?" I asked, but they shook their heads.

"But there's no one out there," I said.

They shrugged.

"Is melted-face man nice or nasty?" I asked, playing along.

"We were frightened the first time we saw him," Rosanna said, winding her light hair around her finger. "But now we think he's a nice man."

"He's a sad man," Jackson corrected.

"Why is he sad?" I asked.

"He lost someone and now he can't find her," Jackson added.

"And why do you call him melted-face man?" I asked.

"Because his face is all melted, silly!" Rosanna replied.

We returned to the puzzle. My need for a drink did not diminish, but neither did I give in to it. I drank several cups of green tea and concentrated on completing the damn puzzle.

When their father arrived, the children dashed to the door, like they hadn't seen him for years. Debbie stayed in the car, as usual.

"We saw melted-face man," Rosanna said as Cliff stepped inside.

"Oh no, not again. What's been going on?" he demanded.

"Nothing," I said. "It's something they've made up."

He turned to the kids. "Did Mum stay with you the whole time?" They nodded. "Did Mum have a friend around?"

They shook their heads.

"See," I said. "It's something they've made up."

He barged past me and went into the living room, the dining room and then the kitchen. He banged doors as he searched through the cupboards.

"I promise you I haven't been drinking," I pleaded. "Come and smell my breath if you don't believe me."

He strode towards me and put his face close to mine. I felt his warm breath as he exhaled. He straightened up to his full height looking down at me.

"Now do you believe me?" I said, shrugging.

He nodded, not taking his eyes off me. Then he did something very strange. He pushed a lock of my hair behind my ear, his hand lingering on my shoulder.

"Hmph," he cleared his throat. "I'd better get going."

He called the children as he walked away.

First Draft

Lydia and Hubert descended the stone stairs of a grand house. They'd been invited for dinner and stayed late. Albert stood by the carriage as Hubert staggered towards him.

"May I?" Alfred offered Hubert his arm.

"Yes you may," Hubert replied, grabbing the offered arm.

Alfred helped him into the carriage and turned to assist Lydia.

"We could have stayed the night," she said as she mounted the steps of the carriage. "It would have been so much better. Alfred's waited for hours and now we've got a six-mile drive along the river road in the dark."

"I wanted to sleep in my own bed," Hubert slurred.

The carriage swayed as the horses broke into a trot along the dark road. Alfred peered behind. Lydia sat as far away from her husband as the narrow seat would allow, her cloak wrapped tightly around her.

The lantern on the carriage swung violently, creating crazy shadows, and Alfred carefully avoided potholes. A broken axle was the last thing they needed on this quiet road.

"Stop here," Hubert demanded as they entered a black tunnel formed by the overhang of ancient trees.

Alfred brought the horses to a halt and jumped down.

"Everything all right, sir?" he asked.

Hubert pulled Lydia roughly towards him. He threw back her cloak, revealing the pale lilac evening dress underneath. The dress was low cut with cream gauze covering her cleavage. Hubert gripped the gauze between his hands as Lydia kicked and scratched at him.

"My wife has beautiful breasts." Hubert smirked as the material ripped. He leered at Alfred as his hand plunged down the front of her dress, squeezing her breasts.

Alfred spun around, grasping his right fist in his left hand.

"Get off me, you beast," Lydia cried.

"You're my wife. I can do exactly what I want with you," Hubert boasted. "Isn't that right, driver?"

Alfred marched to the edge of the road, shaking from head to toe. Never in his life had he so much wanted to kill someone.

He heard a thump and turned. Hubert was sprawled on the ground as Lydia waved a heavy horsewhip over him.

"How dare you insult me in that way," she warned, cracking the horsewhip above her head.

Alfred stomped past the prone figure on the ground, took the whip from Lydia and gently sat her back in the carriage, wrapping the cloak around her with great care.

Hubert sat cross-legged on the cold road, holding his head. Alfred bent and offered his hand.

"It doesn't have to be like this," Hubert said, slapping away Albert's hand and staggering to his feet. "We, all three of us, can be content and satisfied."

Nobody moved as Hubert began to laugh uncontrollably. He doubled over, tears running down his face.

"Don't you see?" Hubert straightened up, grabbing Alfred's sleeve. "She wants you. She longs for you and has no love for me. And I? If I might be granted some comfort with you, I would allow you to sit with her and hold her hand sometimes. That's what you want, isn't it?"

"You are drunk and absurd, Hubert," Lydia said from the carriage. "Come. Let us go home."

"What for, my dear?" Hubert asked, his hand on Alfred's arm. "You turn your head away when I try to kiss you. I know whose kisses you desire. Let us make a pact."

Alfred took his arm and led him to the carriage. "You are married to your wife in the eyes of God," Alfred murmured, looking past him to Lydia. "I fear I could not face the parson on a Sunday if I agreed to what you're suggesting."

Alfred mounted the driver's seat and took up the reins. He was unsettled by the sound of Hubert's laughter all the way home.

CHAPTER TWENTY-ONE

New Beginnings

I asked Mark in for coffee one evening after an AA meeting.

I proudly showed him my emerald dining room and then took him to the top of the house to show off my study.

"These stairs are wet," he said.

"Yeah," I agreed. "They're always wet. I've got a man looking into it."

We sat in my garret and he admired the outside view and commented on the hefty mirror on the back of the door.

"That looks old," he said.

"Mmm," I agreed. "It came with the house."

"Where do you get your inspiration to write?" he asked.

I chuckled. *If only you knew.* "I get ideas from all kinds of things."

"You must have a fertile imagination," he said.

"It's my job to turn my imagination into something that people want to read. And how's your job going?" I asked.

"It's okay," he shrugged. "It's difficult dealing with the general public all day. The worst thing is, I get recognised."

"I can imagine," I sympathised.

"The other day an elderly couple came over and asked for my autograph," he said, curling the side of his mouth. "I signed, 'Mark Walton'. They looked disappointed and said they thought I was someone else."

"That's awful," I said.

"I get it all the time," he said. "People look at me. They're thinking, 'I know him from somewhere'. Sometimes, they say, 'You're that drunk bloke from the telly'. It's so embarrassing."

"I sympathise," I said. "Luckily, I'm not famous enough to be recognised in the street. Sure, I've got devoted fans but I'm not a household name."

"It can be a blessing and a curse," he said.

"Do you think you'll ever get another TV job?" I asked.

"Unlikely," he replied. "I was one of the highest-paid presenters on the station at the time. In the early days, I'd turn up at 3.30 in the morning, hungover from the night before but I was never drunk. Then one night, I arrived straight from a late party. I was pissed, but I could still do the show. From then on I drank all night and got a cab to the TV station. Towards the end, I couldn't read the autocue and I got confused about which guest we had on. I asked a prominent woman MP how long she'd been in *Cabaret!*"

"I bet that pissed her off?" I said.

"She berated me, on air, for being drunk," he remembered. "I've never felt so foolish in all my life."

"Didn't you think to get help then?" I asked.

"I didn't recognise that I had a problem," he replied. "I was convinced that no one noticed when I cocked up."

"I was the same," I said. "I count myself lucky that Charlie has always been completely honest, whilst standing by me. I suppose, like your brother?"

"My brother's getting sick of me living with him." He rubbed his eyes. "We bickered a lot over Christmas."

"That's a shame," I said. "Over anything in particular?"

"It's only a small flat and I'm in the way," he replied.

"I'm sure he only wants to help," I said.

"I know," he said, the smile returning. "I want to make him proud this time. But I don't need to tell you how difficult it is sometimes."

I nodded as he continued. "The knowledge that a couple

of drinks will make all the pain and loneliness go away."

"Only for a while," I said.

"Yeah, I know," he muttered covering his face with his hands.

I pecked him on the cheek as he got ready to leave. He beamed, ruffling my hair as we stood in the passageway.

"I love your hair," he said.

"It's always a bloody mess," I laughed, looking in the mirror.

"It's so natural," he said. "I love its waywardness and the way it catches the light, all amber and russet."

He caressed a curly lock between his fingers. He went to say something, then smiled, thinking better of it and turned to go.

I held onto his arm as we descended the steps to the pavement, not wanting to let him go. A car pulled up at the kerb and I gasped as a man stepped out.

"Moira," Dave, my drunken one-night stand, called out. "Why haven't you answered my calls?"

Mark let go of my arm as Dave, grinning from ear to ear, gave me a loud kiss on the cheek.

"What are you doing here?" I asked.

"I was worried about you when you didn't call," he said, looking Mark up and down.

"Mark, this is a friend of mine, Dave," I said, my jaw clenched.

"A bit more than a friend, eh?" Dave said, nudging me, his bushy eyebrows raised.

"Nice to meet you," Mark mumbled. "I'll see you later."

He quickly got into his old car and drove away.

"What can I do for you?" I asked Dave, looking anywhere but not at him.

"I've got a little gift for you," he said, reaching into his pocket and pulling out a small, gift-wrapped package.

"You'd better come in," I decided, against my better judgement.

Dave removed his shoes and lounged on the sofa. I was sorely tempted to slap his chubby face to remove the leery grin.

The present turned out to be a cheap fountain pen.

"Thanks," I murmured, pulling the lid off and examining the nib.

"I thought it would be handy for book signings," he said. "I told my wife I'd met you. She was very impressed. She chose the pen."

I felt queasy. "Why did you tell your wife about a drunken woman you'd slept with?"

"I didn't tell her that," he answered, the annoying grin replaced with shock.

I leaned against the fireplace. "Thanks for the gift," I said, as pleasantly as possible. "I'm afraid I'm going to have to ask you to leave. I've got plans."

"Moira," he whined. "I'm here for a couple of days. I thought we could spend some time together."

I winced, but he didn't notice.

"You know," he continued, waving his hand like a wind turbine. "Have dinner, drink some wine. Go to bed."

"For fuck's sake." I shook my head.

"What?" he asked, struggling to his feet.

"I mean – I'm busy with the book and such like," I stuttered.

He planted a wet kiss on my lips.

"No," I panicked, pushing him away. "I'm sorry, Dave. Sleeping with you was a mistake."

He planted his hands on his hips.

"Oh, come on," I said. "You don't think I would have slept with you if I was sober?"

He grabbed my shoulders and pressed himself against me, his flaccid lips pressed against my tightly closed mouth.

I twisted away from him. "Get off me!" I shouted.

He grinned. "I know you enjoyed it as much as I did," he leered. "Come on, let's just have a cuddle for now."

He took a step toward me and I shoved my fists hard

against his chest. He staggered backwards.

"I want you to leave," I said, pointing at the door.

"But, sweetheart," he said, the grin returning.

"Please leave," I repeated.

"You can't be serious." He tilted his head, his arms outstretched.

"Sleeping with you was a big mistake," I explained. "I'm sorry, I was very drunk."

"You silly cow," he shouted, his fists clenched at his side. "Do you think you're something special just because you've written a few shitty books?"

I wrapped my arms around my body. "No, it's not..."

"You were fucking hopeless in bed," he said. "Even my wife's better than you."

"Then why are you here?" I asked. "Go home to your wife."

"You're just a has-been," he said, shaking a podgy fist. "An old, drunken hag. I only fucked you because I knew you were easy meat."

I gasped, holding on to the back of the sofa. "I think you should leave now," I repeated.

He strode across the room, bending to retrieve his shoes. "Fucking bitch," was his parting insult.

I sunk into a chair as the door slammed. I brought my knees to my chest and wrapped my arms around them.

First Draft

"What are you doing here?" Alfred asked as Lydia stepped into the stable, her long pearl-coloured dress swishing against the wooden floor.

"I had to see you," she replied, peering over her shoulder.

"You'll get us hung," he sighed, pulling her close and kissing her lips.

"There's going to be an announcement, but I

wanted you to know first," she said, her hands cupped around the back of his neck.

He held his breath.

"I'm going to have a baby." She smiled, but he didn't.

"Oh," he nodded.

"There's a good chance it may be your baby," she added.

"Or his?"

"There's a chance it could be his, but I believe it to be yours," she implored. "It's the only way I can love it."

He took both her hands in his. "It makes it impossible for us to run away," he whispered. "If there's a baby and he thinks it's his, he'll move heaven and earth to find us."

"I'll tell him it's your baby," she said.

"Whatever you do, don't do that!" he said, wringing his hands. "He'll make you and the child suffer, just to get back at me."

"What do we do?" she said, pressing her lips tightly together.

He sighed and leaned on the half door looking out on the yard.

"You'll need to stay here for the birthing," he said at last.

"Why?" she began to say.

"Listen," he said. "You'll get a proper doctor here. If we run, you'll get some simple woman from the nearest village, if we're lucky."

"I suppose I must agree," she said. "But after the birth, we must go. I will write to him from far away and tell him the child is yours. He won't bother us after that. He couldn't bear the shame."

"That might work," he agreed.

He closed the stable door and put his hands around her tiny waist, pulling her close.

Meanwhile, in an obscure country most Englishmen had never heard of, Archduke Ferdinand was being murdered. It was 28th June 1914. No one realised, but the world was about to embark on the bloodiest war it had ever seen.

CHAPTER TWENTY-TWO

Desperation

I'd been sober for a whole month and although I still craved a drink, I was feeling a whole lot better.

"Have a glass of wine if you want one," I said to Charlie as the waiter hovered.

"No. I'll have a Diet Coke too please." She smiled at the waiter, who collected the menus and left us. "I'm so proud of you, Moi."

"It's only been a month. Don't get too excited," I said.

"Still, it's an achievement and you look great," she said. "We haven't met in a restaurant, like this, for years."

"Thank you for suggesting it." I patted her arm.

"Bill mentioned that you'd asked him to do some research for your book," she said.

"Yes," I nodded. "He's researching the residents of my house for the past hundred years. I'm writing an Edwardian saga based on who lived there."

"How fascinating," she said, clapping her hands together.

"It is," I agreed. "I love some of the characters and can't wait to see how things turn out."

"I thought you meticulously planned your books, including knowing the ending?" she asked.

"Usually I do," I replied. "But this time I'm going with the flow. I don't know yet how it ends."

She frowned. "Are your agent and publisher okay with that?"

"Yes," I laughed at her thoughtful concern. "They're loving what I've written so far."

"Good," she said as the Diet Cokes arrived. "How's Freddie taking your sobriety?"

"I dumped Freddie," I said.

She choked. "You dumped Freddie?" she repeated.

"I certainly did," I said. "I saw him for what he is – a conceited parasite."

"That's wonderful news," she said. "I can't say I ever liked him, and look at the grief he's caused."

"You're right," I said, fiddling with a napkin. "I can't explain what I saw in him. I made my children unhappy by destroying our family. I'll never forgive myself for that."

"They're happy enough now," she said.

"You've seen them?" I asked.

"I popped in the other night," she replied. "Debbie was doing homework with them."

"What can she teach them, typing?" I sniped.

"For goodness' sake, Moira, give the woman a break," she cried.

"I'm sorry," I said, pressing my palms against my cheeks. "You're right. Debbie's been great with the kids."

"Her and Cliff are trying to understand who this man is the kids say they've seen at your house," she said.

"Melted-face man?" I asked, and she nodded.

"Debbie got them to draw pictures of him." She snorted. "They're pretty horrible and the children claim he appears in the garden all the time. Your children certainly have your imagination."

"Yes," I agreed, feeling uncomfortable after what I'd also seen in the house.

"Cliff also confided, once Debbie had left the room," she said behind her hand, "that he was sure you were sober that day he and Debbie left the kids and went shopping. He couldn't be more pleased."

I smiled and nodded, feeling very awkward.

She noticed me squirm. "How's Mark getting on with the AA?" She neatly changed the subject.

"He's doing well," I said. "I've been trying to get hold of him but he's not answering his phone."

"Perhaps he's busy. You said he had a job?" she asked.

"Yes, but only part-time," I replied. "I hope he's all right. We had a misunderstanding the last time we met."

First Draft

Alfred leapt down from the carriage and opened the door for his master. He went to the horses, gathering up the reins when he sensed him standing close behind.

"So you've heard the good news?" Hubert spoke with a droll smile on his round face.

"Yes, sir," Alfred said. "Congratulations."

Hubert's breath was hot against his cheek. "You know what this means," he breathed into Alfred's ear. "I've impregnated her like I said I would. Now I can have what I've always wanted. You!"

Alfred turned towards the shorter man, his arm resting on the horse's back.

"You have sinful desires, sir. Which I have no intention of satisfying."

Hubert threw back his head and laughed. "You have no choice," he said, fingering Alfred's coat. "Come. Let us take the steps to the hayloft and lay down together."

Alfred took a step back.

"Yes, I have sinful desires that must be satisfied," Hubert crooned. "I could just go home and make love to my beautiful wife. Can you imagine how she detests me touching her, let alone getting into her undergarments?"

Alfred studied the reins he held tightly in his hands.

"I thought my wealth and power would be a heady aphrodisiac," Hubert continued. "Sorry, aphrodisiac is probably a long word for you. What I mean is, I thought Lydia would moan like a whore every time I came near her. Instead, she lies there with her face turned away. I wonder whom she is thinking of?"

Alfred dearly wanted to wipe the wide grin off of Hubert's fat face.

"So, my dear chap," Hubert said, thrusting out his barrel chest, his hands on his hips. "Do we roll about in the hay for an hour, or shall I claim my marital rights with my loving wife?"

Hubert licked his lips slowly, taking a step towards Alfred.

"And risk your unborn child?" Alfred asked, eyebrows raised.

"Aha," Hubert breathed heavily. "Checkmate."

Hubert strolled towards the house, saying over his shoulder, "Your dignity is safe for now, but once the brat is born I'll come and get what's mine."

Alfred let out a long sigh, burying his head against the horse's warm neck.

"What's amiss with the master?" a young voice piped up over the stable door.

"Toby!" Alfred exclaimed. "Did you see what went on?"

"I heard some," Toby admitted.

"Forget whatever it was you thought you heard," Alfred instructed grimly.

"But Uncle, is Miss Lydia to be afraid of her new husband?" Toby asked.

"You must never speak of it," Alfred replied. "Will do no one no good."

"How can we help Miss Lydia?" Toby said. "She's a good, honest lady and don't deserve to suffer at the hands of such a man as him."

"Don't worry," Alfred reassured. "The lady is safe enough while he believes his child is growing inside her. After that, I will put myself in his way, if it'll protect her."

"You intend to fight with the master?" the boy asked, creasing his forehead.

"Quite the opposite," Alfred replied, biting down hard on his bottom lip. "But it's nothing for you to worry about. Just don't ever find yourself alone with him."

The boy nodded, looking confused.

"For Miss Lydia's sake, we must never speak of this again," Alfred said.

I pushed back from my computer, looking into the mirror for clues, but it was an ordinary mirror, keeping its secrets.

I tried Mark's phone again and got no answer. He hadn't attended our AA meetings and I was worried. The AA would not divulge his address and I was at a loss. Then I remembered my brother-in-law's magic abilities for finding people dead or alive.

I pulled up beside a block of newish flats at the end of a busy high street. There were some sorry-looking rose bushes and littered flowerbeds. I ran up the stairs, where a dark-haired man waited for me.

"Come in," he said. "You must be Moira."

"Thank you. And you're James?" I said.

"Mark told me all about you. You're a writer?" he asked.

"Yes, that's right," I replied. "Is he here?"

"Please sit down," he gestured to a sofa. "I'm afraid

Mark's gone off the rails."

I inhaled deeply.

"He was desperately upset the night he bumped into your boyfriend," he said.

"It wasn't my boyfriend," I said, shaking my head.

"He came storming in here and I'm afraid we quarrelled," James murmured.

"What about?" I asked.

"I thought he was seeing too much of you," he replied. "He is too vulnerable to be falling in love with anyone."

"Falling in love?" I whispered.

"You didn't realise?" he said.

"He told me he wasn't ready for a relationship and we had to focus on the programme," I said, creasing my forehead.

"I think that was his intention." He leant against the windowsill. "When he encountered the rival, he realised he'd already fallen for you. He went down the pub and got in a fight and I haven't seen him since."

"Oh no!" I exclaimed, my hand to my mouth. "The guy he met wasn't a rival, just an awful mistake. I have to talk to Mark. Where can he be?"

James shook his head and stared out of the window. "He could be anywhere."

We drove to the homeless shelter where James had found his brother on a previous occasion, but they hadn't seen him.

A cadaverous-looking woman of about forty watched us, her eyes sunken black orbs. "You looking for Mark?" she screeched, like an out-of-tune violin.

"Do you know where he is?" I asked, seeing in her vacant eyes a possible version of my future.

"He's gone to the slum boats on the river," she slurred, slumping into a chair.

We drove quickly, ditching the car and jogging down the towpath. I'd seen the tatty old houseboats, illegally moored at the side of the river near my home.

Three houseboats rocked gently in unison, moored to trees and stakes in the ground. Strewn around were old deckchairs, gas canisters, crates of beers and general filth.

Mark was slumped against a tree, a can of beer in his hand. His eyes flickered open as I stood over him.

"Mark," I said softly.

"Huh?"

He squinted up.

"Come on, Mark," James said. "Let's get you home."

Mark bent forward, holding his head in his hands.

"Let me take you home," James repeated.

"No!" Mark moaned. "I can see the light."

He pointed down the river where the tall spire of my house stuck out above the trees.

"My house?" I asked.

He nodded and struggled to his feet to have a proper look at me.

"Moira?" he asked.

There was a dark wet patch on his crotch.

"No, no, no," he cried, stumbling backwards.

He fell into the river with a splash, which prompted much laughter from the people on the boats. He spluttered and coughed, staggering to his feet; the river was quite shallow. We hauled him up the bank.

"He can come home with me," I suggested.

After a hot bath and a little soup, I laid him down in one of the kids' bedrooms and he slept for hours. Later, deliberate footsteps descended the stairs and he found me in the kitchen. He wore old tracksuit bottoms and a large t-shirt that I'd left out for him.

"Feeling any better?" I asked.

"I feel like shit," he replied. "And so embarrassed that you found me like that."

"Don't be daft," I said. "I was in exactly the same

condition a month ago."

I pushed a cup of tea towards him.

"Did James leave?" He looked around.

I nodded. "I promised to look after you, so he went home."

"Probably glad to see the back of me," he mumbled.

"James is very worried about you," I said. "He'd do anything to help."

"He's been so good to me and this is how I repay him," he said, dropping his head to his arms on the table.

I ran my fingers through his greying hair. He looked up, his eyes glistening with tears.

"Why am I here?" he asked.

"You were soaking wet, so we walked you back here," I said, stroking his forehead. "Your brother took some convincing before he'd trust me."

"I hope he wasn't too hard on you," he said.

"He has every right to worry about a drunk looking after a drunk!" I grinned.

"Mmm," he murmured. "So here I am."

"You can recover here for a while," I said.

"And then what?" he asked.

"I don't know," I replied. "I'm not sure if my ex-husband would allow my children to visit if you were here."

"I'll only stay until I feel better," he said.

"Let's not worry about that for now," I said, putting my arm around his shoulder.

CHAPTER TWENTY-THREE

Out of the Frying Pan

First Draft
March 1915
My dearest Lydia,

Please forgive me for leaving without warning. Since you've been with child and confined to the house, I couldn't see any way of letting you know without being found out. I couldn't risk being stopped from leaving by a certain person we both know.

Believe me when I say I left for both our sakes. I can only imagine that the same person's behaviour towards us would get worse when the baby arrived.

I have volunteered for the Middlesex Regiment and we are training for war. The officers seem to think I can shoot straight enough and I may join the Rifle Brigade.

I will save my soldier's wages every week so that we may have a stronger state of affairs when I return. The officers say the war will only last about six months or so, and we will have victory over the enemy.

I beg you to take care of yourself and the baby and wish you a safe delivery.

Know that I am your true husband and that I love you with all my heart.

Your loving
Alfred
Lydia, burn this letter as soon as you've read it. I will send more to Mavis, when I may be allowed.

"Don't upset yourself so, Miss," Mavis said. "Think of the baby. It won't do it any good if you carry on. It will only be a short war and the men will soon return."

"He didn't even say goodbye," Lydia sobbed.

"Alfred told me before he left," Mavis said. "If the master got wind of him leaving, he would have been in a great deal of trouble. He joined the army for both your sakes."

"He saw you before he left?" Lydia looked up with wet, red eyes.

"He called in at my lodgings," Mavis admitted. "He was upset at having to leave without seeing you, but we couldn't think of a way to get into the house and past the master. He's replaced all the old servants with his people."

Lydia nodded.

"Alfred also said," Mavis continued. "The last thing in the world he wanted to do was abandon you. But he had no choice in the matter, no choice at all."

Dear Alfred,

I was greatly upset by your leaving, as was a certain person when we heard the news of your surprise departure.

The certain person we know was furious and threatened to turn your family out of their cottage. He was unaware that a different family resided within those walls and that, happily, your family no longer relies on his good opinion (or otherwise) for their welfare

The household has recovered and returned to its old routine. I am still imprisoned in my room and pass my days in boredom, only relieved when I imagine what my true husband is doing and seeing.

I know you left for good reasons, but my heart aches for your return and to see your handsome face again.

Know that I am in the best of health, although as fat as a sow. And I promise to take care of myself and the child so that you may look forward to the day we are all reunited.

All my love, your Lydia.

P.S. Mavis is our guardian angel and has agreed to manage our correspondence.

I sighed, pushing back my hair. I knew it was going to be a long and bloody war and I feared for Alfred.

"Tea?" Mark put his head around the door.

"Yes please," I said, getting up. "Let's have it downstairs."

"Why, in God's name, are these stairs still sopping wet?" he asked, lifting a damp foot.

"I've had half a dozen different tradesmen here," I told him. "No one seems to know. There's no leak in the roof and there's no plumbing in this part of the house. It's a mystery."

"Would it be okay for me to have look?" he asked.

"Be my guest."

I left the door to my study open the next day as Mark pulled up the stair carpet. I carried on writing, forgetting he was there.

"Who're you talking to?" he asked, grinning at me from the door.

"Oh, sorry about that," I replied. "I get so involved with

my characters I sometimes have a conversation with them!"

"I thought you had someone in there with you," he said.

"Any news regarding the soaking steps?" I asked, anxious to change the subject.

"I'm flummoxed," he said, scratching his head. "I just don't understand why it's so wet here."

I shrugged. "Tell me something I don't know."

I leaned on the kitchen sink, waiting for the kettle to boil. The sun was setting and I looked out into the sepia-coloured garden.

A head bobbed from below the windowsill and I jumped out of my skin.

"Jackson," I shouted, rushing to open the back door.

He trudged into the room, frigid air wafting from his winter coat.

"What are you doing here?" I asked.

He scowled and removed his backpack, letting it drop onto the tiles with a thwack.

"That bloody cow Debbie wouldn't let me stay over with my best friend Owen," he said, bottom lip protruding.

"Don't call her that," I said, surprising myself. "Why wouldn't she let you stay?"

"How should I know?" he said, throwing his arms up in the air.

"Does she know where you are?" I asked.

He shrugged and went to look in the refrigerator.

"Jackson," I persisted. "Does she know where you are?"

"No," he said.

Mark entered the room and peered around.

"Everything okay?" he asked, not seeing Jackson who had his head in the fridge.

"Fine," I said. "Jackson's argued with Debbie."

"Oh," Mark said. "Sorry, I didn't see you there. Hi Jackson."

Jackson grabbed a carton of milk, slammed the

refrigerator door and scraped a chair out to sit on.

"That was my friend Mark," I said as Mark made a face and backed out of the room. "Would you phone Debbie, please, and tell her where you are?"

"Why should I?" he said, in between big gulps of milk that left a white moustache above his lip.

"Because she'll be worried about you," I said.

"You're my mum, not that saddo," he said.

"I am your mum," I agreed. "But Debbie has stepped in because I haven't always been a good mum."

"She's the bitch-mum from hell," he said.

"I'm sure that's not true."

"I thought you hated her?"

"I don't hate her," I said. "It's all my fault – the fact that we aren't a family and Daddy went to live with someone else."

He knitted his fair eyebrows together, looking younger than his twelve years.

"Debbie's just trying to do her best in a tricky situation," I explained.

"Why does she have to boss me around all the time?" he asked.

"Parents sometimes have to do unpleasant things and it really shouldn't be Debbie. It should be me," I replied, taking his hand. "I've been a crap mum. I'm sorry."

Jackson rubbed his eyes. "Will you be our proper mum again soon?" he said, watching me closely.

"I'm trying my best," I said. "In the meantime, please be nice to Debbie."

"She still can't tell me what to do," he said.

"While you're living with her and Dad, she has every right to tell you what to do," I said.

"Why can't I come and live here with you?" he asked, banging the milk carton on the table.

"I hope that one day you will be able to," I replied. "But that day is not today. Now get your phone and let Debbie know where you are."

I gave him what Cliff used to call my look of death and he leapt up and got his phone from his bag.

"You talk to her," he murmured, handing me the phone.

"Jack, where are you?" Debbie said crossly, on the other end of the phone.

"It's Moira here," I said.

Silence.

"Hi Debbie, it's Moira here," I repeated.

"Oh sorry. Hi Moira, is Jack there?" she asked.

"He is," I said. "He said there'd been an argument."

"I'm not falling out with you as well," she cried.

"I hope not," I agreed.

Silence.

"Oh, okay then," she eventually said. "Jackson wanted to stay over with Owen. But he has a massive project to do and he hasn't even started it yet and it's got to be handed in on Monday."

I shook my head at a sulky Jackson.

"Is it something I could help with?" I asked.

I heard a sharp intake of breath and imagined her surprise.

"It's about World War One," she said. "He's supposed to learn about the battles."

"That's great timing," I said. "I'm about to do some research for my book. Why don't I get him started on it here and Cliff can pick him up later, on the way home?"

"I guess that would be great," she said uncertainly.

"Thanks, Debbie, we'll get started on it right away," I hung up.

"Upstairs, you," I said to Jackson.

CHAPTER TWENTY-FOUR

Mirage

"I've been texting you for weeks about coming over to collect my stuff," Freddie said as he barged his way into the living room and threw his jacket across a chair.

"You up and left me after the awful fashion show evening," I said, shrugging. "I assumed you and I were done."

I crossed my arms as Freddie wandered around the room picking up random things.

"So, do I get offered a cup of coffee?" he asked.

"I'd rather you just got your gear and left," I replied.

"Come on, darling!" He threw his hands up in the air. "You can't just cut me out of your life. I thought you loved me?"

"Thing is…" I hesitated, even now not wanting to be hurtful. "I manage better without you. I've been six weeks sober and I would've struggled to do that if I was with you."

He leaned against the mantelpiece. "I didn't think you were serious about giving up the booze. I'm sorry."

"I am deadly serious," I said. "I have to get my kids back and I won't let anything stop me."

"I admire your determination," he said, crossing the room and gripping me by the shoulders. "We can still be together."

He ran his hands through my hair, his green eyes staring into mine. My body tingled as he touched my face.

"No, we can't," I murmured, pushing him away.

"I'm sorry you feel like that," he said, his shoulders slumped. "You're such a great person. I know I don't deserve you."

I felt like I'd been hit by a truck. "You've never said anything like that to me before," I said. My voice sounded shrill and unnatural.

"I should've," he sighed.

"It's too late now," I said, with more conviction than I felt.

"Thing is," he said. "I can't stop thinking about you."

"Funny," I said. "We've had long spells when it seemed you'd completely forgotten about me."

"Look," he said, jabbing a finger at me. "When the opportunities come up, I've got to work. Sometimes that means dropping everything."

"You are the biggest disappointment in my life."

"Oh, don't say that, babe," he mumbled, and hid his face with his hands.

"What you offer is never enough," I continued, surprised at my honesty. "It's always, 'Soon, babe. Let's not rush into things, babe.' When you mean, 'I'm never going to love you enough to have a life with you.'"

Had I known this all along? I expect so. But to say it out loud made me feel like I'd stumbled on a kernel of wisdom.

He held his hands, prayer-like to his lips. "You are the only woman who has ever understood me."

"Please!" I said, feeling laughter bubbling up. "You think I'm going to fall for that? Face it, Freddie, if I hadn't been a successful author living in a big house, you never would have given me the time of day."

"How can you say that?" He looked genuinely offended. "I told you when we first met, I am no good at relationships."

"Yes you did," I interrupted, feeling annoyed at more bullshit. "I don't know why I ever thought that was acceptable. But I can assure you that it's unacceptable now."

He nodded, smiling. "I get it, babe. You want more. So

let's find a solution that suits both of us. A compromise."

"I'm sorry, Freddie. Whatever we had together is over," I said.

He turned away. For the first time, he seemed unsure of himself. I felt like a rod of iron was propping up my backbone. I was determined not to back down and throw myself into his arms.

"I'll get my stuff and go," he said, pouting. "Just you remember. I'll always be there for you. All you've got to do is call."

First Draft
1915

Alfred watched the clouds turn pink and a crescent blush of red announcing sunrise. There had been a constant bombardment of the Allied trenches throughout the long night and he felt more exhausted than ever before. He stretched his long legs and looked around at his comrades, some slumped against the mud trench walls, some leaning and looking out across no man's land. He retrieved a letter from his jacket pocket from his father, now living near Weston-super-Mare.

Dear son,

We hope you are keeping well and the British Army is looking after you.

We heard soon after you left that her that was Miss Turner, now Mrs Archer gave birth to a baby boy and both are in good health. It seems like only yesterday Miss Lydia would help with the horses, cleaning tack and so on, until her father came and scolded her for messing up her dress. I suppose she's a grand lady now, wife of him who will one day be the master of Rosebay House.

Your sisters are also doing well and we are blessed

with many grandchildren. So as a family, we have much to be thankful for.

Mother and me are so proud to have a son in The Rifles, fighting the enemy for our King and Country. Mum says to keep safe as she worries about you.

Your loving parents

Alfred sighed and tucked the letter into his khaki uniform. He had been proud and excited to volunteer for the army and sailing to France had been an adventure. The gloomy trench smelled of mud, piss and sweaty bodies. His battalion had been pinned down by bombardment and machine-gun fire for days.

The officers didn't seem to know what action to take next. The men dreaded hearing the shrill whistle which signalled them to go 'over the top' and stage another futile attack against the well-dug-in and armed to the teeth enemy, waiting on the other side of no man's land. He'd seen men shot dead and blown to pieces. He'd listened throughout the night to his comrades dying slowly and in agony, caught up in barbed wire somewhere near the enemy lines.

Homesickness overwhelmed him. He sorely missed stolen glances of Lydia as he passed Rosebay House and even Mavis's constant chatter. He thought about Rosebay's horses, their soft, trusting brown eyes and warm muzzles. The horses commandeered for the war were half starved, worked to the point of exhaustion and terrified of the ear-splitting explosions. He'd tried to calm them, stroking velvety noses, but they trembled and stared at him wide-eyed.

He had thought about walking away and somehow getting back home. He'd known other soldiers who had attempted exactly that. On being captured and tried, they'd been shown no mercy and taken out and shot.

Mark returned just as I'd finished Alfred's account of life in the trenches. I went downstairs feeling dispirited.

"Ah, so you're back," I sighed. "How was it?"

"I'm getting back my part-time job," he said excitedly. "The garden centre has been extraordinarily kind and understanding. James came with me and we were completely honest about my alcoholism and why I hadn't turned up for work. They even offered counselling on the company."

"I'm so pleased," I said.

"You could act pleased," he said.

"Oh, sorry," I smiled. "I've just been writing about the Great War."

"Ah, that's why you look upset."

"Not a pleasant period to have been a young man."

"You'd think our generation would be grateful for what those men went through," he mused. "Instead we take it all for granted."

"Every generation has its drawbacks," I said. "For instance, all the kids from broken homes these days. People stayed together in the past."

"Not always happily," he said.

"For sure," I agreed. "But I do believe it's unsettling for children to be stuck in the middle of warring parents."

"That's one thing my son didn't have to go through," he said, shrugging. "I was never there."

I bustled about in the kitchen and brought two mugs of tea back to the living room.

Mark was examining a jacket slung over the chair.

"Whose is this?" he asked, looking in the pockets.

"Um, I think Freddie left it behind," I replied.

"He's been here?"

"Yes, to pick up his stuff," I said, feeling annoyed at

being questioned in my own home.

"Did you sleep with him?" he demanded, narrowing his eyes.

"That's none of your business," I said.

"You did," he said. "I can see it written all over your face."

"I'm a grown woman and if I had wanted to sleep with him, I would have," I declared.

He wagged his finger at me. "You're a child who needs gratification. You just can't see how this guy messes up your life."

He threw the coat across the room as he stormed out.

I rang James to let him know his brother had gone AWOL again. I went out and walked along the river in case Mark had returned to his boating friends.

It was dusk and the pearly street lights cast a halo of silvery light against an indigo sky. Confused water rushed over the weir, white and foamy as it crashed over the fall. Further downstream the jetty jutted out into the river, sturdy and black against the strong current.

In the periphery of my eye, something shimmered. A woman was standing erect on the jetty, wearing a long trench coat and a hat pulled down over her eyes. She wobbled and I held my breath. She clung to the railing but some force seemed to unbalance her. She fell into the water and was swept away in the strong current.

I grabbed my phone from my pocket and dialled 999.

The police were in a frenzy, running up and down the river bank and launching RIBs on the water. I waited anxiously for them to pull a body out. Someone grabbed my arm and I spun around.

"What are you doing here?" Cliff asked.

"I saw a woman fall in the water," I replied.

He tugged my arm so that I faced him.

"Are you sure?" He held me tightly.

"Yes," I cried, pulling away. "I'm sure. What are you doing here?"

"I was on my way home and saw the police on the towpath. I wondered what was going on. Then I saw you," he said.

"Some poor woman's probably drowned and you're here to spectate," I accused him.

He stared at me for a long time. I felt naked and vulnerable under his gaze.

"Have you been drinking?" he asked eventually.

"No, I bloody haven't," I said, shaking my head.

"Are you okay, madam?" a police officer asked as he approached us.

I nodded and walked away. Cliff spoke to the officer who kept looking over his shoulder at me.

"Now, Miss Delainey," the policeman said, walking slowly towards me. "Your ex-husband tells me there have been occasions when you haven't quite been yourself."

"If you mean drunk," I said, grimacing. "Yes, there have been some occasions. But today I am sober – quite bloody sober!"

"Okay, there's no need to get all het-up," he cautioned.

"Het-up," I cried. "Bloody het-up. I saw a woman fall into the river. What was I supposed to do, just ignore it?"

"The officer would like you to take a breathalyser," Cliff announced.

I shook my head violently. "I don't need to take a breathalyser because I haven't had a drink for six bloody weeks!"

"Then it won't be a problem," Cliff shrugged.

"I don't need this," I cried, striding away from them.

"You could be charged with wasting police time, you know," the policeman called after me.

I got home and slammed the door, tears pouring down my cheeks. The doorbell rang and Cliff stood on the doorstep chewing his lip.

"Why didn't you take the test?" he cried, his hands planted on his hips.

"You're never going to trust me, are you?" I bawled at him.

"After years of lies and betrayal, can you blame me?" he said.

"I'm trying my best to put that right," I screamed. "And you're not helping."

"Let me smell your breath," he said, moving towards me.

"Just fuck off back to your perfect little wife," I pushed him down the steps.

"I don't know what went wrong with you," he said, peering up. "We had everything. Beautiful home, lovely kids and I thought we had a great marriage. What a fool I was."

He strode off down the road, as I sobbed on the doorstep.

My neighbour, Angela, happened to be walking by just at that moment, looking stunning in a white coat. She stared, shook her head and skipped up the steps to her house.

CHAPTER TWENTY-FIVE

Desperate Times

First Draft

Lydia wiped her brow, pushing strands of escaped hair away from her face. Digging potatoes was hard work, but she nearly had a full wheelbarrow after hours of graft.

She heard a holler and saw someone waving and jumping up and down through the open gate to the field.

As she ventured closer she realised it was Hubert.

"What on earth do you think you're doing?" he shrieked, his nose glowing red and bulbous.

"I'm digging potatoes," she answered, wiping her hands on the canvas apron that covered her dress. "I agreed to help and I've almost got a whole wheelbarrow full."

"Digging potatoes?" he repeated. "Digging bloody potatoes? Have you gone out of your mind, woman? What do you mean by spending all day in the middle of a field, when you should be at home looking after our son?"

Lydia tilted her head to one side.

"Well?" he shouted.

"I can't sit at home drinking tea all day while

there's a war on," she said. "And, as you've hired a full-time nanny to look after our son, there's very little left for me to do where he's concerned."

"You're a lady," he said. "It's not your job to get filthy in a muddy field. Leave it to the great unwashed to pull our food out of the ground. Look at your hands."

"Our men are risking their lives, fighting in terrible conditions. I'm sure a little bit of dirt won't hurt me." She pursed her lips. "Besides, there aren't enough women to do this work."

"Our men?" he questioned. "Don't you mean one man in particular?"

"Lots of our friends' husbands and sons have left to fight," she replied. "We have to make our contribution."

"Are you insinuating that I'm not contributing, because I haven't joined the war yet? Let me remind you of the important work that still needs to be done here," he said, pointing at the ground.

"I wasn't suggesting anything of the sort," she murmured.

"Get yourself home. Where you belong," he growled, his pale eyes bulging.

"I've still got a few hours more of daylight," she said, scanning the sky. "I volunteered for the Women's Land Army and I'm not finished."

"Without my permission?" Hubert asked, flinging his arms wide.

"I don't need your permission," she replied, turning away. "There's a war and suddenly England needs its women to leave their parlours and do some work."

"I won't allow it," he shouted after her. "I won't have my wife behaving like a common farmhand. You need to come home at once. Do you hear me?"

"I'll be home later," she said, trudging across the field towards the wheelbarrow.

The policeman, who had suggested the day before that I should take a breathalyser, stood tall and brooding in my living room.

"We've sent down divers and we can't find any trace of a body," he said, clasping his hands together.

"Perhaps the body drifted further down the river," I suggested.

"There's been no report," he said blandly.

I stalked up and down the room to calm my nerves.

"I'm not making this up," I shrilled. "One minute the woman was on the quay, the next she had fallen in the water and was gone!"

"Miss Delainey." He held up his hands in surrender. "I have to ask you some awkward questions."

I knew what was coming. I stopped pacing and held onto the back of the sofa.

"Had you been drinking yesterday?" he asked.

"I told you on the riverbank, I had not been drinking yesterday," I answered.

"So you hadn't had a drink all day?" he persisted.

My nails dug into the soft upholstery.

"I haven't had a drink for six weeks," I said. "You may search the house for booze if you don't believe me."

"I don't think that's necessary." He smiled. "Do you think you might've had a hallucination due to your withdrawal from alcohol?"

My jaw dropped and I was aware of the silly face I was making as I considered what he was saying.

"I'm sorry," I cried. "I have been experiencing some unsettling episodes lately."

I covered my eyes, unable to breathe properly.

"Sit down, Miss Delainey," he said gently and I obeyed. "I

understand from your ex-husband, that you've been making a big effort to ditch the booze. I appreciate how difficult that is; we encounter addicts of one kind or another every day. I think what we're dealing with here is a mix-up of what you thought you saw."

I nodded bleakly as he crossed the room to the door.

"I'll report it as a mistake," he said. "But beware of calling the police again if you get further misperceptions."

I continued to nod, unable to reply with anything useful.

My phone rang as the policeman left.

"I've got some bad news, I'm afraid," James started to say. "Mark tried to commit suicide last night."

"I'm so sorry!" I cried. "What happened?"

"He took pills and booze. The doctor's with him now," James said.

"Which hospital are you in?" I asked.

"Why do you keep going back to your boyfriend when you know how Mark feels about you?" James asked as we waited in the relatives' room in the hospital.

"I don't keep going back to him," I murmured. "I'd arranged for him to come over while Mark spent the day with you. Mark shouldn't have known anything about it."

"Except your bloke decided to leave evidence," he said.

"It wasn't like that," I sighed. "He left in rather a hurry."

He turned to me his lips compressed into a thin line. "You have to decide if you want to be with Mark or this other bloke. You can't have both."

I fidgeted. "Mark and I are friends. But we are both too fragile to embark on a relationship."

"I appreciate that." He shrugged. "But Mark is in love with you."

I could hear trolleys being wheeled about outside and loud voices.

"I'm not sure how I feel about him," I said. "I'm trying to be a good friend to him."

"By fucking your old boyfriend?" he said.

"That's not fair," I cried. "I'm not married to Mark and I'm not his girlfriend. If I want to sleep with someone I will. Who are you to criticise?"

"Sorry," he said, rubbing his forehead. "I didn't mean to preach. It's just that Mark can't stand the thought of you with someone else."

"For the record, I didn't sleep with anyone."

We leapt up as the doctor entered.

"He's stable. You caught him just in time," he said to James.

"Can I see him?" James asked.

"You can see him briefly," the doctor replied.

I followed James to the door, where he held his hand up to my face.

"Don't come with me," he said. "I'll let you know when you can see him."

I backed off and slumped into a hard chair.

Time stood still while James was gone. I was hungry and thirsty and I longed to go and find a pub. My craving was all I could think about as I paced the room, my fist in my mouth.

James returned, avoiding eye contact.

"How is he?" I asked.

"He's weak and confused but he'll live," he replied.

"Can I see him?" I asked.

"He doesn't want to see you," James said.

"But I didn't do anything wrong," I cried.

"He just doesn't want to see you again," he repeated.

I ran my hands through my hair.

"Okay, I'll go," I said. "But please tell him that I'm not seeing anyone, and if he ever wants to be my friend again the door is always open."

First Draft

July 1916

Alfred shook his head.

"Everything all right?" rifleman Peterson asked, squatting down beside him.

"A letter from home," Alfred replied.

"I miss home too, mate," Peterson said. "The missus and the kids. Never thought I would. Three screaming kids causing mayhem and the old lady nagging me."

Alfred swirled a long, thin plait of pale hair between his fingers.

"Your sweetheart?" Peterson asked.

Alfred nodded, winding the hair around his fingers.

"They thought this war would be over in six months," Alfred said. "How wrong they were. We crouch in this mud hole, day in day out, being bombarded by the enemy. There's just no sense to it."

"They don't have a bloody clue." Peterson lit a cigarette.

"Look at us." Alfred held his arms out wide. "Holed up in some godforsaken place in France, awaiting orders from people who don't know what the hell they're doing. Toffs, who would be more at home in a ballroom."

"I always wanted to travel," Peterson said. "Would never have had the chance, being a postman with three kids."

"I'd hardly call this travelling," Alfred pointed out. "More like lambs to the slaughter."

"At least I can tell the folks at home I've been to France," Peterson said. "That's if I make it back to my job as a postie."

"And part-time poacher," Alfred reminded him.

"The poaching was just a sideline to get a decent meal inside the kids," Peterson smiled. "Lord whatever-his-name-is has acres of land. He never noticed a few pheasants going missing and the birds made a lovely dinner."

"Did you ever worry about gamekeepers?" Alfred asked.

"The kids going hungry worried me more," Peterson replied. "It weighs heavy on you if you're a father. Their little faces looking up at you. It was always worth the risk."

Alfred nodded.

"You didn't marry your girl before you left for war?" Peterson asked.

"It wasn't as easy as that," Alfred said turning away and gazing into the distance.

"Didn't her family approve, then?" Peterson persisted.

Alfred snorted. "You could say that."

"You seem like a decent chap. What was the problem?" Peterson said, stubbing out his cigarette.

Alfred screwed up his face and crossed his arms. "She wasn't for me. That's all."

"If you're getting her letters she must have feelings for you," Peterson said. "Perhaps she's waiting for you? Could be when this circus is over, you can go home and make things right with her?"

"I've heard, any day now, we'll push forward at all costs." Alfred stood and stretched, relieved to change the subject.

"God knows why," Peterson shrugged. "Why are we fighting over this shitty place? What's its name? The

Somme?"

CHAPTER TWENTY-SIX

Against the Odds

I was overwhelmed with anxiety, which wasn't helping my quest for sobriety. My leading men in fiction and real life seemed to be in danger.

As usual, I turned to Charlie. She suggested that we take the twins away for a few days to a family activity centre she'd been to before on the west coast of England.

You'd think we'd arrived at Alcatraz when we were shown our large family room in the complex. The children gingerly lifted the bedclothes, screwed their noses up and complained about the shower. It wasn't luxurious, but it would suffice for a few days. And it made me realise how spoilt my children were.

Once we'd unpacked, Charlie and I lounged around the pool as the twins splashed and swum together.

"How did you get Cliff to let them come?" I asked.

"He wasn't very cooperative because of the river incident," she replied.

"I was quite sure I'd seen someone fall in," I said, feeling my bottom lip quiver. "But perhaps I was mistaken."

"Anyhow," she continued. "I told him that you and the children needed to bond and spend time together."

"I have a long hill to climb I suppose until he'll trust me again?" I sighed.

"Don't write him off," she said. "He was saying good

things about you until the river thing. Why on earth didn't you take the breathalyser?"

"I was being stubborn," I admitted. "I haven't had a drink for nearly two months. It's been the hardest thing I've ever done. I was very annoyed that I was immediately labelled the mad alcoholic."

"I understand," she said. "But it would've made it so much easier to take the breathalyser and prove them wrong."

"I know," I laughed. "When have you ever known me to take the easy route?"

The twins and I had signed up for a pottery and clay-making class later in the day, allowing Charlie to escape to the spa for a well-earned break from us.

The teacher plonked big lumps of sticky, grey clay in front of us and informed us that we were going to sculpt a head. She demonstrated for about half an hour and then it was our turn to get stuck in.

I sat in the middle of the children watching them roll the clay into a sphere as the teacher had instructed.

"What are you going to make?" I asked.

They shrugged in unison without looking up.

"I'm going to make a dog," I said.

No answer.

"No, it's going to be a wolf," I corrected.

"Why don't you live with us anymore?" Rosanna asked.

How do you explain your shortcomings to a twelve-year-old, that won't mess them up for life?

"I did something silly," I began. "And the judge said that Daddy should look after you for a while."

She looked up at me with innocent grey eyes.

"Debbie says it was because you couldn't look after us properly," Jackson chimed in.

Bloody Debbie!

"That's true," I agreed. "But I'm much better now and soon I will be able to look after you."

They seemed to accept this and carried on with the clay.

"Was it because we were bad?" Rosanna eventually asked.

My heart broke in two.

"No, darling," I stroked her fair hair. "I've been silly. It was nothing you did."

"And now you're going to stop being silly?" she asked.

"Yes," I agreed. "No more silliness. I promise."

Rosanna smiled and began to carve out eyes and a mouth on her clay ball. Jackson, meanwhile, had a deep frown.

"Is there anything you need to ask me?" I said.

He shook his head.

By the end of the class, Rosanna and I were chatting quite naturally, but I realised Jackson would be a harder nut to crack.

Rosanna had made a sculpture of her daddy and we giggled at the odd clay features. She ran around me to Jackson.

"Melted-face man," Rosanna said, clapping him on the back.

He had fashioned a normal face on one side and a grotesque distortion on the other side.

I pushed back my chair.

"What happened to his face on that side?" I asked.

"It melted," Jackson said, matter-of-factly.

"Why would it melt?" I said.

"Something melted it," Rosanna observed, logically.

"He's certainly been in the wars," I said, and immediately my hand went to my throat.

"What's wrong?" Jackson asked.

"Nothing," I replied. "I just remembered something I'd written about the war in my novel."

"He needs to find the lady upstairs," Jackson explained. "Trouble is, he can never find her."

"Why's that?" I asked.

"'Cos she's not there, silly," Rosanna said, grabbing my shoulder.

"Where is she?" I persisted.

"No one knows where she is," Rosanna said, her palms turned up. "Don't you get it? That's the problem. She's gone and no one knows where."

"Do you know who the lady is?" I asked.

"We don't know her name," Jackson confided.

"But melted-face man 'lourves' her," Rosanna added, grinning from ear to ear.

"Have you seen any other strange things at the house?" I had to know.

"The lady who lives on the stairs," Rosanna said.

"And who's she?" I asked.

Jackson shrugged. "She's stuck on the stairs."

"It's something no one knows," Rosanna said.

"Is she the same lady melted-face man is looking for?" I asked, putting two and two together.

"We're only kids," Jackson replied. "We don't know."

I smiled at that.

"Okay," I said. "But are you frightened when you come to my house?"

They shook their heads.

"Because I'm sure that melted-face man and the lady who lives on the stairs aren't bad people," I added, hoping what I was saying was true.

"Jack and me see lots of things in your house," Rosanna admitted.

"Like what?" I murmured, afraid of what I might hear.

"We saw a pretty lady dancing with a man in your green room," Jackson piped up.

"And I thought they were in 'lourve' too," Rosanna cried, clasping her hands together.

"You think everyone's in love," Jackson said, making faces at her.

"Debbie said it was our imagination," Rosanna said. "And Dad said because you're our mum, we're very imaginative."

"That's probably true," I agreed. "You just need to tell me if anything happens that frightens you."

"We will," they promised.

First Draft

December 1916

"Why hasn't Alfred contacted me?" Lydia asked Mavis as they stood together in the attic room of Rosebay House.

"He told me to tell you..." Mavis began fidgeting with her sleeve and looking at the ground.

"He told you to tell me what?" Lydia asked, taking her gently by the shoulders.

"He told me that he won't be seeing you again." Mavis gulped. "And that he hoped you are happy enough as a married lady."

Lydia turned away, as her heart beat hard against her chest.

"Why doesn't he want to see me?" she whispered.

She was taken back to childhood and the wait for her father to come home. More often than not, he would choose to spend the evening with his associates, rather than his daughter. The feelings of being abandoned and all alone in the world had never left her. That is until she found a connection with Alfred so many years ago.

She turned once more to the awkward girl. "He's returned to England and is staying with his sister about a mile away from here?"

"That's right, Miss," Mavis replied.

"He was injured in the Battle of the Somme?"

"Yes, Miss."

"Badly injured?"

"I couldn't say, Miss," Mavis murmured, rubbing her sweaty palms together.

EYES OF CHINA BLUE

"What do you mean, Mavis? Why won't you tell me?" Lydia's blue eyes blazed as Mavis shrugged.

"I'm sorry," Lydia said, putting an arm around her. "I know your brothers haven't returned from the battle."

"We lost them all," Mavis whispered. "Mum hasn't stopped crying and Dad sits by the fire smoking his pipe and looking into thin air."

"I'm so sorry. Is there anything I can do?" Lydia asked. "I can visit your parents if you think that would help?"

"There's nothing anyone can do," Mavis sighed. "They're all dead."

"What a terrible war this is," Lydia cried. "Our young men killed and injured."

"At least Alfred made it home," Mavis said.

"I'm quite at a loss to know why he won't see me," Lydia said. "Especially if he's injured. Perhaps I can help with his recovery?"

She patted Mavis's arm.

"Tell him Mr Archer has left for France as an officer," Lydia said. "Say that if he's unable to come to the house, I will ride over to see him."

Mavis nodded tearfully.

"Here's some money, Mavis. It's not much but it's all I have right now." She handed her some coins. "Go and see him right away."

Mavis took the money and put it in a secret pocket inside her skirt.

"And Mavis," Lydia added. "I'll get you money. I don't want you walking the towpath late at night."

December 1916
Dearest Lydia,
Please don't be angry with Mavis for delivering this

letter.

While I was away at war, I did a lot of thinking about us. This thinking has led me to believe that now you have a family, your rightful place is with your husband.

We were fanciful in our wish to be together. You are a lady and I am but a common coachman and lately soldier.

I can see now that it is our Christian duty never to see each other again.

Once my health is restored, I will leave this place, never to return.

I wish you a long and happy life.

Alfred

Lydia sat beside Mavis on a bench by the river. Her hand dropped to her side, the letter fluttering in the breeze.

"I don't believe his feelings for me could change so," she stammered through tears.

Mavis stared ahead.

"You've seen him," Lydia said. "Has he changed so entirely that all regard for me has died?"

"He's different," Mavis said, tight-lipped. "What he's been through would change a man."

"Then I am without hope," Lydia sighed.

I turned to the mirror. Lydia had her head in her hands, the letter on the floor beside her.

CHAPTER TWENTY-SEVEN

Don't Give Up

First Draft

Lydia approached the old cottage where Alfred was staying with his sister. A man, his back to her, was chopping wood behind the low, narrow building. He lost balance and nearly fell, saving himself by leaning on the long-handled axe. He swore quietly and swung the axe once more.

She dismounted and led her horse, picking up her skirts as she went. The man turned, glanced at her, dropped the axe and staggered towards the cottage.

"Alfred!" she cried as he disappeared inside.

Lydia tied the horse to the fence as Elspeth, Alfred's sister, opened the door. She looked flustered, twisting her apron between her hands.

"I wish to see Alfred. And don't tell me he's not here; I have already seen him," Lydia said, looking beyond the young woman into the gloomy cottage.

"If you'll 'scuse me, Miss, Alfred's not seeing visitors presently," Elspeth said, squirming.

She had the same blue-grey eyes and light brown hair as her brother.

"I'm not a visitor. I am his... friend," Lydia cried.

"Please tell him I wish to see him at once!"

Elspeth wrung her hands and peered into the darkness behind her.

"If you please, Miss," she said. "I will go and speak to my brother to see what's to be done."

"Ask him to come outside," Lydia begged. "I'll not take up much of his time."

Elspeth closed the door softly.

Lydia heard raised voices coming from inside. She tugged at her lacy gloves, pulling them out of shape as she waited for the outcome of the exchange.

The door creaked and Alfred sidled out, facing away from her and flattening himself against the cottage wall. Lydia took a step towards him, grabbing his shoulders. A small gasp escaped from her lips as he straightened up to face her.

The left side of his face was puckered and raw. The hair was scorched and thinned on that side of his scalp. His left eye was partially closed. His ear was no more than a small crescent of burnt flesh. She reached out and touched the scar tissue; it hung in puckered layers, distorting his chin and mouth.

"God in heaven," Lydia whispered.

"Don't touch me," he cried, stepping away.

"What happened to you?" she asked, tears welling in her eyes.

"Why did you have to come?" he asked. "Go away and leave me be."

"You can't mean that?" she said. "You need me more than ever."

"What, to remind me of what can never be?" he groaned.

"To remind you of the love I bear for you," she

said, grasping his shoulders tighter. "Your injury doesn't change how I feel about you. You must think I'm an inconstant woman if you think it does."

"You must forget about me," he said, turning the injured side of his face away. "You and me being together, it wasn't real before. You'd soon regret choosing a life with me. People would shun us, wherever we went."

"I don't care about people, I only care about you," she said.

Alfred slumped against the wall, tears falling freely, soaking his shirt. Lydia let him go, stepping back, her hands hanging loosely by her side.

"My love for you runs so deep that it isn't changed by your scars," she said. "My life means nothing if there is no chance of you being in it."

"Please don't," he begged her. "I can't bear it."

"Listen to me," she said, taking his hand. "I don't see your wounds. I see the man I love. My dear Alfred. I've waited and prayed for you every day and night."

"I'm broken. Not just on the surface but inside too," he cried. "I'm not the man you knew. I'm changed by the things I've seen and the things I've done."

"Let me take good care of you and help you mend," she begged. "However long it takes, let me help you."

"It's not as easy as that," he said, breaking away.

"You have to give me a chance," she said, holding her hands out to him.

"Lydia," he turned to her. "I've shot someone in the face at close range and watched him fall to his knees, crying for his mother. I've closed my ears to men dying in agony in no man's land. When I go to sleep at night, I feel the bullet hitting me and knocking me sideways, over and over again."

"Is that what happened?" she asked.

"I got hit by a sniper's bullet," he murmured, staring at the ground. "It went in at the jaw and destroyed my facial muscles. It emerged singeing my ear and my scalp. The surgeon said I was lucky, I could've been killed if it had been half an inch to the right."

"Oh, my love," she said. "I can only thank God you're alive."

He stared at her. "Thank God? I'm disfigured for life. Children will scream and run from me."

"I don't care what you look like. You are my true husband," she said, approaching him.

"No," he cried, backing away along the cottage.

Lydia reached out and took his hand again.

"I've prayed for your safe return every day. It's all I've lived for," she sobbed.

"You must forget about me and the dreams we had," he said, pushing her hand away. "We were foolish to think we could make any kind of a life before my injury. But now!"

"How can I? Do you think I can live with my vile husband, knowing you are out in the world somewhere, alone?" she cried.

"Look at me," he murmured, his hands shaking. "I'm no longer a man. I'm a wretched freak."

"You are still my beloved Alfred," she said. "Please let me care for you. It's all I've lived for since you left for war."

"Go home, Lydia," he shouted, making her jump. "Go home to your husband and your baby. There's nothing for you here."

He strode past her into the cottage.

Alfred appeared in the mirror, leaning on a table in the

gloomy cottage, his head hidden in his arms. I heard Lydia knocking gently on the door and calling his name. Eventually, she must have given up, as silence descended on the unhappy figure.

He lifted his head and stared out at me. The undamaged side of his face was a poignant reminder of how arrestingly handsome he had been. At least I now knew who the melted-face man was.

I sat at my desk for a long time after the image faded, feeling upset and distressed. I had read on the internet about the appalling injuries WW1 soldiers had returned home with; and early attempts at plastic surgery to treat facial wounds.

My phone disturbed my contemplation.

"Hi Charlie, how are you?" I asked.

"Fine thanks," she replied. "I just wondered how you're getting on with things?"

"I've been invited to a lavish party in London for the launch of someone's book," I said.

"Amazing! The only thing I've been invited to is a bring-and-buy sale at the church hall," she replied.

"Except," I cautioned. "It will be a massive challenge for me. The champagne will flow all night and the waiters almost force you to take a glass. And if I feel stressed or if someone pisses me off, the first thing I'll do is reach for a drink."

"In the past, you might have done," she said. "You're a different person now. You don't drink anymore, remember? Anyway, you didn't touch a drop while we were away with the kids and they were pretty demanding at times."

"I don't intend to drink," I agreed. "But you know how people insist? Almost to make them feel better. It will be an over-the-top, drink as much as you like and don't leave until you're completely rat-arsed, kind of affair."

She giggled, but I could tell she was also thinking about my predicament and that was usually a good sign.

"You'll have to deal with people who'll want to press alcohol on you all of the time," she eventually said. "That's the nature of your business, right?"

"I suppose," I mumbled.

"Then approach this event as a test," she suggested.

"What can I say – I'm pregnant or training for the marathon?" I sighed.

"Why don't you be honest and tell people you don't drink anymore?" she suggested. "You'd be surprised how many people have given up drinking. Many of our friends for instance."

"I don't want to answer awkward questions," I admitted. "You know how nosey people can be? Especially writers. I'm not solid enough yet to fend off other people's curiosity."

"Thing is Moi, this has got to be you now," she said. "You have to think of yourself as a non-drinker. You have to say 'no thank you' every time you're offered a drink."

"Hmm," I breathed. "That is a discomforting thought. I'm still determined not to drink, but that doesn't mean I don't crave it. I hoped the longing would have faded by now. But every day I'm tempted. When I'm in the supermarket or walking past a pub. Just one drink, that's all to get that feeling of—"

"You're doing so well; I'm so proud of you," she interrupted, and I smiled. "Tell you what. If you're tempted to drink while you're at the party, call me. I'm on lates so I don't care what time it is. Promise?"

"I promise."

CHAPTER TWENTY-EIGHT

Encounters

First Draft

Lydia followed Mavis along the dark towpath by the river. The old oak trees that lined the path were bare and still in the cold night air. An owl flew low over their heads, hooting in annoyance at their presence.

"Is it much further?" Lydia asked.

"No, Miss. Along here a bit," Mavis replied.

They passed the weir, leaving the tumultuous sound of water cascading behind them. Ahead, two black figures were outlined against the gently flowing river.

"Alfred!" Lydia called, and the taller of the two looked up.

As the women got closer they could see the other figure, a child of ten or eleven, fishing with a long pole.

"What are you doing here?" Alfred asked, shaking his head.

"I had to see you," Lydia replied.

"Mavis, take Miss Lydia back home," Alfred demanded. "What are you thinking about, bringing a lady to the river in the middle of the night? It's not safe."

"I couldn't stop her," Mavis mumbled. "What the lady wants, the lady gets."

"Don't blame Mavis," Lydia said, approaching him. "I want to talk to you."

"Toby," Alfred called to the child. "Keep an eye on the float."

He took Lydia by the arm and led her towards the racecourse. In the dim light, with his left side facing away, he looked no different from when he'd left for war and she couldn't help but stroke his cheek.

"Please don't," he objected. "I can't tolerate it."

"Alfred," she said, her palms held out to him. "I have only lived for your return. I've longed to be reunited with you. I simply don't care about your injuries."

"You don't know what you're saying," he murmured. "I had very little to offer you before, but now I'm disfigured. I have nothing to offer you."

She took a step towards him.

"No." He held his hand up to her face. "Go and don't come back. Whatever fantasy we had of being together as man and wife somewhere far away from here is dead and gone. I cannot be a husband to you. My life is over, as would yours be."

"Please don't push me away," she declared, grabbing his hand. "I've loved you for most of my life and that hasn't changed. I am convinced we may still make a life for ourselves somehow."

"You have no idea of what lies ahead," he whispered. "We cannot survive without a man's work and no one will employ me looking like this."

"That's just not true," she said. "You're a war hero and people will be honoured to offer you employment. Besides, I can teach or copy legal documents. I can sew and set myself up as a dressmaker."

He shook his head. "You don't know what it is to

be poor. The cold, the hunger, the poverty. You'd end working your fingers to the bone for a pittance and into the bargain, hating me and our life together."

He broke away. Lydia followed, putting her arms around him, her cheek resting on his shoulder. He felt thin and undernourished in her embrace.

"If you leave me here I will have to endure a lifetime of misery with Hubert," she reasoned. "He has made it clear that he wants more children when the war's over. Can you imagine going to bed with a man you despise?"

Alfred shook his head to dispel the disturbing images parading through his mind.

"Then you must speak of him to your father," he said.

"I haven't seen my father in weeks," she said. "He knows how unhappy I am and he feels responsible. I know for sure he would not interfere between a man and his wife. Even if the wife is me."

"I'm desperately sorry for you," he said. "But I know that sooner or later you'd be equally unhappy if you were with me."

"I would not," she said. "I would be the happiest woman alive."

He turned and held her gaze. His arms reached out as he pulled her close, burying his face in her lavender-smelling hair.

"You are the most determined woman I have ever met," he said, lifting her chin.

"I won't ever give up on you." She smiled.

He rested the handsome side of his face against hers, but she lifted her hands to his face and kissed him on the lips.

"I love you," she said.

"You know how much I love you," he said.

"I have good news," she said. "Your son was born, hale and hearty."

"My son?" he asked. "How can you be sure?"

"He has the same eyes as you," she smiled.

Alfred nodded and kissed her again.

A shout rang out and Alfred took her by the hand and limped across the grass to where the boy was waving the rod around as if he were conducting an orchestra.

"Be still, Toby," Alfred commanded, steadying the rod.

"It's a biggun'," the boy cried, planting his feet.

Alfred and Toby carefully reeled the fish in towards the bank as Mavis pushed a net under the thrashing, silver creature.

"Well done, boy," Alfred said, holding the large, flapping fish up by the gills. "That's a good-sized chub."

The boy grinned from ear to ear. "Mother will be so pleased to have something big and plentiful for the cooking pot."

"She won't be all that pleased," Alfred added. "The blighter's full of bones."

He dropped the fish into a bucket, smiling down at the boy.

"This is one of my eldest sister's boys," he said to Lydia.

"Oh, your nephew," she said, noticing the boy's floppy brown hair.

Alfred nodded.

"How do you do?" Lydia said as the boy lifted his cap.

"You'd better escort Miss Lydia home, Mavis,"

EYES OF CHINA BLUE

Alfred said.

I caught my reflection in a mirror as I strode into the upmarket restaurant, where the book launch party was being held. I'd invested in a mannish black jacket with wide trousers and I looked good in an Annie Hall kind of style.

My agent Lucy and I air kissed in greeting.

"Moira, it's so great to see you," she said. "You look wonderful, darling. Drink?"

She beckoned a waiter.

"No, thanks," I said, biting my lip. "A glass of water, please?"

Lucy smiled. "Not drinking?"

"I've given up," I said, and it felt surprisingly good. "For the time being."

She nodded and smiled. "Good for you."

That was easy.

"How's the novel coming along?" she asked.

"It's great," I said.

"Have you decided what the ending should be yet?"

"No. It hasn't materialised," I said, pursing my lips.

"You sound like you're waiting for divine intervention," she laughed.

"Something like that," I chuckled.

The smile was wiped off my face when I noticed Freddie, his arm around a middle-aged woman I recognised.

"Isn't that—?" I stuttered.

"Yes," Lucy interrupted. "Freddie is with Marie Lamarr, the Editor of *New York's Fashion Bible*."

I shook my head as I watched Freddie grinning and prancing around the famous socialite.

"How long has that been going on?" I asked.

"Only a couple of months," she answered.

I laughed, clapping my hands together and he looked over.

"He hedged his bets," I whispered in her ear. "He must

have been dating her whilst begging me to take him back."

"He's a dickhead," she said. "He's tried it on with every wealthy woman here. I didn't like to say anything when you were with him, but you're better off without him."

I felt sick to my stomach. Everyone must have known what a fool he was making of me at the time. I excused myself and went to the other side of the room to a table laden with food. Usually being completely pissed, I'd never eaten at these functions. I picked at the sumptuous array of food until I felt a tap on the shoulder.

Freddie stood before me, an amused look on his handsome face.

"You look great," he said.

"I know," I replied, walking away.

"Can I get you a drink?" he offered, catching up.

How I wanted to say yes.

My phone vibrated in my bag and I glanced to see an encouraging message from Charlie. She was psychic.

"No thanks," I murmured, picking up a prawn on a stick. "I don't drink anymore."

"Still on the wagon?" he frowned, thrusting his hands deep into his pockets.

"I am," I confirmed, and left the table.

"Wait," he urged.

I stopped, feeling mildly amused at the panic in his voice.

"There's something weird going on in your house," he said, raising his eyebrows.

"Nothing I can't handle," I shrugged.

"I'm sorry," he said. "You deserved better than me,"

"You're right," I said, twirling a tassel on my bag.

"We were great together," he added.

"No," I disagreed. "I was great for you. That's why you're here and not photographing some darts match in a grotty pub."

He shifted awkwardly from foot to foot as I continued.

"I lost everything precious in my life: my kids, my house. I'd worked so hard for it all. And on top of that, I almost lost my sanity."

I'd never been brave enough to be honest, and for once he was silent, staring down at the floor.

"You were the biggest mistake of my life, Freddie," I said triumphantly. "I'll never be stupid enough to love someone as selfish and self-centred as you ever again."

His eyes flicked up.

"I'm pleased for you, babe," he said huskily.

"So you can go back to your fifty-year-old celebrity," I said, pointing in her direction. "Because this ship has sailed for good."

I turned on my heel and wove in and out of the crowd. Freddie's new sugar mummy watched as I departed, so I flung her a sarcastic air kiss.

CHAPTER TWENTY-NINE

Destiny Calling

First Draft

Summer 1917

Alfred held the wriggling child on his lap, noticing his grey-blue eyes. The child stared back at him, pouting and sticking a thumb between his cherry-like lips.

"He's a beauty," Alfred said, choking on the words.

"He takes after his father," Lydia said proudly.

"Is he big for a two-year-old?" Alfred asked.

"You're not accustomed to seeing a well-fed child, that's all," Lydia replied.

They had moored the small sailing craft against an uninhabited island in the Thames and the vessel rocked gently to and fro.

"He has something of my family's look about him," Alfred said.

"Unfortunately he was christened Hubert, John," Lydia frowned. "But we'll call him Alfred when we leave."

"Mmm," he nodded. "You're still planning on leaving?"

"Very much so!" she cried, making the child wince. "We must leave soon. Hubert could return home at any minute if there's a decisive battle."

"There's no chance of that, my love," he said, kissing the top of the boy's head. "We've fought over the same muddy, potholed bit of ground for years. No one gets to win. Good men die is all."

"Is it that bad?" she asked.

"Men live in mud holes like worms. The bombardment never ends and you feel like you might go mad with the thunderous noise and the continuous threat of being blown to pieces," he murmured.

The child began to squirm and Lydia took him from Alfred.

"We can't imagine what it's like," she said. "Sleeping soundly in our beds every night while our men are away fighting."

"It's a nightmare I still haven't woken up from," he said. "My sister dropped a big iron pot on the floor yesterday and I nearly jumped out of my skin. It took all day for me to calm down."

The boy snuggled in her arms and closed his eyes.

"I suspect it's something you'll carry with you forever," she said. "You have not told me exactly how you got shot. If it is not too painful to recount, I would like to know."

"It's not a pretty story," he began, leaning back in the boat. "We'd been under constant bombardment for days. The Rifles were given orders to move forward and pick off the enemy if they attacked," he gulped. "As we hurried along the trenches to our position, a German sniper came out of nowhere and began firing at us."

Lydia held his hand as he continued. "I was hit and fell. I must have been out cold for a while and that probably saved me. The sniper took no notice of me, thinking I was dead. When I came to, I couldn't believe the carnage," he murmured. "Most of the soldiers, my friends, had been shot and were either dead or injured. I couldn't see very well. My face swelled up like a football, the pain was unbearable."

He squeezed his eyes closed, covering his face with his hands. Lydia laid the sleepy child down on her coat in the curved bow of the boat and pulled Alfred close.

"I was one of the lucky buggers who lived," he cried. "Others, men with families most of them, were slaughtered."

"I thank God you survived," Lydia said. "I feel very sorry for the other men, but I thank God that you returned to me. Despite your injuries."

"The wounds are healing and it's not as painful, but I'll always have to face the world with these ugly scars," he said. "Oh Lydia, why are you here with me? It just don't make sense."

"Because I love you and so will our son when he gets to know you," she said.

"I will give you the money I saved," he said, dropping his hands in his lap. "You must leave here and make a life for yourself and the boy far away, where Hubert can't find you."

"I'm not going without you." She stood and rocked the boat. The child whimpered, staring up at her.

"You'll have no life with me and neither will he." Alfred pointed at the boy. "We won't be able to give him a good home, or decent clothes. And he won't have a proper education like you've had."

She hesitated.

"I'll educate him," she said, sitting back down. "I will give him lessons every day in all I know."

"He won't be a gentleman," Alfred continued.

"He'll be the son of a poor man and live a life of just getting by."

She frowned. "I had not given any thought to his life and how it would be," she admitted, lifting the child and cuddling him.

"It'll be kinder to leave him here with Hubert if you're set on going away," Alfred muttered.

"Abandon our son?" Lydia whispered, turning the child around to face Alfred. "We won't be able to give him riches, that's true. But we will love and cherish him. Besides, times are changing. There will be more opportunities for him as he gets older. I am convinced of it."

"Is Hubert a good father?" Alfred asked.

"Gentlemen are superfluous to the raising of their children," Lydia said, a wry smile on her lips. "As my father did with me, Hubert employs someone else to bring up his child and rarely sees him."

The boy's face creased and he began to cry. Alfred took the child in his arms, softly singing to him.

"When he's older," Lydia continued. "He will be sent away to boarding school where he will be beaten and bullied or 'made to be a man', as my father calls it. He will grow up to be a man without empathy or the ability to love."

"That's a harsh view of the gentry," Alfred said, still bouncing the boy on his knee.

"It's my experience of people in my class," she said, tidying her hair. "Why do you think I prefer you and Mavis?"

"My family were often surprised at how much time you spent with us and the servants," Alfred said. "Mother used to say you'd grow up wielding a bucket rather than a looking glass."

"I suppose she was right. I am not comfortable arranging afternoon tea parties and spending hours embroidering," she agreed. "However much Hubert expects it of me."

"We cannot escape the truth," Alfred said, looking deep into the child's eyes. "Being raised in a poor household will be tough on the little fellow and no mistake."

"We may only leave if we leave together as a family," Lydia asserted.

"I can't fight you," Alfred whispered.

After my AA meeting, I got home and worked long into the night. I must have dozed off because I awoke laying awkwardly on the sofa in my garret.

The sky was magenta in the east and tiny wisps of pink clouds hung above the horizon. I rubbed my tired eyes as I yawned in front of the mirror.

I heard scratching on the other side of the door. My hand shot to my throat, imagining a large rat determined to get into the room. As the solid door rattled in its frame, I understood something more substantial than a rodent was agitating it. It stopped and the room was silent again apart from the sound of my labouring breath. Then a rhythmic pounding on the door vibrated around the hexagonal room as I sank to my knees, which were shaking uncontrollably.

A shadow stained the bottom edge of the mirror, grainy and out of focus at first. As it became clearer, I saw a figure crawling towards me on all fours, the head hanging down. Long hair hung in dirty ribbons as the creature raised black, claw-like, withered hands and clung onto the frame of the mirror. With a massive effort, it hauled itself into the room and flopped, sodden onto the floor.

It slowly raised its face – what was left of it. Rotting

skin and the absence of lips revealed a full set of teeth and the underlying bleached bones of the skull. Black eye sockets stared, as if, despite the lack of eyeballs, it was watching me intensely.

I clambered onto the desk, pinning myself against the window as the repugnant creature struggled to its feet. An injured shoulder hung low, causing the gaunt head to loll to one side. A tattered gown, covered in mud and trailing dripping vegetation, draped to the floor. Raising its putrid arms, it stretched rotting fingers towards me. It was perfectly still as if locked in this grotesque pose.

The mirror reflected a pallid face, the skin stretched taut across the cheekbones, the eyes wide with fear. A high-pitched squeal rang loudly in my ears.

Golden shafts of sunlight cut across the room creating a bright glare from the sunrise. I could see nothing for a few moments before I tugged the easterly shutter closed, plunging the room into gloominess. The mirror, I realised, reflected me, my mouth wide open, screaming at the top of my voice.

"It's okay," I whimpered, clasping my hands to my chest and realising the corpse-like figure was gone.

I climbed down from the desk, shaking from head to toe as my teeth chattered in my head. The room was thankfully back to normal as fingers of sunlight crept around the shutter. I rested the palm of my hand on the cool surface of the mirror. My reflection resembled some wild, mad creature, blinking and jerking its head from side to side.

I got a hold of myself, breathing slowly and deeply as the colour came back to my cheeks and my eyes resumed their normal size.

The carpet felt wet as I slid to the floor. My mind struggled to comprehend the soaking, decayed presence I'd seen in my garret. I wondered if she was a regular visitor. The permanently soggy stairs and what Freddie claimed to have seen would back this up. I dearly hoped the twins hadn't seen the awful decaying corpse that had crawled out of the mirror and joined me that morning.

My nerves jangled as I searched for my car keys, desperate to get out of the house and whatever was lurking there. I drove around for ages as the rising sun lit up the landscape, casting a reassuring glow. Subconsciously, I headed for sanctuary and reassurance. I found myself parking outside a large hospital; Charlie would finish her shift at seven.

"This is a nice surprise," she said as I leaned against her car.

"Have you got time to talk?" I asked.

"Seeing you've come all this way, how can I refuse?" she replied.

We found a petrol station cafe and bought coffee and croissants.

"You look terrible. Have you been drinking?" she asked.

"No," I replied. "Thanks to you and my AA meetings, I'm still doing okay."

"I'm glad," she said, patting my hand.

"It's my house," I said, scratching my head. "There's weird stuff going on."

"What do you mean?" She tried to hide a yawn behind her hand.

"You remember that the twins were frightened by melted-face man?" I reminded her. "I've seen him too. And today a corpse-like thing crept out of the mirror."

"Huh?" She raised her eyebrows.

"My house is haunted," I proclaimed.

"Are you sure you haven't been drinking?" she asked again.

"No— I— have— not," I replied. "Even Freddie saw something that scared the bejesus out of him."

"He was most likely high." She pursed her lips, just like our mum used to when we were kids in trouble.

"I'm telling you," I said. "The house is haunted by its former occupants."

"Are you serious?" She leaned on the table, supporting her chin in her hands.

"The book I'm writing," I began, even though a voice in my head told me to shut up. "It's being dictated by Lydia, the woman who lived in Rosebay House in the 1900s."

"Of course it is," she muttered.

"I had writer's block for two years," I cried. "I was struggling until I saw a pair of china blue eyes reflected on my computer. I started writing and I haven't stopped."

"I think you should see your doctor," she said. "You're having more hallucinations."

"No, Charlie," I begged. "You've got to listen."

"You're not making sense and I've got to get home and have some sleep," she sighed, getting up to leave. "Call me later."

CHAPTER THIRTY

Retribution

First Draft

Alfred tossed pebbles up at Lydia's window from the garden of Rosebay House. He heard a cough coming from the shrubs and he turned to see Hubert striding across the garden, smoking a cigar.

"My God. You're not a pretty sight," Hubert said, grinning. "Did you argue with a bullet?"

Alfred went to leave.

"What are you doing here?" Hubert asked, adopting a wide-leg stance, his hands planted on his hips.

"I've given Cook some rabbits I caught earlier," he said, partially telling the truth.

"So you've not come to see my loving wife?" Hubert smirked. "I don't suppose she's so fond of you now. God, you're an ugly beast."

Alfred's hand instinctively covered his scarred face.

"It's no good trying to cover it, boy," Hubert chuckled. "How I desired you and your pretty face. Well, you need not worry, I'll not be bothering you again."

"Pleased to hear it, sir," Alfred said as he left by the side entrance.

As Alfred strode along the towpath towards his sister's cottage, he was nearly bowled over by Mavis as she ran out of the trees, adjusting her clothes.

"You're not up to your old tricks?" he asked, noticing her flushed face.

"What's it got to do with you if I am?" she cried.

"I was of the notion that Miss Lydia gave you money to keep you from meeting chaps on the towpath?" he said.

"She does," Mavis admitted. "But it's not enough to feed me and Mum and Dad. Now the boys have gone I have to take care of them."

Alfred sighed and smiled his twisted smile.

"Here, take this," he said, thrusting some coins into her hand.

"Thanks," she said, reaching up and kissing him.

"Promise me you'll stop hanging around the towpath," he said. "It's not safe."

"It's nice of you to worry about me," she said.

She leaned her head against his chest, encircling him with her arms.

"Have you heard?" he asked. "The master has returned home."

"Miss Lydia told me," Mavis replied. "He came home the day before yesterday. Something about a disgrace in France and him being sent home to do a desk job."

"So he's home for good?" Alfred murmured.

"I believe so," Mavis replied.

I'd spent half an hour sitting outside a grotty pub. The temptation to go in and buy a bottle of wine and snuggle in a corner and drink it all still tormented me.

The person I was waiting for staggered out, unzipped his trousers and urinated against the wall.

"They have toilets, you know," I said.

E W GRANT

He held onto the wall, zipping his trousers as he focussed on me.

"You!" Mark accused, staggering over and holding onto the table.

His clothes were grubby and he was unshaven.

"How did you find me?" he slurred.

"James," I sighed.

He lowered himself onto the bench, still grasping the table.

"Have you come to gloat?" he mumbled.

"James was worried about you," I said.

"He should have let me finish it," he cried. "He should've let me die."

"He loves you."

"He's a fool."

"We keep letting down the people we love," I said.

He nodded and began to weep.

"I know how hard it is," I said. "I constantly have to remind myself that I'm an alcoholic. I wrestle with the pain every day."

He looked up, his face wet with tears.

"I have to stop. I feel like shit. I hate myself. Trouble is— trouble is… I don't believe it's possible," he whispered.

"There are no guarantees," I said. "But I'm into my third month of sobriety and although some days I could kill for a drink, I fight it. I fight it because I wake up in the morning and feel healthy and full of energy. I fight it because I get to spend time with my kids and they're not terrified of what I'll get up to. But most of all, it's because I remember the look on the faces of the people I love when they've had to rescue me from some shit hole I've got pissed in."

He rubbed his face, closing his eyes. "Help me, Moira."

Mark's head lolled from side to side as if his neck were made of jelly and his mouth hung open on the car journey back to the house. The stale smell of alcohol was nauseating. I was shocked to think I had undoubtedly looked the same every time my sister had rescued me from some drunken escapade.

I let James know his brother was safely passed out on my sofa. I opened my laptop and continued writing as Mark snored and mumbled in his drunken sleep.

First Draft

"We have no one to saddle the horses with all of the men at war," Lydia said, standing by the stable door.

"That's all right my dear," Hubert said. "I know how to saddle a horse."

"I'd rather not ride today," she admitted. "I think baby Hubert is slightly under the weather. I should get back and see that he is comfortable."

"Nonsense," Hubert smirked. "That's why we have a nanny so that we don't worry about such trivia. Come, you know how to put on a bridle and I'll do the saddles."

Lydia went ahead to the tack room and stretched up to get a bridle off the hook. She felt Hubert's breath on her neck as he grabbed her and lifted her skirts.

"Get away from me!" she cried, struggling.

He held her firmly around the waist, pulling her frilly undergarments down. She gritted her teeth as he forced her legs apart, thrusting against her and grunting in satisfaction.

"Lydia," Alfred called from the yard.

"Go on, cry out for him," Hubert whispered in her ear.

She clamped her lips tightly together.

Alfred entered the tack room. "Lydia!" he cried.

"She detests my lovemaking. I have to force her," Hubert said to Alfred, his hands grasping Lydia's bare hips. "It makes me desire her even more."

Alfred flew across the stable, thumping Hubert on

the side of the head and sending him crashing into a bench. He grabbed Lydia, pushing her behind him as she rearranged her clothes.

Hubert lay laughing in a heap on the floor. "She's my wife." He grinned. "You can't stop me from fucking her."

"Touch her again and I'll kill you," Alfred seethed.

"Do you mean that?" Hubert got up, buttoning his fly. "Are you going to kill me for bedding my wife? You once had the chance of taking her place but you refused."

"What does he mean?" Lydia asked.

"You couldn't begin to understand," Hubert said, pointing at Lydia. "The companionship and affection men have for each other, I wanted with Alfred. I was so enamoured by his handsome face and strong body."

"Some of the soldiers in the trenches partook of the companionship you describe," Alfred said, Lydia, clutching his arm. "But they had become good friends before anything happened. You thought you could claim me and I would submit, just because you're rich and I'm poor."

"If you had accommodated me, life would have been very pleasant for us all," Hubert surmised.

Lydia pushed past Alfred. "You are a filthy beast," she confronted Hubert. "If you come near me again, I'll make sure you'll regret it, I promise you!"

Hubert laughed. "What will you do? Set your cripple on me? Come, my dear, be realistic."

He spat on the floor and strode out of the room laughing, a deeply disturbing sound.

"Why did you threaten to kill him?" Lydia demanded as she held onto Alfred's coat. "He might tell someone in authority and get you arrested."

"I will kill him," Alfred said. "If he touches you again in front of me, I will kill him."

"I know you must have been very shocked, seeing what he was doing to me," she said, her face hot and flustered. "But it did not happen by chance. I am sure he did it on purpose."

"I know it," Alfred said. "He sent a boy to fetch me to help with the horses. So I came."

"He wanted to provoke you," she agreed. "We have to leave now, there's not a moment to waste. We have to make plans and quickly."

"How can we if he's watching our every move?" Alfred said. "We stood a chance of leaving while he was in France, but now he's returned it makes it much harder to get away."

"We'll find a way," Lydia said, clasping her hands together. "Give me time to think. I can stand it no longer."

"He'll come looking if we take the child," he added. "You mark my words. He won't let the child go."

"You must leave first," Lydia said, bright spots of colour on her cheeks. "You go and make a home for us far away from here. Hubert will find out you've gone and think you've abandoned me and that's the end of it. We let the dust settle and later you can write to Elspeth and let me know where you are."

"I can't leave you with him," Alfred objected. "God only knows what he'll do next."

"I will deal with him," Lydia said through gritted teeth. "I'll pretend to settle down so he'll never suspect anything. The boy and I will join you later. We'll go to the West Country. He'll never look for us there."

CHAPTER THIRTY-ONE

Reap What You Sow

"It's a sizeable basement," I pointed out to a bleary-eyed Mark. "There are two rooms. You can use one as a living room and the other as a bedroom."

"Why would you want me here?" he asked, frowning.

"We can help each other," I replied. "We'll have our own space but we can give each other support too."

"But you're far ahead of me in recovering," he sighed, leaning against the doorframe.

"Step up!" I said. "Do you want to get better?"

"I do," he nodded. "I'm going to try hard this time."

"There are rules." I put on my school teacher's voice. "No booze in the house and weekly attendance at the AA."

"Absolutely," he agreed.

"I'll do whatever it takes to help you stay sober." I smiled.

"That's a huge commitment," he said. "You might regret it."

"Was there ever a time when you managed to stay sober?" I asked.

He ran a hand through his hair and walked across the room to the window, staring out at the garden.

"When my son Joshua was born," he said. "Maria, my ex-wife, and I hadn't planned to have a child. I was far too unreliable for that. But when she found out she was pregnant,

206

she was determined to have the baby, with or without my support."

He shook his head. "I didn't touch a drop while she was pregnant or for a good few months after Josh was born."

"What happened?" I asked.

"I loved being a dad," he replied. "I changed nappies and did the nighttime feed sometimes. I still had my presenting job and early mornings, so it was pretty tiring."

He grinned. "Joshua was so gorgeous: blond-haired like his mum and always smiling. I'd rush home from work to give him his bath."

He sighed, rubbing the back of his neck.

"Was Maria the weather woman on your programme?" I asked.

"That's right," he replied. "We met on the show. Our romance was in all the newspapers and we sold the rights to our wedding to *Hello* magazine. I regret that now, but Maria wanted it."

"I remember thinking how happy you looked together. I often watched the show, whilst getting the kids ready for school," I said.

"We were so happy for a while," he said. "I became friendly with a researcher on the show, Sue. She was an attractive woman who confided in me about a difficult, unhappy marriage she was trapped in. At first, I was a friendly ear, but later..."

He grimaced as if he had a bad taste in his mouth. "I foolishly agreed to meet her in a pub for a chat. I thought one beer couldn't hurt – after all, I'd been sober for months."

"It's easily done," I murmured.

"We got pissed and ended up having sex in the back of my car," he said. "Not exactly classy."

"Did your wife find out?" I asked.

"Not that time," he replied. "My wife thought I went to meetings after the show. Sue and I would go to a hotel for the afternoon. Once, when her husband was away, we had sex in her marital bed."

I nodded remembering, painfully, my shameful behaviour.

"I was drinking every day by then," he continued. "I'm sure Maria knew but she never said anything."

"How long did this go on for?" I asked.

"Our sordid little affair lasted about six months," he replied. "We were stupid. We used the same hotel all the time. A picture appeared in one of the tabloids of us snogging, my hand on her arse."

"How awful!" I exclaimed.

"I still presented the show the next day despite the newspaper report," he sighed, rubbing his eyes. "The producers wanted me to make a public apology. It was so humiliating. I hadn't even spoken to my wife about it. There I was, admitting my guilt and asking for forgiveness live on breakfast TV."

"Poor you," I said.

"Worse, so much worse for Maria," he cried. "I was a coward. I didn't go home after the show. I headed for a seedy bar and got drunk. Someone recognised me and made fun of my disgrace. I lashed out. Not being much of a fighter, he managed to beat me unconscious."

"You're kidding," I said.

"Maria picked me up from the hospital. The paparazzi were crowded outside our house in St. Johns Wood." He wrung his hands. "She asked no questions. She took care of me until I recovered. The police asked if I wanted to press charges – of course, I didn't."

"What happened to your lover?" I asked.

"She was sacked from the show and I never heard from her again," he replied. "I was a popular presenter and the public couldn't get enough of me, despite my affair."

"And your marriage?"

"We led separate lives even though we lived under the same roof," he said. "She never forgave me but didn't want to deprive Josh of a father. I continued to drink – sometimes

EYES OF CHINA BLUE

dropping into the pub on the way home, but often downing ten or twelve beers while I watched the TV at home. She never left Josh alone with me and some weekends she went to her parents with him and then I'd go on a proper bender."

I rested my hand on his shoulder.

"As Josh got older," he murmured. "He learnt to ignore drunken daddy. At the time it all seemed normal to me."

"I know how that feels," I said.

"Then I got prosecuted for drunken driving," he cried. "And presented the show drunk more than once."

He snorted, shaking his head.

"Being sacked from the show was the last straw as far as my wife was concerned," he said. "She asked me to leave."

"Where did you go?" I asked.

"I went to Spain for a bit to get away from the furore," he replied, biting his lip. "I ran out of money quite quickly. I was spending a fortune in the bar all day and night buying drinks for my new 'friends'." He raised his eyebrows. "I lived with James when I returned to the UK. I looked for work, even advertising, but no one would touch me with a barge pole."

"I guess you quickly learnt who your real friends were," I said.

"I stupidly began to steal from James to finance my drinking," he said, shaking his head. "That, my dear, was the beginning of my homeless phase. James threw me out and I lived in my car under the underpass."

"How awful!" I said.

"Not really," he smiled wryly. "At least I was dry and could run the engine to keep warm. The other poor buggers only had cardboard and old blankets."

"How long were you there for?"

"After two bloody freezing winter months, James came looking for me," he said. "He insisted I went home with him again and I've been there ever since."

"He's an angel, like my sister," I said.

Mark nodded, putting his arm around my waist.

209

"I've tried to stay in contact with my son but he wants nothing to do with me," he said.

"I'm sorry to hear that," I said. "I hope the twins will forgive me in time. It's the one thing that keeps me on the straight and narrow."

"I don't blame Josh," he said, pulling away and running a finger along the mantlepiece.

"He may change his mind, once you've been sober for a while?" I said looking on the bright side.

"Mmm," he answered. "What are we going to do about furniture then?"

"Let's have a mooch in the junk shops," I suggested. "That will be fun."

"Will it?" he laughed.

First Draft

Alfred and Toby cast the float out into the dark river. Frost was beginning to form sparkling patches on the tree bark and stars twinkled against a black velvet sky.

"Keep the rod still," Alfred instructed.

Heavy footsteps echoed from the towpath above and Alfred peered up to see two thick-set men scrambling down the bank.

"Get lost, kid," one of them said to Toby.

Alfred nodded and Toby ran.

One of them pinned Alfred's arms behind his back, while the other man beat him again and again with his big fists, favouring the injured side of his face. They left him with a final jab to the ribs and he crumpled into a heap by the water.

Alfred gasped for breath, holding his bruised ribs. He heard a swoosh of skirts and Mavis was beside him.

"Who were those men?" she cried, trying to help

him up.

"It don't matter," Alfred breathed. "Just get me home."

Despite Mark's reservations, we did enjoy walking around the junk shops. We bought a desk and a large chest of drawers and I found a large hat with extravagant ostrich feathers sticking out of it. It was similar to one I'd seen Lydia wearing, although this one wasn't particularly old.

We bravely visited a pub and ordered coffee, sitting together on a large sofa by the window. It was only early evening but some of the pub's patrons were clearly drunk and had probably been there for most of the afternoon.

"Gosh, don't drunk people look ridiculous," Mark said, reading my mind.

One man was flat out on a wooden bench, his arms hanging on either side of him, while another sat astride him singing an unrecognisable song at the top of his voice. It was like watching a horrible play.

"I used to wake up from a night on the tiles," I confided, "and glimpses of my drunken behaviour would sear into my memory. Awful things I'd done or said."

"Those recollections are almost as painful as an aching head or repeat vomiting," Mark sighed.

"I agree," I continued. "So was it ever worth it? I mean, you always pay the price if you're an alcoholic, right?"

"For me, it's the only time I feel alive," he said. "Some people climb mountains or ride motorbikes. I have to get pissed before I feel dynamic or animated."

"That's awful," I said, cupping my face. "Does that suggest your life is meaningless without a drink?"

"Not at all." He smiled, taking my hand. "I realise drinking is the easy way out. It takes a lot of effort to build a good life, and maybe you and I in the past haven't always been willing to put in the work."

"But I had put in the work and built a good life," I said. "I threw it away without a moment's hesitation."

"You had the addition of being infatuated by someone who seemed exciting," he said. "But in reality, he was only in it for himself."

"That's true," I agreed. "I felt my life with Cliff was boring and I was missing out on something."

"And Freddie was fun and made you feel great?" he asked.

"At first," I replied. "He was very complimentary and claimed he'd never met anyone as clever or as attractive as me. I'm five years older than him, so I was hugely flattered. Cliff was busy all the time; I hardly saw him."

"So you risked everything," he surmised.

"I was a fool," I admitted. "Freddie and I started seeing each other, secretly at first. But as I got more pissed every day, we became quite blatant about our affair. Cliff found out and begged me to split up with Freddie. I wouldn't, so he left. As soon as Freddie realised I wanted our affair to become something more serious, he backed off and lost interest."

Mark put his arm around my shoulders.

"I even paid the deposit on Freddie's house, thinking it would make him want me," I said. "Of course, it didn't work and I felt like such a loser."

"Hey!" he exclaimed. "You made a mistake, but Freddie was the one in the wrong."

"I had no judgement," I sighed. "I was either drunk or hungover. I felt wonderful when Freddie was with me. But he always had something on and would disappear for days on end. Then I felt like shit."

I sat up straight, grasping my hands together in my lap.

"Sorry, have I been too nosy?" he asked.

"No, not at all," I answered, turning to him. "It's just that Charlie is the only one who has ever been so honest with me. It's refreshing having someone I can be completely open with. Even if it doesn't cast me in a particularly good light."

CHAPTER THIRTY-TWO

The Price

First Draft

"How badly hurt is he?" Lydia asked Mavis, as they met by the side entrance to the garden.

"He's bruised and has a nasty cut above his left eye, where the beasts punched him on the poorly side of his face!" cried Mavis.

"My poor Alfred," Lydia held a handkerchief to her nose.

"He's being cared for by his sister. He sent me to warn you," Mavis said.

"Warn me?"

"He says 'tis the master's doing and that you must be careful." Mavis's face creased as she wiped her nose on her sleeve.

"Don't fret," Lydia said. "I will make sure Alfred is safe from now on. Tell him I'll come by and see him when I can get away."

"Oh no, Miss," Mavis wailed. "He 'specially said you weren't to come."

"Where do you think you're going?" Hubert said, grabbing Lydia's arm just as she was about to climb into the waiting carriage.

"We have leftovers from the kitchen and I am going to give them to a poor family who live near the church," Lydia said.

"That's very charitable of you, my dear," he said. "I've never known you to distribute our leftovers to the poor before."

"That's not true," she objected. "I've kept quite a few families going through the war with leftovers and vegetables from the garden."

"Is that so?" He smiled menacingly. "Perhaps I should take a closer look at the household accounts if we've got such an abundance."

Lydia wrenched her arm from his grip and mounted the carriage steps.

"Don't be so absurd, Hubert," she hissed. "We have more than enough for our needs."

She arranged her voluminous skirt on the carriage seat.

"Maybe I should get my hat and coat and come with you?" he suggested, grinning. "After all, I expect the peasants would be honoured to meet the master of the house."

"No, thank you," she answered. "I can manage on my own."

The driver flicked his whip and the carriage creaked into life.

"Who is that lad driving the carriage?" Hubert asked the housekeeper as the carriage swayed gently away.

"That's Adam, another of young Alfred's nephews," the housekeeper answered.

Hubert sucked on his cigar.

The carriage drove through leafy lanes and past

heavy horses working in fields. Finally, they stopped at Elspeth's cottage. Lydia asked Adam to stay with the horses as she stepped down.

The cottage door was open and Lydia entered. The smell of freshly baked bread made the gloomy interior feel more welcoming.

"I told you not to come," Alfred muttered as she made out his shadowy figure slumped in a chair in the corner of the room.

Lydia caught her breath. His face was unrecognisable.

"What did they do to you?" she cried, kneeling before him. "The beasts, the absolute beasts!"

"If he finds you here, God only knows what he'll do next," Alfred mumbled through bruised lips. "You're not safe. You must leave at once."

Lydia stroked his hair.

"He won't find me," she assured him. "He doesn't like the countryside; too rustic, he says. And he doesn't know his way around the county even now."

"What if one of his henchmen followed you?" he said.

"We were very careful," she said. "Adam turned and looked behind several times to check we were not followed."

"You mustn't take risks," he cried, holding her arms. "If anything happened to you, I'd never forgive myself."

"I had to come to see you," she said. "But we must act quickly to remove you from the district. Who knows what Hubert might be planning next."

"What do you have in mind?" he asked.

"I have brought money," she said, pulling a large

wallet from her pocket. "There's more than enough to get you to the West Country and sustain you for a while."

"How can I leave you and the child with such a devil?" he cried.

"You must," she said, placing the wallet in his hands. "Your life is in danger if you stay."

"I don't care about my life. I only care about you," he murmured, holding his head.

"And I care about you," she declared. "That's why you have to leave and make provision for the child and me."

"How will you escape?" he asked.

"I'll think of something," she said brightly. "Then we can be together and forget the misery we've had to endure over the years."

"You will find it's too difficult to escape with a child," he said. "And the West Country is a long journey for a lady on her own."

"I'm not the genteel lady I was before the war," she confided. "I've worked in fields, I've driven a motorcar. I'm capable of travelling on my own."

Alfred smiled, despite his injuries. "You were never a fine lady," he said. "You preferred grooming horses and picking out their feet rather than playing with your dollies."

"My father despaired," she recollected. "I'd come home, my shoes all muddy, bits of straw sticking out of my hair."

"I had to lead you home on your pony, otherwise you wouldn't leave the stables of a night." He stroked her hair. "I always loved that time of day. Just you and me and the sunset."

"Please promise you'll leave," she begged him.

"I promise," he agreed.

"Hubert is due to stay in London with his mother a few times a week, to fulfil his new role at the ministry," she said. "It may give me the opportunity I need to escape."

Alfred sat up. "You'd have to catch the train from here to London and then travel on to wherever I'm living."

"The problem will be getting our son out of the house," she said, rubbing her lip with a finger. "He has a full-time nanny. I'm never alone with him, except at night."

"That may prove difficult if she's been instructed not to let him out of her sight," he said.

"You leave Mavis and me to sort something out," Lydia said. "You must leave as soon as your injuries have healed. And don't give your full address when you write, just a local railway station or inn. We don't want your whereabouts falling into the wrong hands."

Lydia had her back to me in the mirror, wisps of platinum hair escaping from under her hat. A full yellow skirt billowed across the floor from her tiny waist. Alfred's head leant against her shoulder, and the bruised features of his right side turned to face me. It was a tender moment and I wished I could freeze the image and use it for the book cover, but as usual, the figures faded.

"What're you finding so fascinating in that mirror?" Mark's voice brought me back to the present.

"I'm thinking about the next bit of the plot," I lied.

"I doubt you'll find it there," he snorted.

Wanna bet? I thought to myself.

"I was just mulling over what my heroine will do next," I explained.

"What are her options?" he asked.

"She could stay with her brutal husband in a comfortable house, never having to worry about money and ensuring her son gets a privileged upbringing," I replied. "Or she can run off with the man she loves, a poor World War One soldier, and live a life of hard work and poverty."

"Oh well," he said. "No contest."

"Really?" I asked.

"Which would you do?" he replied.

"I'd like to think I'd go for love," I shrugged. "But being poor's no fun."

He laughed.

"What's so funny?" I said.

"The fact you even have to think about it." He raised his eyebrows. "How often do you fall in love?"

"Not often," I admitted. "It doesn't alter the fact that being poor is miserable."

"So you'd prefer to be rich and miserable?" he said.

"Yes," I said. "If I was destined to be miserable, I'd prefer to be rich."

"Congratulations." He smiled. "Your runaway literary success and fabulous income allowed you to be rich and miserable. You did it!"

I wasn't sure whether to be offended or intrigued, so I chose the latter.

"Are you suggesting I would have been happier if my books hadn't sold and I'd remained a stay-at-home mum?" I asked.

"What do you think?" he replied.

I squeezed my eyes shut imagining being with Cliff and the kids in our old semi-detached and a sudden longing for my old life overwhelmed me.

"Whoa!" he said, touching my arm. "I'm sorry, I shouldn't have brought it up."

"It's fine," I said, patting his hand. "You're right. It all went to my head and I lost everything precious to me."

He nodded. "We can't turn back the clock."

"Indeed we can't," I agreed. "We can strive towards a better future though. How are you feeling?"

"Much better," he said, looking healthier than I'd seen him in a long while.

"We've got our AA meeting later so I'd better finish up."

CHAPTER THIRTY-THREE

An Understanding

First Draft

Lydia brushed her long blonde hair, her child asleep in the cot beside her.

"I hear your stable lad has abandoned you," Hubert said as he entered the room and slammed the door behind him.

"Ssh, you'll wake the child." Lydia put her finger to her lips. "Why are you in my bedroom?"

"He isn't going to kill me to protect your honour after all," he said, smirking. "I didn't think he would have the courage."

"You could've killed him with your hired bullies," she said, continuing to brush her hair. "I have no idea where Alfred has gone, but I'm glad he's out of your reach."

"And out of yours," Hubert said. "No more furtive glances at each other when you think I'm not looking."

"What nonsense you spout," she said.

"You think me a fool?" he asked. "I know that you love each other and have done so for a long time. I hear the rumours."

"They are exactly that, rumours," she replied.

"I don't care," he shrugged. "I know Alfred will always put your safety above his own. That's why he's gone."

"He left because you paid someone to beat him," she said, a slight quiver in her voice. "I hope you are proud of injuring a war veteran and mistreating him in such a dreadful way."

Hubert laughed, taking the brush from her and holding the skein of bright hair in the other hand. He dropped the brush and stroked her long neck; Lydia twisted away from him.

"Please go," she requested. "I don't want baby Hubert to wake, I've only just got him to sleep."

"Then you'll need to be quiet," Hubert said, grabbing her wrist and hauling her to the bed.

He clambered on top of her, pinning her down, and lifted her skirts. Lydia squirmed, stretching her arms above her head and retrieving a large bayonet from under the pillow. The blade glinted wickedly in the lamplight.

"Get off of me," she said through gritted teeth.

Hubert, the point of the blade near his face, held up his hands and leant back, kneeling.

"Something Alfred left as a parting gift?" he asked. "So now you are going to kill me?"

"I'll make a mess of your face if you come any closer," she said as his grin faded.

"If you injure me I will have you committed to a lunatic asylum and you'll never see your child again," he threatened, keeping his distance.

"Can you imagine the shame on your family?" she grinned. "Hubert Archer, horribly scarred by his mad wife. Your mother would be pleased."

"Go ahead and cut my face. Would it make you love me the way you love Alfred?" he asked, pressing his cheek against the blade and drawing blood.

"You don't want my love," she said.

"I wanted to be part of you and Alfred," he whimpered. "I wanted to be part of the love you had for each other. Would it have hurt you to have included me?"

She shook her head. "You have made our lives so unbearable, how can you imagine that Alfred or I could have any affection for you?"

"You shut me out," he whispered. "You have a look of distaste every time I come near you and your stable boy wouldn't accommodate me, however hard I tried."

"Alfred would have respected you if you had treated him better," she said.

"I wanted more than respect," he said.

"You think you can force people to like you?" she said. "You have to earn friendship."

"I am accustomed to being obeyed." He sulked. "Why wouldn't Alfred obey me?"

"You have driven Alfred away and you are left with me," she said, still pointing the bayonet at him. "We can either continue to make each other unhappy or find a compromise."

"I want you to think of me as a good husband and father," he said.

"Why do you care what I think?" she asked.

"You are my wife and the mother of my son," he replied. "I require a civilised marriage to raise my child."

"You may have that," she acquiesced.

"I enjoy immensely, walking into a room with you on my arm." He grinned. "Every single man looks at you and thinks what a lucky chap I am."

"I am happy to walk into a room with you," she agreed.

"And we may have more children?" he asked.

"No."

It was satisfying to see an Edwardian lady taking a stand against her abusive husband. I still had no idea how my novel ended, but I would need a conclusion soon.

Charlie was convinced that I could be trusted to have the twins overnight. Cliff, understandably, was reluctant at first to agree. After much discussion between them, Cliff gave way and didn't even insist on Charlie's presence. Charlie surmised that Cliff and Debbie probably needed a night without the children. I didn't care as long as I would be able to spend time with my dear children.

"Can we play on the iPad?" the children asked as soon as they arrived. I agreed.

Cliff brought their bags in and looked out of the kitchen window.

"Who's that?" he asked.

Mark was busy in the garden chopping down bind-weed.

"That's Mark, a friend of mine," I replied.

"From the pub?" Cliff asked.

"From the AA actually," I sighed. "I haven't had a drink in months."

"I know, Charlie told me," he said. "I've seen him somewhere before."

"He used to be on the telly," I said.

"I remember." He scratched his head. "Mark someone or other from breakfast television."

"That's right," I agreed.

"Didn't he have an affair that became very public?" he asked.

"That's him," I replied.

"So you've got quite a lot in common then?" he said,

E W GRANT

smirking.

"We're both alcoholics if that's what you mean?" I said, refusing to rise to his insult.

"Sorry," he said. "That was uncalled for."

"It's all right," I said. "He's staying in the basement at the moment."

"Goodness me," he said, looking once more at the busy gardener. "How did a celebrity like him become an alcoholic?"

I shook my head. "You wouldn't believe the mixture of people at my AA meetings. It could happen to anyone." I pointed at him. "Even a respected member of society like you."

"We've recently cut back on the drinking," he admitted. "We were having a bottle of wine every day with our evening meal."

"There you go," I said. "That's how it starts."

"I guess so," he agreed.

"How's Debbie?" I asked.

He looked confused. "Hang on, are you asking, with sincerity, how my wife is?"

"I'm sorry I've been so shitty about her. I suppose I was jealous," I said.

"You left me, remember?" He smiled.

"Can you ever forgive me?" I asked, feeling a lump rising in my throat.

He tilted his head. "I loved being married to you. When I realised you were having an affair it broke my heart."

I laid my hand on his arm.

"I hoped it was a fling," he continued. "I knew it wasn't when I caught you looking at him across the room with such intensity. It was at one of those ridiculous parties you insisted on having."

I looped my arm through his. "He was a big mistake," I said.

"You need to understand," he said, taking my hand. "Debbie was there for me. We were just friends at first. I still hoped you'd come back to me."

"I'm sorry." I shook my head.

"I'm happy now," he said, dropping my hand. "It's not the same as being married to you. It's predictable and stable and I've found that I like that. We've been desperate to start a family, but there's no hope."

"None at all?" I asked.

"No." His mouth turned down at the corners. "Debbie's due for a hysterectomy soon."

"That's a shame," I said. "Debbie would make a great mum."

"Yes, she's a great step-mum to Rosie and Jack," he said.

I wasn't churlish enough to remind him of our children's names.

"Let me know if there's anything I can do to help," I offered.

After Cliff left, the children and I played Monopoly for a couple of hours, until they became hungry.

"You promised us takeaway," Rosanna squealed.

I went to the kitchen to get menus and found Mark hugging a coffee cup in his hands.

"That's the noisiest game of Monopoly ever," he said.

"Why don't you come and join us for takeaway?" I suggested.

We tucked into doughy pizzas, garlic bread and ginger beer in the dining room.

"Do you like having a sleepover with your mum?" Mark asked the children before stuffing a huge bit of pizza into his mouth.

"We didn't like it at first," Jackson replied. "We were scared of melted-face man."

"Melted-face man?" Mark asked, glancing at me.

"When we found out he was a soldier we were okay," Rosanna said.

"Who's melted-face man?" Mark asked Jackson.

"He used to live here," Jackson replied.

"Not in this house," interrupted Rosanna. "But in this town."

"He's looking for someone," Jackson continued. "He can never find her though."

"He 'lourves' her." Rosanna giggled.

Mark shrugged at me. "They have their mother's ability to make up stories."

"It's not a story," Rosanna said, shaking her head.

"It happened. A long, long, long time ago," Jackson agreed.

"Huh," Mark muttered.

The children went to watch TV and Mark helped me clear up.

"What were they talking about?" he asked.

"There have been some strange things going on," I replied, stacking the dishwasher. "The children have seen a soldier in the garden and I..."

Mark stared at me in disbelief.

"I know it's hard to believe," I said. "But I'm convinced I'm writing Lydia's story."

"You believe in that paranormal stuff?" he asked.

"Not until I lived here," I replied. "I found Lydia's photograph in that ugly old sideboard in the dining room. And..." I hesitated, his expression changed from disbelief to cynicism.

"You can believe whatever you want," he said. "But the children are at such an impressionable age."

"They saw a soldier in the garden quite independently of me," I said. "I hadn't told them anything about Lydia."

"Children pick up on things," he said.

"I know," I agreed. "I assure you I haven't mentioned the novel or the people who lived here. It was them who told me about the soldier without any prompting."

"Sorry, I shouldn't interfere." He walked away. "Thanks for the pizza and have a good night with your kids."

CHAPTER THIRTY-FOUR

Vanquished

Cliff picked the children up the next day. I even managed a cheery wave at Debbie waiting in the car.

I was desperate to know the final plot of my novel and decided to empty the sideboard to see if it held any more clues. I tipped the drawers onto the floor, creating a heap of paperwork, champagne corks and a large magnifying glass. I picked up a green, leather-bound album with "H.J.A." embossed in gold on the front. Hubert, John Archer, Lydia's son. I flicked through pages of a stamp collection and was just about to discard it when a photograph fell out. It was a hand-coloured print of Lydia, wearing an elaborate hat with satin ruffles and large feathers sprouting out of the top. I flicked it over. 'Mummy' was written in a childish hand.

There were several Bibles. One large tome bound in magenta leather, the initials on the inside, 'H.J.A', and a small white leather-bound prayer book with the initials 'L.T.': Lydia Turner.

I put them to one side. I opened a stiff white envelope, finding two letters inside. One was written on smooth vellum notepaper and the other was scrawled on what looked like brown packing paper. I read the scrawled letter first.

June 1939
Dear Mr Archer,

E W GRANT

I was nicely surprised to get your letter. Please forgive my attempt at writing I was not schooled proper.

You wanted to know about your dear mother. Let me say that she was indeed a great lady that we all looked up to in the district.

We was all very sad when she moved to your Grandma's house in London and never thought to return to the house she was born in. We guessed that life was very grand and our little town was unappealing.

As you say, some thought she went to join my brother Alfred in Cornwall. I can put your mind at rest. Even though my brother always held a flame for Miss Lydia, nothing ever came of it. Miss Lydia was a lady and Alfred was just a poor working man. I know this to be true because my brother wrote now and then and always asked about Miss Lydia's health. I told him that as far as I knew she were living a cheery life in London and he would do well not to think of her.

It is very nice that you have moved into Rosebay House and the old place is lived in once again.

Thank you for asking about my health. I don't do laundry anymore, but my husband and myself have been blessed with many grandchildren.

Kind wishes,
Mrs Elspeth Dodds

Alfred's sister. I was perplexed. Why would Lydia have finished up living in London when she was so determined to join Alfred in Cornwall?

I unfolded the second letter.

Dear Mrs Dodds,
I am in your debt for your swift reply to my letter. I hope I am not putting you under pressure to answer more questions about my dear mother.

When my father and I moved to the family home in

Northumberland following Grandpa's death in 1921 I was just a small child.

As I grew up, I dearly wished to know my mother's whereabouts and Father always said that she wasn't well and she lived in Rosebay House. Yes, my present house! He promised that we would go and see her when she was better. Sadly, that day never materialised.

Mother was never at Granny's house in London. I know that for sure, having spent Christmas and summer holidays there. Granny also maintained that my mother lived in Rosebay House by the River Thames.

So you see, when I returned to the district, I was intrigued by the rumours regarding your brother and my mother. Now you have put me straight on that, however, and it seems the mystery of my mother's final whereabouts remains, as there is no grave that I know of.

I remain indebted to you

The letter ended without a signature and clearly hadn't left Rosebay House so I surmised that H.J.A. had changed his mind about sending it. I threw the letter back on the pile and a bright oval brooch tumbled out. It was an embossed silhouette of a woman in lapis lazuli on a pale pearly surface. The long neck, fine bone structure and piled-up hair convinced me that I was looking at an image of Lydia.

"Damn," I said, folding my fingers around the smooth brooch.

"What's up?" Mark asked, entering the room and looking at the mess I'd made.

"I was hoping to get some idea of what happened to my heroine, but all I've found are more mysteries."

"So you're convinced she's a real person?" he asked.

"Bill, my brother-in-law, looked her up on the census thing. She was living here in 1911 before the war," I replied.

"I suppose the war changed a lot of people's lives," he remarked. "Especially women's lives."

E W GRANT

"You're so clever," I said. "Of course. Lydia was a suffragette before the war so she may have moved away and got a job."

My spirits lifted and then took a nosedive. "But why would she leave her child? And why didn't she join Alfred when she had the chance?"

"You're not making any sense," he said.

"No." I rubbed my temples. "Because you don't know the whole story."

I leapt to my feet, spilling Mark's tea.

"You need to read the novel," I shrilled, running out of the room and taking the stairs two at a time.

Mark and I peeked over Bill's shoulder as he tapped the computer keyboard.

"Alfred's living in Falmouth from 1918 onwards. He's a labourer." Bill pointed to some documents.

"And here," Bill jumped to a different tab. "Is his death certificate."

"1935 – cause of death pneumonia," Mark read.

"He's not very old," Bill murmured. "Fifty."

"Is there any trace of Lydia Archer, née Turner?" I asked.

"I've looked," Bill replied. "There's just no trace of her at all after the baby's birth certificate."

"She may have changed her name," Mark suggested.

"Moira has clearly involved you in the research for her latest novel," Bill snorted.

"I've read the rough manuscript," Mark confirmed. "She knew that would be enough for me to be fascinated by the characters."

"Mark's my chief researcher," I remarked.

"I'm not getting paid though," Mark laughed.

"You live rent-free, what else do you want?" I said, patting him on the back.

"There's something else," Bill said, switching to another tab. "Hubert Archer."

230

EYES OF CHINA BLUE

August 1935
The London Evening Standard
Murder in Soho

The body of businessman and former army officer Hubert Archer was discovered this morning in Soho Square. His throat had been cut. Mr Archer was last seen leaving the notorious Popes Club with a young male companion at about 2 a.m. on Saturday.

Mr Archer had fallen on hard times in recent years. He, unfortunately, lost his fortune after the Wall Street Crash and was forced to sell his family home in Northumberland to cover his debts.

He leaves behind a son, Hubert, John Archer (20).

Any witnesses to the crime should contact the police immediately.

"He came to an undignified end," I said.

"There's no mention of him leaving a wife behind, just his son," Bill said. "So we have to assume Lydia was long gone."

"Gone where?" I asked, exhaling loudly.

"Do you want to stay for dinner?" Charlie shouted from the kitchen.

"We'd love to," I answered, winking at Mark.

"I could do with some help," she added.

"You're getting on well with Mark," Charlie observed as she stirred gravy.

"He's great company," I said. "I didn't realise how lonely I was."

"Unrequited love will do that," she said, waving a wooden spoon in the air.

"You mean Freddie?" I asked, and she nodded. "You need not concern yourself. I have no intention of ruining my life again for a worthless man."

"I'm glad," she grinned. "Wasn't Mark once on breakfast

TV?"

"You recognise him?" I said. "Unfortunately, he ruined his career because of drinking."

"I don't remember," she said. "It's just that his face looked familiar."

Bill and Mark seemed to hit it off over dinner. I smiled contentedly at Charlie.

"Bill, have a beer if you want one," Mark said.

"Nah," Bill said. "We only drink at weekends. Apart from anything else, it piles the weight on."

"Hugely," Charlie chimed in. "We've both lost about seven pounds since we cut down our drinking."

"I think we're being humoured," I said. "These two are skinny as rakes!"

"If what Moira says is true, I can only thank you for your thoughtfulness," Mark said.

"Hey," Bill said. "We're very pleased to see Moira with a decent bloke, so not drinking doesn't matter."

"We're not a couple," I said. "For now, we're close friends and fellow AA members."

Mark pushed his fork around his plate.

"We decided to take things slowly," I added.

Mark tapped his fork against the plate until I covered his hand with mine.

"That's right." He looked up. "We're taking things slowly."

"Anyway, thanks for having us to dinner," I said. "We only came over to pick your brains, Bill."

"Pick away." He smiled. "Perhaps you would find out more about Alfred if you went to Falmouth?"

CHAPTER THIRTY-FIVE

Step-Back

"This is the house where Alfred lived." I pointed at a narrow building, one street back from Falmouth Harbour.

"It looks very chic now," Mark said, his hair blowing in the brisk wind.

The house had a cheerful, modern front door, UPVC windows and gaily painted window boxes that held marigolds and herbs.

"It was likely cheap accommodation in Alfred's day," I remarked.

I had arranged a meeting with a local historian Bill had put me in touch with, so I took the car while Mark went off to buy lunch to have in our bed and breakfast accommodation later.

I had googled Willow Jenner and as I entered the library I saw a hippie-type woman matching her description, with red hair even wilder than mine.

"Hi. You must be Willow?"

"Moira Delainey." She smiled. "How lovely to meet you. I've read all of your books. I can't wait for the new one. It's been quite a while, hasn't it?"

"I've been busy with the children and such like," I declared untruthfully.

Willow pulled a sheath of papers from her bag and

E W GRANT

arranged them on the table.

"You were interested in Alfred Johns?" she asked.

I nodded.

"He was a bit of a celebrity in Falmouth for a while," she said. "I have a picture of him from the local paper. It's a bit grainy."

She placed an A4 sheet in front of me and there he was. His face was oddly distorted on one side and perfect on the other, just as I'd seen in the mirror.

"He was injured in the war," I said.

"It says so here," she pointed. "And he rescued a young woman when her horse bolted. It took fright and galloped down the high street. Alfred stepped out and managed to calm the animal before it threw its rider."

"He was always good with horses," I said.

"You know something about him already?" she asked.

"Only what I've read back home," I replied.

"The rider was the local magistrate's daughter." She pulled out another article. "It says here that he awarded Alfred fifty pounds."

"Wow," I said. "A fortune in those days."

"It also mentions that Alfred was a reluctant hero who would have preferred to remain anonymous," she said.

"I can understand why," I sighed.

"The article goes on to say, 'We felt it appropriate to mention the brave hero who put life and limb at risk to stop the out-of-control horse from causing serious injury to the young lady.'" She squinted at the small print.

"What else do you know about him?" I asked.

"Not much," she admitted. "He worked around the harbour and he died of pneumonia in 1935."

"We found his death certificate," I said.

"Interestingly," she held up a legal document. "He left his modest worldly goods to a Mavis Titmuss."

"Mavis," I shrieked, getting stern looks from the other library users. "Sorry. I'm just surprised Mavis is here; if it's the

234

same Mavis that Alfred knew back home."

"Mavis must have thought herself very lucky," Willow said. "Alfred left her fifty pounds and tenure to the cottage."

I hurried back to bed and breakfast to share my news with Mark. The door was locked, he hadn't returned. It was quite a large town, he could be anywhere. I feared the worst.

Two hours later:
Text message: Mark
I'm so so sorry.
Waiting outside The Lobster Pot.
Don't know my way home.

I found Mark outside the large pub, slumped against the harbour wall with two drunken companions.

"Don't be mad at him, he's that famous geezer off the telly," one of them slurred.

"Come on," I said, pulling Mark up.

It was slow progress hauling him up the steep hill to our accommodation. He slumped onto his single bed as I removed his shoes.

"So sorry," he whimpered.

I shook my head, looking down at him. "You need to sleep it off."

He began to sob. "I'm such an idiot."

"You are," I agreed, folding my arms.

"Please forgive me,"

"We'll talk about it later," I said. "Go to sleep now."

Mark surfaced when I was eating breakfast the next day. His hair stuck up in spikes and his face looked lined and dehydrated.

"Ah, so there you are," I said.

"I'm so sorry," he repeated.

"Here, have some orange juice." I poured a glass and handed it to him. "What on earth happened?"

"I was going to the supermarket. Honestly," he declared. "But it was such a nice day I decided to stop for an alcohol-free beer and sit in the pub garden for a bit."

He closed his eyes and I thought he'd dropped off. I poked him.

"I got talking to an interesting bloke," he continued. "I can't remember what we said, but he remembered me from the show. He offered me a beer and I was too embarrassed to ask for an alcohol-free one. I thought one beer wouldn't hurt."

"I can imagine the rest," I interrupted.

"I can't believe what an idiot I've been," he said, covering his face with his hands.

"You can't have just one drink," I said. "You're an alcoholic and there's no such thing as just one drink."

He nodded.

"Listen, Mark," I continued. "I want a drink every day and do you know what stops me?"

He shrugged.

"I remember what it was like to wake up feeling like you do now," I said.

He peered through his fingers.

"Also, because I'm sober, my kids have been allowed to stay overnight with me. And most of all, life is worth living."

He looked more miserable. "I don't know if you can forgive me?" he muttered.

"I've been given more chances by the people who love me than you can imagine," I told him as I took his hand.

"I… want to… stop drinking," he stammered.

"Will I be sober forever?" I asked. "I hope so. But any day I could fail – as you have. We take one day at a time."

"You're so much stronger than I am," he said, squeezing my hand.

"No," I insisted. "I'm not. But we are stronger together."

"I love you," he cried.

"And I love you too," I confessed.

EYES OF CHINA BLUE

Based on information Bill had given me on the phone the night before, I left Mark in the bed and breakfast and drove to Veryan, a Cornish village on the coastal Roseland Peninsula.

I tramped around the graveyard next to St. Symphorian Church. It was overgrown in places and some of the gravestones were so old the wording was no longer legible.

In a quiet corner under a yew tree, I found what I was looking for:

Alfred David Johns
Born 1885 - Died 1935
A brave soldier in WW1
Rest in Peace.

I'd never met Alfred, but I couldn't stop crying. I spied more engraving at the bottom of the stone and pushed the vegetation aside.

Mavis, Victoria Titmuss
Born 1889 - Died 1959

"Did you know Gran?" a voice behind me hollered.

I stood as a tall, slim man of around fifty approached.

"Not really," I said, wiping the tears away. "I'm doing some research for a book I'm writing."

"About Mavis?" he asked.

"More about Alfred," I replied. "Mavis was your grandmother?"

"She was," he nodded. "And a bit of a character by all accounts."

"What was she like?" I asked.

"I never met her," he said. "She died in 1959 and I was born in 1960. I only know what Mum said about her."

"I'd love to hear it if you've got the time," I said.

We let ourselves into the church and sat on a pew.

"I'm Ed, by the way," he smiled.

"Sorry. I'm Moira Delainey and I'm writing a novel

E W GRANT

about the house I live in," I said. "Mavis was a maid there for a while, that's why I'm interested in her."

"Was she?" he asked, tilting his head. "Mum didn't mention that. She did say that Mavis had an interesting past. She was a suffragette and that she fled to Cornwall because she was in some kind of trouble."

"She was a suffragette," I confirmed. "Who was your grandfather?"

"Alfred Johns was named on my father's birth certificate. Although he and Mavis never married." He sighed. He didn't resemble either Alfred or Mavis, which was annoying.

"He waited for Lydia," I said.

"Sorry?" he said.

"Nothing," I said. "It's just that Alfred was in love with a grand lady who lived in my house. I think she must have let him down though."

"Alfred was a bit of a celebrity around here," he said.

"Yes. I heard about the bolting horse incident."

"A reluctant celebrity, I should add," he said. "Dad said Grandad wouldn't leave the house for days, wary of the newspaper reporters."

"I can imagine he'd want to keep a low profile," I said. "Are your parents still living hereabouts?"

"Dad passed away and Mum lives in a care home." He pursed his lips. "She has dementia."

"Oh, I'm sorry," I said.

"Mavis paid for Alfred's burial," he continued. "He'd been injured in the war and his face was disfigured and Gran thought he deserved a proper burial."

"And so he did," I agreed.

We parted exchanging email addresses.

CHAPTER THIRTY-SIX

Retribution

First Draft

Small stones tapped against the pane as Lydia quietly lifted the window, to find Toby staring up from the garden.

"What is it, Toby?" she whispered.

"Please, Miss. Mavis was set about by two men on the towpath. They beat her up proper bad," he said, peering around nervously. "She sent me to tell you. They took a letter she was delivering to you. It was from Uncle Alfred."

Lydia held her hands to her head. "Wait here a moment," she said and went to her desk to retrieve a purse.

"Here." She threw the purse. "There's ten pounds. Give it to Mavis and tell her to leave at once."

Lydia managed to close the window just before Hubert burst into the bedroom. He grabbed her by the hair and dragged her along the landing and up the short flight of stairs to the attic.

"Now I know for sure what you've been planning with that half-witted scarface," he shouted as he dumped her on the floor.

"I have no idea what you're talking about," Lydia cried.

"It's all here," he shouted, waving a letter in her

E W GRANT

face. "You're planning on leaving me and taking my son."

"That's just Alfred's fantasy," she declared, clutching at straws. "You don't think I could leave and live like a pauper?"

"You are most convincing," he smiled. "But I know you're lying. Listen to this..."

My dearest Lydia,

I was relieved to receive your letter and to know you and the boy will soon make your escape and travel to be with me.

Be sure to check and double-check the train timetable. It would be troublesome if you missed the train.

I have rented a decent cottage for us all to live in. It's small, my love, but dry and comfortable. I've even made a bed for the boy, so you need not worry about his comfort.

I have the money you gave me, plus my soldiers' pay safely hidden away. We will not be rich but we will not want for much either.

Please make haste. I worry so about your safety.

Your faithful Alfred.

Hubert glared at her, his eyes ugly and protruding. "What have you got to say, you scheming harlot?" he screamed. "After agreeing to a mutually beneficial marriage for our son's sake, you were conniving behind my back."

"I am planning to leave you." She got to her feet. "Our marriage is a farce and I can't wait to get away."

He hit her across the face with the back of his hand and she crashed into the large mirror on the back of the door.

240

"Get up," he said, clenching his fists. "I've not finished with you."

Lydia slowly got to her feet, clutching the side of her face.

"I have made some important decisions to safeguard the future of our son and indeed your future." He jabbed a fat finger in her face. "You will write to Alfred and tell him you've changed your mind about leaving me."

"Never," she whispered.

"Oh, but you will," he insisted. "For his letter is proof that you have both been scheming to kidnap my child."

Lydia's head snapped up.

"I can see to it that Alfred goes to prison for a very long time," he said. "Not only Alfred. I believe your faithful courier is wanted by the authorities for an undischarged prison sentence?"

"You wouldn't," she moaned.

"You know very well that it would amuse me no end to see your precious Alfred thrown in prison," he said, grabbing her wrist. "You will write to Alfred, wherever he's hiding, and tell him that you've changed your mind and intend to stay with your loving husband. Wait a minute; he'll know that's a lie. Tell him you could not face leaving Rosebay House and your comfortable life. That's far more realistic. You must also promise never to see or contact him or the woman again."

He shook her.

"Do I make myself clear?" he screamed in her face.

Lydia felt an icy chill up and down her backbone; it was the chill of defeat.

"Do you promise to leave him alone?" she asked.

"Where's he hiding?" Hubert demanded. "One of my men said his parents had moved to Somerset."

"I don't know," she said truthfully, her hand covering her mouth.

"You were going to steal my son and run away," he said, digging his thumbs into her shoulders.

"You gave me no choice," she cried.

"Don't fool yourself, my dear," he said between gritted teeth. "We could have lived a comfortable life and raised our son. You just can't get Alfred out of your head."

He shook his head. "I thought we'd come to an accommodation that day you so elegantly thrust a bayonet in my face. I was a fool. You will never give up loving Alfred, however hard I try."

He released her and she fell backwards, thumping her head against the mirror.

"Wait a minute," he said, stroking his chin. "Alfred was replying to your letter. You must have an address for him."

"I don't," she said. "I give the letter to Mavis and she addresses it 'care of' to a boarding house in the West Country."

"I couldn't care less about him. He's nothing to me now," Hubert said. "As long as my son is safe, you may keep the secret of his whereabouts until the day you die."

Lydia looked him in the eye. "I agree to your terms, but don't expect me to be your loving wife."

"Never fear, my dear." He grinned. "As long as I have this letter I have every intention to resume my conjugal rights. You will have no choice but to accommodate my needs. Loving or not, it makes no difference to me."

Dear Alfred,

It is with great difficulty that I write this letter.

You reminded me once of how baby Hubert would be forced to grow up in poverty, because of the selfish decision I was considering making on his behalf.

I have had time to dwell on this and have concluded that I must abide by my husband and remain in a safe and stable home.

I realise this will come as a great disappointment. It seems our different positions in life do make any hope of being together incompatible.

As recompense please keep the money I gave you.

I implore you not to try to contact me by any means.

Yours sincerely,
Lydia Archer (Mrs)

I decided to return Mark to the scene of his disgrace, to have dinner. It was a way of exorcising his demons.

"Would you like the wine list?" the waitress asked.

"No, thank you," I said. "Just a bottle of water, please."

"Did we have to come here?" Mark moaned.

"We're righting a wrong," I said.

"If you say so," he said, making a face.

"Did you read the latest chapter?" I asked.

"I did," he nodded. "So now we know why Lydia didn't join Alfred. I guess the ending is in sight?"

"Maybe," I shrugged.

"Maybe?" he echoed.

"We still don't know what happened to Lydia," I said.

"I suppose she wasted away in Rosebay House," he suggested.

"There's no trace of her," I said.

"Perhaps Hubert carried out his earlier threat and had her committed to an asylum?" He arched his eyebrows.

"That's an idea," I agreed. "I'll get Bill to check."

"It's sad that Alfred and Lydia never got to be together," he said.

"I was hoping for a happy ending," I sighed.

"You're not famous for that," he said. "I read that some of your readers live in fear of what you've got in store for your characters."

I laughed. "One reader complained bitterly when I killed off his favourite character in my last book."

"It's quite a responsibility." He grinned.

"That it is," I agreed.

We had enjoyed our meal and were just about to order coffee when a scruffy old man approached Mark.

"That the wife, mate?" he slurred.

"What?" Mark looked confused.

"Don't you remember me?" the man asked. "We bought each other shots at the bar."

"Vaguely," Mark said.

"I get it. You don't want to say hello with the little woman around." The man grinned, showing missing teeth.

"It's not that," Mark said. "I made a promise to this lovely lady that I wouldn't drink because I'm an alcoholic. And then I went and ruined it all."

The look of surprise on the man's face is something I'll never forget.

"I don't remember you, I'm sorry," Mark continued. "And I don't drink anymore so I wouldn't be good company."

I clapped my hands as the man staggered back to his companions at the bar.

"That was a heartfelt confession," I said.

"I took a good look at him and thought, 'that could be me', and it frightens me to death," he said.

"Fear is good," I said.

CHAPTER THIRTY-SEVEN

Disgrace

First Draft

Rays of sunshine lit up the attic room as Lydia stared out of the window. Since the letter was discovered it felt like the longest twenty-four hours of her life. She'd been imprisoned in the attic with only the insult of a chamber pot for company. A stony-faced woman, a stranger to Lydia, had brought food on a tray but refused to let Lydia know anything about the well-being of her son.

She leaned her forehead against the cool window, imagining how devastated Alfred would be when he read her letter. Bile arose in her throat as she imagined the hurt in his blue eyes.

Below her, in the street, Mavis stepped out from behind a tree, looking to her left and right and waving furiously up at Lydia.

"My God! Mavis, why are you still here?" Lydia whispered to herself.

Dear Mavis,

I am so sorry you were hurt by those awful men. I sent money to enable you to leave. Did you not get it? You must leave soon. Mr Archer has somehow found out that you have a prison sentence to complete. You are not safe here.

I thought you might join Alfred. You know more-or-less where he is. I beg you, do not ever communicate his whereabouts in a letter or conversation. I could not bear for him to suffer and my husband has a vengeful temperament.

I am locked in the attic during the day and in my bedroom at night. I understand my husband is telling people that I am unwell and not able to see anyone.

Additionally, I am removed from my son. My heart is broken, for I hear him crying and long to go to him.

So you see, Mavis, my dear friend, I am a miserable prisoner. Please do not worry for one moment about my situation. You must see to your safety and welfare.

Your friend Lydia

Toby ran as fast as his legs would carry him. Night had fallen and he knew only bad people hung around the towpath. He pushed against the door of the mill and ran up the stairs.

"What have you got there, a message from Miss Lydia?" Mavis asked as he entered the small room.

"From the lady," he panted.

She read it slowly, phonetically, saying the long words out loud.

"How did Miss Lydia get the letter to you?" she asked when she'd read it all.

"She threw it out of her bedroom window as I waited in the garden. Nobody saw," he said.

"And can you get a letter back to her?" Mavis asked.

"She gave me this." He produced a large silver hairbrush with bright hair caught between the bristles. "I'm to tie the letter to it and throw it up to her. I've been practising throwing it up at the trees on the way over."

Mavis smiled at the boy's dedication. "You're very fond of her, aren't you?"

"She's always been good to me." He smiled. "She always says 'thank you'. Some of the rich folk don't even know I exist. And sometimes, when no one is looking she gives me a penny!"

"She's a proper lady," Mavis agreed. "Now hush. I need to write this letter and I'm not so good with my letters."

We returned to Rosebay House after our eventful trip to Cornwall. I ventured downstairs after a full day of writing to find Mark busy at the hob in the kitchen.

"I thought I smelled something nice," I said, sitting at the table.

"I need to do something to pay for my keep," he smiled, stirring a saucepan. "How is Lydia's story going?"

"She's not in a good place," I admitted. "I can't see how this ends well at the moment."

"You still don't have an ending?" he asked, slurping from the spoon.

"I know you're sceptical, but I truly believe Lydia hasn't revealed the ending yet," I replied.

"It's hard to believe what you're saying if, like me, you don't believe in an afterlife or ghosts," he said.

"I agree," I said. "But so many odd things have happened in this house. I have to believe what I've seen with my own eyes."

"They say as you recover from alcoholism, your body reacts in many different ways." He waved the spoon around. "Maybe that's what you're experiencing."

"But my twins aren't recovering from anything and they've seen melted-face man – I mean, Alfred – in the garden," I said.

"Don't you think they might just be picking something up from you?" he suggested.

"My rational head would agree with you," I said. "But, something instinctive, something I can't explain, convinces me that Lydia is desperate to have her true story told. I have committed to putting the record straight about what happened to her."

"Which is?" he asked.

"I don't know yet."

He served up chicken curry and rice.

"Mmm," I said, tucking in. "This is so good."

"I'm glad you like it." He grinned. "It's one of two dishes I can cook."

"And the other is…?"

"Beef curry," he said.

"Another classic," I said, raising my eyebrows.

"It's what I managed to cook for my son when I used to get a rare visit from him," he said.

"How long ago was that?" I asked.

"I haven't seen my son in three years," he replied, shaking his head.

"Perhaps once you're feeling stronger you could contact him?" I suggested.

"He wouldn't be interested in seeing me," he said. "The last time I saw him, he was fifteen. He's a grown man by now."

"Even if you were sober?" I asked.

"He'll never forgive me," he said, cupping his face with his hands.

"You'd be surprised how resourceful kids can be," I said. "My two, for instance. A couple of months ago they didn't want to see me, but now I hope we're on our way to having a great relationship."

"Yes, but your kids are only twelve," he sighed. "I've been drunk all of Joshua's life. I've let him down, turning up at school sports days drunk and falling over. My disgrace is out there on the internet for all to see. That's hard for him to forgive."

"I understand," I said. "That's what keeps me sober, the thought of my kids looking forward to seeing me and spending time here."

He exhaled a deep sigh. "I couldn't bear to see disappointment and fear in his eyes again. I'll never forgive myself for what I put him and his mum through."

"There's no going back." I reached for his hand. "We're going to make it this time."

CHAPTER THIRTY-EIGHT

A Leap of Faith

First Draft

November 1918

Lydia closed the door as Mavis crept into the attic, checking her appearance in the mirror.

"Cook smuggled me in," Mavis confided, curling a dark strand of hair around her finger. "We made sure no one else saw me."

"Good." Lydia smiled. "Hubert has gone to London on important business. He'll be gone for a few days, thank goodness. Something about the war ending."

"Everyone would be grateful if that were true," Mavis said. "There's been talk of our side winning, though no one's sure."

"Thanks for coming. I know it's a big risk and I appreciate it," Lydia said, hugging her. "Has Elspeth heard from Alfred lately?"

"Yes," Mavis nodded. "He's not happy at all since getting your letter. Elspeth said he was pretty much heartbroken."

"I had no choice in the matter," Lydia shook her head.

"But Elspeth says he readily accepts your reasons,"

Mavis said. "He never could understand why you thought so highly of him. 'Specially since his face was ruined."

"I love him and for me, there can be no other," Lydia sighed. "But I had to make it clear to him that we could not, under any circumstances, be together. It is to keep him safe. I greatly feared what my husband might do if I had not agreed to break with Alfred."

Mavis nodded, admiring a large black hat hanging on the back of a chair.

"Try it on." Lydia smiled.

Mavis placed the hat on her head, posing in the mirror.

"Keep it," Lydia said. "It suits you and I'm sure you'll make better use of it."

Mavis peered through the window, adjusting the hat.

"Your husband's men are watching the house. I'd better get out of view." Mavis stepped back.

"They stomp about out there all day," Lydia said. "I'm a prisoner in this house."

"It's not right, keeping you here," Mavis said. "This was your home long before you got married. It's unforgivable, your husband throwing his weight about and telling you what to do."

"There is no solution I'm afraid," Lydia sighed. "I even smuggled a letter out to my father, but he said he would not come between Hubert and me."

"I've got an idea, Miss," Mavis confided, patting the seat beside her. "It's risky and it might not work at all. But I think I know how we might trick your husband."

I'd cooked a proper Sunday roast lunch and Mark and I flopped out in the living room. I had just closed my eyes for a nap when I heard a motorbike pull up outside.

"Oh no," I muttered, going to the window.

"Who is it?" he asked.

"Let me deal with this," I said.

Freddie pushed past me into the living room, coming to a halt when he saw Mark.

"You didn't wait long then," Freddie grinned, throwing his helmet onto a chair.

"You're not welcome here," I said.

"You haven't answered my calls or texts, so what was I supposed to do?" he asked.

"Do you think I even care what the fuck you do?" I shouted.

"Darling," he continued. "You have to admit we had some good times?"

"No," I pointed at him. "I got drunk and paid the consequences."

"I'm sure we had a better time than you're having with a has-been like him?" He jabbed a finger at Mark. "Aren't you that dodgy bloke off the telly?"

"She doesn't want you here, mate." Mark shrugged.

"Please leave," I said, pointing at the door.

"You can't mean that?" Freddie said, shaking his head.

"I thought you were with the lovely and very rich Marie Lamarr?" I reminded him.

"That's over," he said. "She doesn't compare to you."

"You mean, you've been replaced already," I snorted, knowing Miss Lamarr's reputation.

"It was mutual." He shrugged.

"Whatever." I waved my arms in the air. "I don't want to see you anymore. Can't you get that into your big head?"

He smiled, his green eyes devouring me. "You're looking good, babe. Really good."

Mark laughed out loud. "That's original."

"Now I remember. You're that drunk off the telly from years ago," Freddie said.

"That's me," Mark admitted. "What do you want, an autograph?"

"I want to talk to Moira, privately," Freddie said.

"We have nothing to say," I said.

"I just want to have a proper conversation," Freddie begged, his hands stretching towards me.

"You need to go," I repeated.

"You can't be serious!" Freddie exploded. "I thought you were ditching the booze? This guy's a joke and a drunk."

"Actually," I smiled at Mark. "He's very special to me."

Freddie looked from me to Mark and back again.

"But it's me you love," he murmured.

"No," I shook my head. "It's him."

"You heard the lady," Mark said, pushing Freddie toward the door. "Now bugger off."

Freddie must have left, but I have no recollection of it. I threw my arms around Mark, looking up at his dear face. His lips were on mine as he returned my embrace.

Later, our legs entwined on the messy bed, as we lay in each other's arms.

"I haven't done that in a very long time," he said, out of breath. "I thought it was bloody marvellous. I hope it was the same for you?"

I pushed my hair out of my eyes, nodding furiously. "Let me get my breath back," I giggled.

"How I adore your laugh and your brown hair," he said, curling a lock around his finger.

"My hair is a mess even when I've been to the hairdresser," I said.

"It's soft and shiny and I love it," he said, kissing me.

"I'm so happy. I never thought I'd be able to say that again," I said, biting a fingernail.

"I've dreamt of this." His strong face softened.

"Now you don't have to dream." I laid my head on his chest.

"Goodness, I hope you don't regret this?" he said, stroking my arm.

"Make sure I don't," I suggested.

"You don't think it was too soon in our recovery?" he asked.

I sat up. "Seeing Freddie again made me realise how much happier I am with you. I have no regrets."

"Before today," he said. "I thought you regarded me as your hopeless friend. I was so surprised and thrilled when you told whatshisface that you loved me."

"I do love you," I said. "And whatever life throws at us, we'll deal with it. I feel we've been given a second chance."

He pulled me close and kissed the top of my head. "I'm a lucky man."

First Draft

Dressed in a long black coat, a hat jammed over her head and a black veil covering her face, a tall woman gently closed the door as she left Rosebay House. She carried a small suitcase and walked quickly towards the station.

When two men appeared from out of the trees, she turned onto the bridge and headed along the towpath.

Small birds trilled and flapped their wings as she hurried by. She noticed that only one of the men had followed her and was catching up. Then the second man appeared ahead of her, out of the trees, grinning and blocking the path. They moved closer, trapping her between them. She dropped the suitcase and mounted the rickety jetty across the effusive, brown water. The men grabbed hold of the wooden structure, rocking it, making it buckle and recoil.

She wobbled, clinging on desperately. The men laughed uproariously, reinvigorating their efforts as she teetered over the end. Without a sound, she plunged into the swirling water and was swept away.

The men dusted off their hands and one of them grabbed the suitcase. Lady's garments, a silver hairbrush, a pair of lacy gloves and an oval brooch spilt out onto the muddy ground.

I hadn't realised it at the time, but I had witnessed Lydia's demise the day I saw the woman fall from the pontoon on the river. I held my breath as I typed, exhaling with a whoosh. My readers would not be surprised at the sorrowful ending to my novel.

"Hello," Mark said, entering. "Bloody wet there again. I've put some towels down."

"Oh thanks," I smiled. "It's always soaking."

"Must be a leak from somewhere," he said, scratching his head.

I nodded, pursing my lips.

"Everything all right?" he asked.

"I know the ending of my novel," I sighed. "Lydia was pursued by Hubert's thugs and fell into the river."

"Oh, I'm sorry," he said. "But it explains why Bill can't find a death certificate for her. I mean, I doubt her husband would report it."

"I 'spose not," I agreed. "But her body would've washed up somewhere, surely."

"Maybe," he said, rubbing his chin. "But if the current was strong, she could've been swept quite a long way. If she wasn't reported missing, who would know it was her? She'd be a bit of a mess by the time she was found and they didn't have dental records in those days."

"Horrible," I said, covering my eyes with my hands.

"I know you wanted things to work out between Alfred and Lydia," he said. "They still can. You can write the ending you want."

"I could," I said. "But I need to tell Lydia's story. If she was murdered on her husband's orders, I want the world to

E W GRANT

know."

"Your publisher has insisted you change all the names though?" he asked.

"Yes," I replied. "We don't want any living relative to accuse us of libel."

"If you can change names, why can't you change the ending?" He rubbed my back; it felt nice.

"I have a duty towards Lydia," I insisted.

He took my hands and kissed my fingers.

"I understand," he said. "Poor Lydia."

CHAPTER THIRTY-NINE

Sink or Swim

Mark was fast asleep as I pulled the curtain back. A creeper had grown up the side of the house and was knocking against the glass in the breeze.

I pictured Lydia standing on the jetty, wobbling back and forth as her tormentors shook the wooden structure. I had mechanically typed, as images of the awful scene appeared in my head. I'd been surprised that Lydia fell. She'd been holding onto the railing, but inexplicably let go. Everything happened so quickly that I'd missed a minute movement as she fell through the gap in the railing and hit the water.

"She pushed off with her feet," I squealed.

"What?" Mark sat up, bleary-eyed.

"She launched herself off the jetty," I said.

"Who?" Mark looked around.

"Lydia," I exclaimed. "She meant to jump into the river."

"How can you be so sure?" he asked.

"I can picture it in my head. Like rewinding a film," I replied. "She wobbled for a bit, then her posture changed like she was preparing."

Mark yawned and swung his legs out of the bed.

"She committed suicide," he said.

"That hadn't occurred to me," I said.

"Oh, you thought she'd jumped to stage her death?" he suggested.

E W GRANT

"Yes," I said. "And swum to safety."

"Can we talk about this tomorrow, love?" he said, yawning.

"No," I said. "I have to know."

"All right then," he said, getting up. "Do you know if Lydia could swim or not?"

"No," I admitted. "I think it would be unusual for an Edwardian lady to be able to swim."

"You'd have to be a really good swimmer," he said. "The current is very strong in the middle of the river."

"I haven't got any information on Lydia's swimming ability," I said.

A memory of earlier dialogue exploded into my brain and I grabbed Mark by his t-shirt.

"The person who is a good swimmer. Who spoke about swimming off the jetty with her brothers when she was a child..."

I grinned, still clutching his t-shirt.

"Please, Moira," he begged. "You've woken us up at 3 a.m. Tell me what you're on about?"

"Mavis," I said.

We negotiated the sodden carpet to my garret and switched on the computer.

"What are we looking for?" he asked.

"A woman jumped into the river. Let's still assume it was Lydia and her husband never reported it," I said. "There's no death certificate and no trace of her. What could've happened?"

"She drowned and only her husband and his thugs knew," Mark suggested.

"But the servants would notice she was gone," I said.

"Hubert would say she'd gone to his mother's in London," he said.

"Mavis would know," I said.

"You're right." He beamed at me. "Mavis is the key."

"She would've searched for the truth if Lydia had gone missing," I said. "She would've alerted Alfred too."

"But according to his sister, Alfred thought Lydia was living in Rosebay House," Mark said.

I leaned back in my chair, my hands clasped behind my head. Mark began to sift through the folder of information Bill had given us. He pulled out the Falmouth newspaper cutting of Alfred and studied it through a large magnifying glass, I kept on my desk.

"There's a woman behind him," he muttered. "They are holding hands. See at the side of the picture?"

"Are you sure?" I shuffled closer.

"You can't see her face. She's looking in the opposite direction. But there's definitely hand holding."

He handed the glass to me and sure enough, there was a woman's blurry figure behind Alfred.

"Was Mavis blonde?" Mark asked.

"No," I replied. "Mavis was dark-haired."

"Lydia was blonde though?" He smiled. "The woman next to Alfred has light hair against a dark dress and hat."

"Are you sure?" I asked, squinting through the spyglass. "Yes, I can see now she's fair-haired."

"I think we've figured out the end of your novel," he grinned. "Now can we go back to bed?"

First Draft

Mavis swam to the opposite bank, out of sight of her pursuers. She hauled herself out of the river and jogged through the trees to a boathouse. She was shivering with cold and quickly changed into dry clothes she'd left there earlier.

Alfred leaned against the harbour wall. He frowned as he repaired a large fishing net. His fingers were red raw and his eyes strained from fiddling with the threads. He looked up when he heard the swish of a lady's skirt.

She was wearing a dowdy brown dress and an old knitted shawl, but her posture and blonde hair, expertly wound on top of her head implied refinement.

"Lydia," he cried, dropping the net.

"Shh." She put her finger to her lips. "Mavis Titmuss."

He took her hand, leading her to the far end of the harbour, where they wouldn't be heard.

"How did you get here?" he asked, holding her hands.

"Mavis planned it all," she replied, tears falling down her cheeks. "Dear Mavis wore my clothes and took a suitcase full of my things. She tricked Hubert's men into thinking she was me and heading for the railway station. She made sure they chased her to the jetty. They, true to form, tried to frighten her by rocking the structure. Next, she pretended to fall in and they believed her."

"I know she can swim, but was she saved?" Alfred searched her face.

"I worried about her safety too, but she wouldn't be talked out of it," she said. "Mavis used to swim off the jetty with her brothers when she was a child. She's an excellent swimmer. While the men were pursuing her, thinking it was me, I ran to the station and caught the London train and later the Cornish Express."

"My love," he embraced her. "How grateful I am to Mavis. I knew she was a quick-witted, clever girl, but jumping into the river to help you get away was a very brave thing to do. I can't believe you're here."

"Elspeth told Mavis you were in Falmouth," she said. "I didn't know where you lived. It's taken me all day to find you."

He held her at arm's length.

"But won't Hubert search for you if they don't find a body?" His crooked mouth turned down at the corners.

"Mavis says that loads of people drown in the river every week and quite often no one ever claims them." She smiled. "Hubert won't worry too much over what became of me. He will see it as a great way of getting rid of me."

"I can't believe you're here after the letter you sent me." His eyes filled with pain. "I thought that was the end. The letter did say as much."

"Hubert made me write the letter after he intercepted a letter from you," she explained. "Your letter clearly showed that I planned to leave him and take the boy with me. He threatened to have you charged with kidnap."

"The boy?" he asked.

Lydia sobbed. "I deeply regret, that I had no way of bringing our son. He was taken from my care and I rarely saw him. I only managed to escape because the cook let me out of the attic."

"I'm so sorry," Alfred pulled her close. "I know that will be difficult for us to come to terms with."

"I couldn't stay," she whispered. "Hubert set out to make my life a misery. You cannot imagine what it's been like."

"I greatly feared leaving you with him," Alfred said, wringing his hands. "I feel so wretched about the child being left behind, but taking him was always going to be difficult. This way nobody will be looking for you."

"You must call me Mavis and if anyone asks, say I am a dear cousin," Lydia said.

"And what of Mavis?" he asked.

"Mavis will lay low for a while and then join us here," Lydia said, smiling. "I gave her sufficient money to travel. Once she gets here we can find out what she wants to do next."

"There will be work for a young lady such as Mavis in the wealthy houses around here," Alfred said.

"I owe much to her and will do everything in my power to see her decently provided for," she said.

"Dear Mavis," he said. "What would we do without her?"

"You must remember my love," she said. "I am Mavis."

"That will take a bit of getting used to," he said.

"We must be cautious. Hubert may still attempt to find out where you are," she said. "I imagine though, once he thinks I'm no longer a thorn in his side, he will forget about you too."

"I hope you're right," Alfred agreed.

"At long last, I can forget about Hubert and his cruelty and carve out a life with my true husband." She held his hand.

"We will get married?" he asked.

"We can't," she replied. "We must not draw attention to ourselves."

"We will live in sin?" He raised his good eyebrow, the damaged side of his face expressionless.

"If we tell lies on official documents and get found out, we put our whereabouts at risk," she said. "We will say I am your cousin and you kindly let me lodge with you."

"I understand the sensible thinking," he agreed. "But I'd much rather we were wed."

"I want that with all my heart too. But you forget I am already married," she said, patting his arm.

"To a monster," he sighed.

"Let us put all that we've been through behind us," she said, slipping her arm through his. "We will think of our son on his birthday. But at all other times, we must put him out of our minds, or we shall go mad with grief."

"I fear we must do as you say," he nodded. "We will try, with God's will, to make a joyful life together."

It was beginning to rain as they strolled arm-in-arm towards their home.

CHAPTER FORTY

New Beginnings

"So what happens now the book is finished?" Mark asked as we strolled past the modern version of the jetty Mavis had leapt from a hundred years ago.

"The first draft is with my agent," I replied. "I always let her read it before I start the rewrite. She has such a good eye for detail and continuity."

"So will she make massive changes?" he said.

"Unlikely," I said. "But she will say if she thinks any of the characters are unrealistic or weak. Or if the storyline is confusing or messy. I tend to write whatever comes to mind and in this case, what Lydia wanted me to write."

He glanced sideways at me, narrowing his eyes.

"You still believe that Lydia wrote her story through you?" He stopped to face me.

"I do," I laughed. "You may mock, but how would I know all of these people unless someone was telling me about their lives?"

He shrugged, squinting in the sunlight. "You're a very creative person."

"I'm not a historian though, and the people I've written about actually lived," I said.

"So you've created a story around them," he said.

We stepped aside to let a whole family on mountain bikes plough past us.

"I'll never convince you," I said, shaking my head. "Lydia and Alfred were real people and the events I've written about happened."

"You're not the first author to take real life and write fiction," he pointed out.

"I'm telling you: this is Lydia and Alfred's story," I insisted. "I'm certain Lydia wants her version told. Wouldn't you, if someone had abused you the way Hubert abused her?"

"Let me get this straight," he said. "A woman who died a hundred-odd years ago, is telling the world what happened to her – through you?"

"I know how it sounds," I laughed mirthlessly. "But you have to trust me."

"I want to," he shrugged. "But I just don't believe in the supernatural."

"And neither did I," I agreed. "Until I moved into Rosebay House. After two years of staring at a blank screen, suddenly my head was full of ideas and Lydia's amazing story unfolded before my eyes."

"Which I can appreciate," he conceded, leaping over a large puddle. "Don't you think moving into an old house filled with character would inspire you to write?"

"Of course," I sighed. "But other people have seen things in the house that can't be explained."

"The twins are influenced by you," he said.

"Not just the twins," I remarked.

"Who else?" he asked.

"Freddie saw something in a photo he took of the attic one night," I said.

Mark marched ahead, his shoulders tensing.

"He was probably just humouring you so that he could get in your knickers," he murmured, talking to himself.

I stopped and put my hands on my hips as he turned around.

"Sorry," he said, approaching me. "That was a stupid thing to say."

"Yes, it bloody was," I said.

E W GRANT

The early autumn leaves on the large oak trees were turning to shades of lemon, amber and russet. They reflected the sunlight in a kaleidoscope of colour. I pondered that younger versions of these trees would have been growing here in Lydia and Alfred's lifetime.

We stopped at a busy outdoor cafe near the river. I blew on my black coffee, watching the steam curling in spirals. Out of the corner of my eye, I spied my next-door neighbour, Angela, sitting on her own at one of the tables.

"I'll be back," I told Mark, as I pushed back my chair.

Angela looked away as I approached.

"May I sit for a moment?" I asked.

She looked at me suspiciously under heavily mascaraed eyelashes.

"I don't think we have anything to say to each other," she replied.

"I've come to apologise," I said.

She raked long fingernails through her thick auburn hair.

"I won't take up much of your time," I promised.

"Why would I want to hear anything you've got to say?" she said quite loudly, causing others to look up from their coffee and Mark to give me a concerned shrug.

"You have every right to tell me to piss off," I said, narrowing my eyes. "But if you could spare me just a moment?"

I waited under her harsh gaze, fanning my hot face and butterflies in my stomach.

"Okay then," she nodded. "I haven't got long though."

I hoisted a leg over the wooden bench and sat facing her. Despite my agitation, I marvelled at her perfect make-up. The glossy lips, strategic blusher and subtle eyeliner. It must take her hours to get ready every day. My routine consisted of cleaning my teeth and splashing my face with water.

I took a deep inhale. "I'm so sorry about my behaviour at your party," I began. "I was— I am an alcoholic."

She pursed her lips.

"The way I acted was unforgivable. I don't expect you to excuse what I did," I continued. "I wish I could turn the clock back."

"It was so awful," she sneered. "You acted like a mad woman."

"I'm so sorry," I repeated.

"I was hoping we might be friends," she murmured. "Until you made a fool of me in front of my guests."

"I thought we might be friends too," I agreed. "I made a bigger fool of myself and in addition, I nearly scarred my face for life."

She leaned her arms on the table.

"You seemed so normal when we had coffee in your kitchen."

"I am normal," I said. "But not when I've had a drink. I turn into an uncontrollable, selfish monster, as you witnessed at your party."

"I was very upset and so was Steve," she said, putting her hand to her mouth.

"I have a sickness, it's called alcoholism," I said. "I have taken serious steps to overcome my addiction, including joining Alcoholics Anonymous and attending weekly meetings."

"I appreciate you coming over, that can't have been easy," she said, patting my arm.

"I've apologised to a lot of people, including my family," I confessed. "I'm three months sober and working hard to make amends."

"Good for you," she said, a faint smile on her shiny lips. "I sincerely wish you all the best for the future."

I returned to Mark. I had a large lump in my throat and couldn't speak at first.

"What was that all about?" he asked.

I waved my hand about until I could manage an answer.

"She's my next-door neighbour. Unfortunately, she

witnessed my mad, drunken behaviour in her home last Christmas," I croaked.

"You let her know that you've given up the booze?" he asked.

"Indeed," I confirmed. "She won't be the last person I grovel to."

Mark kissed my hand, making me feel so much better until I noticed Angela coming toward us.

"Hi." She smiled.

"Angela." I sat up straight. "This is Mark, my... lodger."

They exchanged nods, although I noticed Mark's jaw tighten.

"What you did just then was very brave," she said. "I don't bear grudges and I hope we can try to be friends again."

"I'd like that too," I said.

"Perhaps you'd like to meet for coffee one day?" she said, beaming at me and then at Mark.

I nodded.

"Wow!" Mark breathed as she walked away.

"Do you mean 'wow' at what she said or how she looks?" I made a face at him.

"She's lovely," he said. "But she's a bit overdone. I love your naturalness and your dark eyes. Except, now you're staring at me making me feel uncomfortable."

I laughed. "I didn't expect such a generous reaction from her," I said. "I thought she'd tell me to piss off."

"Just shows you how understanding people can be," he said.

I nodded vigorously.

"So I'm your lodger?" He leaned forward, supporting his chin with his hands.

"Sorry," I replied. "She surprised me."

"That's okay." He sighed, looking anything but okay. "I suppose I should be grateful that you even admitted to that."

"You're my lover and my best friend," I said, grabbing

his arm.

He shrugged, turning to watch the rowing boats on the river gliding through the choppy water.

CHAPTER FORTY-ONE

Disquiet

Large church candles glowed softly on the table as the sparkling chandelier reflected splinters of light off the emerald green walls.

Mark and I fussed over and rearranged the table settings several times before we were satisfied. We wore silly grins as we stood back to admire our work. We even placed name cards on side plates, just as a humorous touch.

Normal things become a major obstacle if you're an alcoholic. Mark and I discussed at length the pros and cons of entertaining Charlie and Bill in our home for the evening. It would be a challenge to have alcohol in the house and offer our guests a drink, whilst abstaining ourselves.

Even walking around the supermarket and choosing our favourite wine was difficult, knowing we would never get to pour a glass for ourselves.

Charlie and Bill stood awkwardly in the dining room as we offered them a glass of champagne.

"We're happy to have soft drinks," Charlie said, smiling brightly.

"We live in a world of alcohol and we have to get used to other people drinking, even if we don't," Mark said, handing them a glass of champagne and me a glass of fizzy mineral water.

"That's very decent of you," Bill said. "We're very proud

of you both for ditching the booze."

"We can only imagine how hard it must be," Charlie finished his sentence.

"Thank you," I said. "And thank you for all the times you've rescued me from mad, drunken escapades."

"Let's hope you'll never need to again," Mark chipped in.

We raised our glasses, followed by an awkward silence.

"And here's to the former occupants of Rosebay House," Bill said eventually, raising his glass once more. "To the ghost of Miss Lydia Turner."

I could feel Mark's eyes boring into me but I didn't give him the satisfaction of returning his gaze.

My efforts roasting a chicken and cooking vegetables turned out rather well and Mark's Eton mess was greatly admired. I winked at Mark as the last morsel of sugary meringue and cream was divided evenly between himself and Bill.

"It's nice to see you both looking so happy," Charlie observed.

'We're getting there,' I said. "We give each other support and encouragement to stay sober. And the book's finished, apart from the editing and rewrites."

"That's brilliant," she cooed.

"And are we allowed to know the ending of the novel?" Bill asked

I briefly explained the outline of the plot.

"That could be the reason why, in real life, there's no death certificate for Lydia," Bill said. "Clever you, finding a scenario that explains her disappearance."

"You're happy with the ending?" Charlie asked.

"We discussed two or three options we thought possible," Mark replied.

"You've taken a great interest in Moira's novel," Charlie said.

"It's been a revelation," Mark admitted. "I've found the whole process fascinating."

"It must be nice to have someone to bounce ideas off." Charlie turned to me.

"He's been great," I told her, holding Mark's hand across the table. "Writing can be a lonely pursuit."

"I hear your readers are in a state of high anticipation for the release of the new book," Bill said. "I've been following their reaction on Instagram."

"I'm getting loads of new followers every day," I said. "That's nice, but I hope my traditional readers will enjoy the book too."

"They'll certainly be surprised at the upbeat ending," Bill said.

"Oh well, it's good to be unpredictable," I laughed.

"So now comes the really hard work," Bill said,

"You won't see much of her," Charlie said to Mark.

"I don't mind," he said. "I'm happy to get the shopping and cook the meals."

"You lucky thing!" Charlie grinned at me.

It was late by the time we showed Charlie and Bill to the basement bedroom. Mark had given it a lick of paint and I'd arranged lots of cushions on the bed just the way my sister liked it.

"I haven't organised a dinner party in years," I said, pulling on my pyjamas in my bedroom. "In the old house, I got caterers and spent the whole evening pissed. It's bloody hard work doing it all yourself and staying sober."

"I'm quite proud of myself," Mark said. "I didn't fancy a drink all night, even though there was wine and beer freely available on the table. I was quite happy to stay sane and sober."

"I wish I could say the same," I said. "I fancied a nice glass of champagne. Just the thought of the bubbles in my mouth and that casting off of inhibition."

"You don't have inhibitions," he said. "You're always you. With your opinions and outrageous fashion sense."

EYES OF CHINA BLUE

"There's a part of me that envies Charlie's steadfastness," I admitted. "The way she manages to do everything properly. The marriage, the mortgage. Even being a midwife. I mean, how selfless and public-spirited."

"You're just different people," Mark remarked, pulling me down beside him on the bed. "She is so proud of your writing, she even told me so."

"I'm such a loser compared to her," I sighed.

"Nonsense," he said, stroking my hair. "You create something thousands of people love. That's equally public-spirited."

"I suppose," I said snuggling up and laying my head on his chest as he switched off the light.

Had the evening been overwhelming or perhaps I had too much coffee? I was wide awake for ages, listening to Mark breathing deeply and evenly. Eventually, I slipped out of bed and tip-toed to my study.

I scrolled through emails, my sleepy eyes adjusting to the brightness. Bill was right: my fans were in a state of high excitement over the prospect of my latest novel.

The sound of rushing water suddenly engulfed the room, assaulting my hearing. I spun around; the sound came from the old mirror that now resembled a muddy aquarium. The water rippled cloudy green and grey as sunlight sparkled on the surface. Above the waterline, trees and shrubs swayed in a breeze under a leaden sky.

Long tendrils of hair waved to and fro among the aquatic plants in the current. I rushed to escape, not wanting to encounter the face beneath the hair. I wrestled with the door handle but it stayed stubbornly closed.

I backed away as a scarred brow, followed by two huge black eye sockets appeared out of the water. The nose, a bony septum, was revealed and the exposed bony jaw rhythmically opened and closed as if it was guffawing.

Black stubby fingers beckoned as the skull leaned in, so

very close to my face. The smell of decaying flesh and river mud was overwhelming and I gagged as I grasped the edge of the desk. My decayed visitor reached out and wrapped putrid fingers around my trembling hand. The chill from the dead hand seeped throughout my body. As much as I wanted to snatch my hand away, I was completely paralysed.

I can't explain if some psychic exchange took place between the creature and me or if it was pure imagination, but I knew that I had to discover something vital that could not be ignored. Something crucial to Lydia's story that was, so far, a mystery and unknown. The awful presence insisted on it.

The corpse's grip suddenly released and I fell back, knocking my printer over. It hit the floor with a loud thud.

Moments later the door flew open.

"What's wrong?" Mark asked, coming towards me.

He lifted his feet. "Did you spill something?"

"A drowned corpse crawled out of the mirror," I whimpered.

"You what?" he asked, scratching his head.

"I saw swirling water and then eye sockets, a nose, a jaw…" I was speaking too fast but I couldn't stop. "It had weed and twigs caught in its hair and its jaw flapped." I imitated the jaw action with my hands.

Mark closed the door.

"This mirror?" He pointed.

I nodded.

"Moira," he reasoned. "It's just a mirror."

I saw my reflection as I pressed myself against the wall, my hair sticking up in clumps and my mouth wide open.

He tilted his head. "Have you had a drink?"

"No," I squealed, shaking my head.

Charlie put her head around the door.

"Everything all right?" she asked.

"I think Moira's been drinking," Mark accused.

"I haven't," I shrieked.

"Why are you up here?" Charlie asked, pointing at me.

"I saw something terrible," I cried, tears and snot sliding down my face.

"Okay, love," she said, opening her arms. "Let's get you downstairs."

They each took one of my arms and escorted me to the bedroom where I slumped on the bed.

"I'll go and check on the alcohol," Charlie said, leaving the room.

"If you've had a drink it's okay," Mark said, stroking my back. "You said you fancied a glass of champagne."

"I haven't had a drink," I muttered.

"I believe you," he said, his eyes watching me like a hawk.

"Look," I said leaping off the bed. "I can walk in a straight line."

I strode up and down, intending to demonstrate my balance but actually looking more like a deranged penguin.

Charlie returned, shrugging at Mark.

"There's half a bottle of champagne in the kitchen, just as I left it," she said.

"Did you taste it?" Mark asked. "Because I used to fill the bottle with water after I'd drunk it."

"I – did – not – drink," I insisted.

"Does she have a stash hidden somewhere?" Charlie asked.

"No," Mark shook his head. "We haven't allowed drink into the house before today."

"Excuse me," I bawled. "I am here in the room."

They turned their attention to me.

"I did not drink, I promise," I pleaded. "I saw something horrible in the mirror and it freaked me out. But I did not drink."

"There's nothing we can do tonight," Mark addressed Charlie. "Let's all go back to bed and we'll deal with it in the morning."

Charlie nodded and left the room. Mark smiled at me, following her out.

"I think she wet herself. The floor up there is wet and stinky," I heard him say quietly.

"Let's not upset her," Charlie replied. "I'll clean it up in the morning."

Mark came back into the room, closing the door softly behind him.

"Let's go to bed," he encouraged, patting my bottom and pulling the duvet back.

"I haven't had a drink," I repeated. "And I haven't wet myself."

"I know, love."

CHAPTER FORTY-TWO

Looks Can Be Deceiving

A couple of weeks later my twelve-year-old daughter turned up looking like Britney Spears. She wore a mini skirt and black tights. Without my knowledge, her ears had been pierced and large gold rings glinted from them. Her light-coloured hair was fastened in a high ponytail by a pink bow. Cliff had dropped the children off to stay overnight.

"Are you wearing make-up?" I asked.

"Debbie lets me wear her blue mascara," she replied.

"Aren't you a bit young for make-up?"

She raised her eyebrows and let out a big sigh.

"What do you know?" she said, running up the stairs. "You never look nice."

My face stung as if she'd slapped me as I watched her disappear into her room.

"Take no notice," Jackson said. "Lately she's behaving like a spoilt brat, even with Dad and Debbie."

Rosanna watched TV in her room, while Jackson played cards with Mark and me.

"What's up with Rosanna?" I asked.

"I don't know," Jackson shrugged. "She's always in a bad mood and she never wants to play with me anymore."

"It's probably growing pains," I said.

"What's that?" Jackson asked.

"It's when women begin to get moody and

unreasonable," Mark replied. "Generally, they stay that way."

I made a face at him.

"She's just growing up, Jackson," I said. "You need to be patient with her."

"Forever," Mark grinned.

"Do you have any children?" Jackson asked Mark.

"I do," Mark replied. "I have a son of eighteen. But unfortunately, we're not in touch."

"Why's that?" Jackson said.

"It's none of your business," I said to Jackson, shaking my head.

"It's all right," Mark said. "I wasn't a good father. I let my son down."

"Like Mum did with us?" Jackson looked up under his fair brows.

"Similar," Mark said. "But your mum was sensible enough to sort herself out before any lasting damage was done. You should be proud of her."

I fiddled with a button on my jacket.

"She's the best mum," Jackson smiled.

My mouth dropped open.

"She's great," Mark agreed.

I hadn't remembered to breathe for about thirty seconds and I exhaled noisily.

"You all right, Mum?" Jackson asked.

"Yes, yes. I'm fine," I replied. "I want to apologise for the times I did let you down."

"Okay," he said, dealing the cards.

My heart swelled as I grinned at Mark.

"Melted-face man is in the garden," Rosanna shrilled as she burst through the door.

Rosanna and Jackson ran back up to her room and we followed. They were staring out of the window when we got there.

"What can you see?" I asked, joining them on the bed.

EYES OF CHINA BLUE

"He's gone now," Rosanna said.

"Tell me what you saw?" I stroked her hair and she pulled away.

"I saw melted-face man," she whined.

"What was he doing?" I persisted.

"Don't encourage this," Mark said, standing by the door.

"She saw Alfred," I said. "I'm just interested."

Mark threw his hands up in the air.

"He was looking for the woman who lives on the stairs," Rosanna cried.

"Was he looking for Lydia?" I asked.

"For Christ's sake, Moira," Mark frowned.

"I don't know," Rosanna continued. "But he's very sad he can't find her."

"He's gone now," I said. "He's nothing to be frightened of."

Rosanna nodded.

"He's an old soldier," Jackson said, putting an arm around his sister. "We've seen him loads of times before. He just stares up at the window. He's not scary at all. Is he, Rosie?"

Rosanna smiled up at her brother.

"Okay, you two, time for bed," I said. "Jackson, you sleep in the other room tonight. You're too old to share a room."

Mark had disappeared downstairs and was staring out of the dining room window.

"You really shouldn't encourage them," he said, arms folded tightly across his chest.

"I've told you before: odd things are going on in this house," I said. "The children and I have seen them."

"Can you hear yourself?" he said, turning to face me. "You can't be convinced Lydia and Alfred still inhabit this house?"

"I know it sounds absurd," I said. "But I know that Lydia guided me the whole way through the plot of my novel."

"You've embellished the information that was out

there," he insisted. "I mean, that's your job. You get an idea and weave an amazing narrative and hey presto! You have a bestseller."

"I sat in front of a blank screen for two years," I said. "I didn't have a clue until a pair of china blue eyes appeared on my screen."

He frowned holding me at arm's length. "Perhaps you need to talk to a professional about what you're imagining?"

"What, and take the kids with me?" I asked. "Because they're seeing stuff too."

His arms dropped to his sides as he sighed. "None of this makes any sense."

Mark and I agreed he would sleep in the basement when the children visited, so I didn't sleep well. I was awake when frantic screams came from the landing.

Rosanna was screaming her head off at the bottom of the short staircase to my study. I grabbed her by the shoulders and she spun around.

She was wide-eyed, her complexion pale and waxy. Jackson came out of his room yawning and rubbing his eyes.

"What is it?" I cried.

"She was on the stairs," she wailed.

"Who was?" Jackson asked, putting his hand on her shoulder.

"The soaking wet woman," she replied.

I slumped against the doorframe as Mark appeared, rushing up the stairs towards us.

"What have you been telling her?" Mark demanded, holding me by the shoulders.

"Nothing," I shrilled. "I've told her nothing."

"She lives at the bottom of the river. She can't see nothing, she's got no eyes," Rosanna shrieked.

"Okay," I soothed, putting my arm around her shoulders. "You've had a fright. Let's go downstairs and have a drink. You'll feel better."

EYES OF CHINA BLUE

Rosanna was fiddling with her phone when I put a mug of hot chocolate in front of her.

"Dad's coming," she said, sticking out her bottom lip.

"Please tell me you haven't contacted him?" I said.

"He's coming." She shoved the phone in my face. "I told him."

"Get in the car," Cliff said to the children as I opened the front door.

"You've got to listen," I said as Rosanna pushed past and ran to the car.

"I've spent a lifetime listening to you," he said. "Most of the time it's a pack of lies."

"Dad," Jackson cried. "It wasn't Mum's fault."

"Get in the car, son," Cliff repeated.

"Rosanna saw something inexplicable," I began.

"Was it him? Drunk in the garden?" Cliff shouted, pointing at Mark.

"No one's had a drink," Mark said, calmly coming to my side.

"Pull the other one," Cliff said.

"Do we look drunk?" Mark asked. "There's not a drop of booze in the house. Come and search if you like."

"It's true, Dad," Jackson said.

"Get in the bloody car, Jack," Cliff hissed, jabbing a finger at Mark. "Don't you ever frighten my kids again." And then he turned to me. "You were doing so well and now this."

"You have to believe me," I begged. "We haven't been drinking. There's been some peculiar activity in this house and Rosanna got frightened."

"She's telling the truth," Jackson said.

"It'll be a long time before I trust my kids with you again," Cliff pointed at me. "And you," he said, pointing at Mark. "Keep away from my kids."

"I understand you're angry," Mark began.

Cliff charged forward and punched him on the chin,

sending Mark tumbling to the floor.

I grabbed Cliff and pulled him back. "What the bloody hell do you think you're doing?" I cried.

"Because you're upset about the kids, I'm going to let that one go," Mark said as he staggered to his feet.

"Now perhaps we understand each other," Cliff said.

He grabbed Jackson and hauled him to the car.

"Why doesn't he believe me?" I wailed, watching helplessly as they drove away.

"Because you've lied to him so many times before," Mark answered.

CHAPTER FORTY-THREE

Abstinence

"You don't believe there are ghosts in the house?" Charlie said as we ate lunch in her home.

"What else could it be?" I frowned.

She suspended her fork in the air.

"It's like the children pick up on whatever's going on in your head," she said. "Like the night we came to dinner and you had a fright in your attic. We never really got to the bottom of what happened, but I'm convinced you were sober."

"Thank you, but it's more than that," I said. "I've never explained the plot of my novel to the kids. So how do they know about a World War One soldier?"

"They are much more internet savvy than we are. Perhaps they've been doing research?" she said.

"Do you believe I've been sober for months?" It was a difficult question but I had to ask it.

"You look awful when you're on a drinking binge," she said. "You're pasty and your eyes stare. You don't look like that now. You are confident and happy."

The tension in my shoulders was released for the first time in days.

"I just wish Cliff had a bit more faith in me," I sighed.

"He will. Give him time," Charlie encouraged.

"The first thing he did was accuse Mark and me of being drunk," I said.

"You can't blame him," she reasoned. "Rosanna claims to see a strange man in the garden and later a mad woman is creeping up the stairs. What do you expect?"

"I can't explain what's going on," I shrugged. "But it's certainly not drink-related."

"You've always had a very vivid imagination," she continued. "You frightened me to death on more than one occasion when we were children. Do you remember when you held the torch under the bedclothes and told me stories about kidnappers and murderers?"

I laughed. "And the time I told you a witch lived in the cupboard under the stairs and she was keen on eating little girls."

"I refused to go in there when Mum asked me to do the vacuuming and she told me off!" she said.

"What are you two laughing about?" Bill said, entering the room and kissing Charlie.

"Moira's vivid imagination and how she got me into trouble when we were kids," Charlie said.

"I found something that might be of interest to you," Bill said, addressing me and rooting around in a computer bag. "Ah, here it is."

He put an A4 photocopy of the *London Evening Standard*, November 1920, on the table.

An Altercation Between Two Gentlemen

Hubert Archer and Joseph Turner were arrested yesterday afternoon after exchanging blows outside Mr Turner's place of work in Cheapside.

The men, both respectable gentlemen, were reported as having a heated argument that escalated into a full-scale fight. It took four policemen to break up the shameful scuffle.

The reason for the fight is unknown, although Mr Archer is married to Mr Turner's daughter and they have a son together.

No charges were brought against either man and they were later released.

"Of course," I cried. "Lydia's father would be curious about what happened to her."

"I'm afraid he wouldn't have had long to find out," Bill sighed. "He died in 1921. He was beaten to death on the way to his club one evening. The police reported it as a robbery."

"I wonder if that was the true motive?" I pondered. "Or if something far more sinister took place."

I didn't have time to stay and discuss the demise of Joseph Turner with Charlie and Bill. I had an important lunch appointment to attend.

The Art Deco restaurant had large windows overlooking the Thames. The handsome bow-tied waiters discreetly attended to diners, including an A-list Hollywood actor dining with a rowdy bunch of people at one table, whilst a controversial politician ate alone at another. I felt comfortably insignificant.

"The publisher is questioning why you've written an uncharacteristically happy ending to this novel," Lucy, my agent asked, revealing immaculate white teeth.

"It was instinctive," I replied, pulling at the sagging neck of my old blouse.

Her beautiful diamond stud earrings sparkled as she tilted her head.

"It's good to keep your readers on their toes," she said. "Why don't we order some champagne? We've got a lot to celebrate."

"No, thank you," I said, rubbing the back of my hand across my mouth. "I'll stick to water."

"Don't be daft," she said. "After the terrible struggle you've endured, having writer's block and so on, you deserve champagne! Waiter."

"I'd rather not," I replied.

"Why ever not?" she chortled. "Are you on the wagon?"

A Thames tugboat heaved two huge barges, creating V-shaped waves as it negotiated the narrow arch of the bridge.

"I'm an alcoholic," I said at last.

She twirled her long highlighted hair around her finger.

"I knew, of course," she said.

"I think everyone did," I admitted. "I've been sober for three months. It's early days, but I feel so much better. Although I still find it a huge challenge to come to a place like this and not drink."

"That's very courageous of you," she smiled. "Waiter. A large bottle of water and two glasses please."

Lunch was very pleasant, even more so because I didn't go on a London bender like I would have done in the past, ending up in some hellhole, unsure of how I was going to get home.

Mark was out when I returned home, so I ran a bath. I was getting undressed when my phone rang.

"Hi Mark," I answered.

"Can you come and get me?" he asked, his voice high and scratchy.

"Of course," I replied. "Where are you?"

He gave me the address of a pub twenty miles away.

He was sitting on a wall outside a grotty pub, his head in his hands.

"Mark," I called, and he looked up.

"I'm so pleased you're here," he said, coming over.

"Have you been drinking?" I asked.

"No, but I came close to weakening," he said, taking my arm.

We got into the car and I waited patiently for an explanation.

"I had a phone call earlier today from my son," he said, clasping his hands together.

"Oh," I said. "What did he say?"

"He wanted to see me so we arranged to meet in this pub." He pointed out of the window. "He's had a good job offer in Australia and he wanted to see me before he left."

"How long will he be away?" I asked.

"He doesn't have any idea at the moment, but it sounds like a really good opportunity for him," he replied.

"It's great he wanted to see you before he left," I said.

He nodded.

"I nearly had a drink," he snorted. "Josh offered to buy me a beer. When I hesitated he asked me what was wrong so I told him everything."

"How did he take it?" I asked.

"I don't think he believed me at first." He held his hand to his mouth. "But I told him about you and the AA and then... I said how sorry I was for everything I'd done."

I held his hand, giving him a moment to collect his thoughts.

"He said he forgave me for being a rubbish father," he continued. "And that he hoped I would give up the drink for good. He also hoped that I'd visit him once he got settled in his new life."

"That's brilliant," I said.

"I couldn't believe how much he'd grown up," he said. "He's at least six foot."

"So you didn't have a drink?" I asked.

"It took all of my willpower," he said, thumping the dashboard. "I wanted Josh to see I was determined to be sober. So I've had about six cups of coffee."

"Well done," I said.

"I also thought of you and how disappointed you'd be," he said.

"I definitely would have been," I agreed. "What else did your son have to say?"

"That he and his mother had done all right without me." He stroked his chin. "I felt like the lowliest piece of shit."

"Don't do that to yourself," I told him, stroking his cheek.

"He's a fine young man," he said. "Good-looking and fair, like his mother. I missed all those years of him growing up. I just left her to get on with it."

"What's she like?" Most writers are nosey.

"I was the star of the show and she was the weather girl," he reminisced. "Unbeknown to me, she had a degree in meteorology and at first wasn't keen to do the weather forecast on the show."

"I remember she was very attractive," I recalled.

"She was," he agreed. "Everyone fancied her. Once I realised how clever and educated she was, I thought she was out of my league. It took me ages to ask her out."

"It was front-page news," I said, feeling a pang of jealously

"Ridiculous really," he chuckled. "The paparazzi followed us everywhere, we didn't get a moment's peace."

He stared into the distance.

"She used to put me to bed drunk every night." He pursed his lips.

"Did she marry again after you divorced?" I asked.

"No," he shook his head. "Josh said she's been on her own all these years. I guess I put her off getting married again."

His mouth attempted a smile but his eyes remained sad.

"What about your ex-husband?" he asked.

"We both worked for a publisher," I replied. "Cliff was the man who fixed your computer when it packed up. He was helpful and funny and all the girls fancied him."

Mark raised his eyebrows.

"I asked him out," I admitted. "It was the nineties and women did that sort of thing."

"I remember," he said.

"We dated for a couple of years, got married, and had kids," I reeled off. "I gave up work and stayed at home while the children were young. I had an idea for a novel and started writing in-between school runs. Cliff became head of a large IT department and spent hours at work."

"Were you happy?" he asked.

"I thought I was," I replied. "I made a fortune from my second novel and we bought a massive house in Holland Park. I thought it was what we wanted, but looking back I don't think Cliff wanted it at all. Our lives changed and so did I, and not for the better."

"It's tough, isn't it?" He spoke softly. "When you have to live with so many regrets. I have massive chains of self-remorse tied around my shoulders weighing me down."

"Me too," I agreed.

"This is just too hard," he said, staring at me, tears brimming in his eyes.

"What's the alternative?" I asked, dreading the answer.

He shrugged, wiping his eyes with his sleeve.

"You achieved something huge today. You decided not to blank out the pain with a drink," I said.

"I've wasted my life and made my family's lives a misery. I never gave her a penny you know," he admitted. "She got the house, but by that time I'd squandered every penny I'd ever earned. She had to work and bring him up all on her own."

"She must be a good mum if he's all you say he is," I said.

"She was the best," he sighed. "She tried to save our marriage, but I acted like I couldn't give a shit. And worse still, I was short-tempered with Joshua because I was always hungover."

"Perhaps you should write to her and apologise," I suggested. "You know how cathartic that can be."

"She'd probably tell me to bugger off." He slumped against the car seat.

"She might," I agreed. "But you'd be surprised how generous people can be."

"Take me home, please." He closed his eyes.

CHAPTER FORTY-FOUR

Life and Death

"Hi Lucy," I said, my phone on speaker. "Thanks for lunch yesterday. It was great to see you."

"You too," she cooed. "And looking lovely."

I knew she was being generous. I'd caught sight of myself in a shop window on the way home. My baggy old scoop-neck frock, made me look like an old frump – perhaps Rosanna was right about me.

"I wanted to talk to you about the conclusion of the novel," I said. "I'm having second thoughts. Something feels not quite right."

"Hmm," she said. "There's still a heck of a lot of work to do, so you've got time to change it if you want to."

Mark, sitting close by, gave the thumbs up.

"Let me think about it for a few days and I'll let you know," I suggested.

"That sounded positive," Mark said as squally rain battered the windows of the garret.

"As she says, there's a ton of work left to do," I said.

"Explain to me why you want to change the novel?" he asked, leaning forward.

"I've just got this gut feeling that the ending isn't what happened," I sighed.

"Let's assume Lydia was pretending to be Mavis and lived in Cornwall with Alfred," he said. "They would want to

290

EYES OF CHINA BLUE

keep it a secret just in case Hubert ever got wind of it. He'd already given Alfred a beating and arranged for Lydia to be murdered."

"Mmm," I said, wracking my brain for answers. "I imagine Elspeth to be a simple, God-fearing woman. A typical rural person of the time. Would she have lied to Lydia's son in her letter? She would realise how important it was for him to find out what happened to his mother."

"I very much doubt that she would lie," he said. "But I guess we'll never know for sure."

"I'm sensing there's more to Lydia's story." I frowned. "Why have I seen a drowned woman crawling out of the mirror?"

He made a face and folded his arms.

"I know you're sceptical, but I truly believe she's trying to tell me something," I insisted.

"Okay, if I put aside my scepticism for a moment," he said. "Who is this woman and what does she want?"

"I'm not sure who she is. She's too decayed to be recognisable," I said, making a face.

"Yuck, thanks for sharing." He stuck out his tongue. "We have to assume that she's either Lydia or Mavis."

I nodded as the wind rattled the window frames.

"The woman behind Alfred in the newspaper cutting definitely had fair hair and therefore is probably Lydia," he surmised. "Mavis had dark hair. Maybe she died jumping into the river? Think about it. She's wearing swathes of Edwardian clothing, the river has a strong current and it's cold."

"That would account for the dripping cadaver climbing out of the mirror," I said, feeling icy fingers running up and down my spine.

"Perhaps deep down, you suspected that Mavis drowned and your imagination filled in the rest," he surmised.

"Then why did I write a whole chapter about Mavis swimming to the bank and climbing out of the water?" I asked.

"Wishful thinking," he replied.

"Either Mavis Titmuss is buried with Alfred, or it's Lydia pretending to be Mavis," I said. "Having one death certificate that could belong to either woman, doesn't categorically point to which of them finished up with Alfred."

"Titmuss is an unusual name," Mark remarked. "What if Mavis did survive and moved away to a different part of the country? Wouldn't there be another death certificate for Mavis Titmuss?"

"It's possible." I bit my lip. "It's also possible she moved away and changed her name completely. It would have been easy in those days and remember, Mavis had a prison sentence awaiting her."

It felt like we were going round and round in circles. I turned to the mirror, wondering why its secrets were never revealed when Mark was in the room. Did it want only me to know? I jumped as a searing flash lit up the room.

"It's just the storm," Mark said, stroking my arm.

"We have missed something important," I said, recovering and closing the shutter.

"Lydia was the wife of a prominent, important man," he recalled, tapping the desk with a pencil. "There must be some record of what happened to her. Only poor people went missing without a trace."

"Lord Lucan?" I joked. "Bill's looked at census reports, birth, marriage and death certificates. The truth is, not even Lydia's son knows what happened to her."

"It does point to some kind of cover-up," he conceded.

"At last," I said, punching the air.

"Don't think for a minute I'm convinced about the dripping corpse," he added.

Lightning blazed across the sky as thunder shook the round turret, like a giant's fist thumping the roof.

"Let's get out of here," I said.

We adjourned to the safety of the kitchen and the delights of the coffee machine.

"Did you look through the stuff Bill gave you?" Mark

asked, chewing the end of a pencil.

"Here," I handed him the sheaf of papers.

"What do we have?" he murmured, fanning the pages on the table. "1911 census.

Mr Abraham Titmuss, Head,

Amy Titmuss, Wife,

Kenneth Titmuss,

Arthur Titmuss,

William Titmuss,

Walter Titmuss, all sons,

Mavis Titmuss, daughter. All residing at number 2 St. Peter's Way."

"Wow, four sons," I said. "Poor Mrs Titmuss must have been knackered after giving birth to that lot."

"I bet they lived in terrible, cramped conditions," he remarked. "Mavis probably came a very long way down the pecking order with four big brothers."

"Either that or she was taken care of by her brothers," I said. "They taught her to swim."

"There's a local newspaper report, dated September 1916." He followed the text with his finger. "Brothers Kenneth, Arthur, William and Walter Titmuss were eager to volunteer for the army at the beginning of the war. They have bravely fought for their King and country. It is our sad duty to report the deaths of the brothers, within days of each other. These courageous men lost their lives in the trenches of the Somme."

"All of the brothers?" I asked, feeling my jaw drop.

"I'm afraid so," he confirmed, carrying on. "Our condolences go to the family."

"How tragic," I whispered, feeling as if I knew them.

"It must have been a real blow for Mavis," he said.

"Poor Mavis," I cried. "She had a tough life."

"It gets worse," he murmured, holding up another sheet. "Death certificates for Abraham Titmuss, 1920, died of Spanish Flu and Amy Titmuss, also 1920 and Spanish Flu."

"Good grief," I said. "So Mavis loses all her family and is

left entirely on her own."

"It looks that way," he confirmed.

We sat in silence, while the thunder rumbled overhead making the old house tremble.

Mark continued leafing through the documents. "Ah. A birth certificate for Arthur, Alfred Johns," he said at last. "Born 5th May 1929 to Mavis, Victoria Titmuss, spinster and Alfred Johns, labourer."

"I wonder why Alfred didn't marry the mother of his child?" I questioned.

"He wouldn't if Mavis was Lydia," he answered. "Because Lydia wouldn't commit bigamy and risk getting caught."

"So that suggests that Lydia took Mavis Titmuss's name and it was her who gave birth to his child," I said. "And they lived happily ever after."

"Unless Alfred always held out hope that Lydia would find him," he sighed. "He wouldn't have wanted to marry Mavis if he was waiting for Lydia."

"That's not helping," I said.

He resumed rummaging through the papers.

"A marriage certificate for Arthur, Alfred's son and spinster of this parish, Florence, Dorothy in 1947."

"After World War Two," I interrupted. "Their boy grew up!"

"Mmm, horrible word: spinster," he said, making a face. "Aha, and Bill's found a formal black and white photo of a young Mavis, a portrait, but not very good quality. What a round face she had; a wide mouth and lots of dark hair."

"It looks like an official photograph. It may have been taken when she was arrested," I pondered.

"She's attractive in a provocative kind of way," he remarked. "She looks like trouble."

"You're right," I said. "And she was a woman ahead of her time. The suffragettes were seen as terrorists before the war – causing mayhem and destruction of property. Of course,

Lydia had the same beliefs, but being from a respectable family she always got bailed out of trouble."

"Not poor Mavis though," he sighed. "Here's her criminal record: vandalism, causing an affray, arson. There's quite a list."

"I wonder what she'd be like if she lived now?" I asked.

"She'd be Prime Minister," he replied.

CHAPTER FORTY-FIVE

Reconciliation

I smiled at the tiny camera positioned above me as Debbie opened the door. Her perfect pert boobs were outlined under a tight sweater and I averted my gaze, realising I was staring.

"Cliff's not here." She pursed her lips.

"Mummy!" Jackson squealed as he pushed her aside and jumped into my arms.

I held him tightly, spotting Rosanna standing in the hallway biting her nails.

"I've come to see you, Debbie," I said.

She frowned as she assimilated my request.

"I don't think we've got anything to say to each other," she murmured.

"I'll not take up much of your time," I added, stepping inside.

I'd never been to their house before. It resembled a John Lewis showroom. White leather sofas faced each other, lining up precisely with a long smoked glass coffee table, laden with art and design books. A massive television took up most of the wall and was showing an Australian soap opera. The loud volume exaggerated the Australian accents. Large ferns and palms lurked in the corners, reminding me of our doctor's surgery.

"It's very nice," I murmured, taking a seat as Debbie turned off the TV.

"Rosanna was very upset the other night," she accused.

296

"I know, and that's why I'm here," I said. "I owe you an apology, Debbie."

She blinked rapidly in disbelief.

"I mean it," I continued. "I've been an unfit mother and you've done a great job of looking after my kids all this time."

She nodded in agreement, her perfect blonde hair bouncing.

"But the other night was different," I said. "Mark and I hadn't had a drink. We were stone cold sober. Rosanna must have had a bad dream or imagined something."

Four fidgeting, skinny legs were visible on the slatted stairs, where the children were listening.

"Why should we believe you when you've behaved so badly in the past?" she asked.

"Because I'm trying my best to make amends," I replied. "I know it will take time, but I'm determined to overcome my problems."

"Charlie's told me," she admitted. "The thing is, it will be a long time before Cliff trusts you again."

I nodded, feeling exposed and helpless. "I realise that," I whispered.

"Let's face it," she continued. "We've bent over backwards trying to accommodate you. We've let you have the children against our better judgement only because we think it's important for the children to see you."

"I'm grateful," I sighed.

"But you let the children down," she said. "And we have to pick up the pieces."

"I'm sorry," I mumbled, my hand over my mouth.

"The twins have terrible nightmares," she said, shaking her head. "Terrible, screaming and shouting in their sleep."

"I didn't know," I said, biting my lip.

"We thought you had enough to cope with so we didn't tell you," she said. "Jack and Rosie both have recurring dreams of drowning."

"I can't believe it," I whimpered.

"We've arranged counselling," she said.

I must have looked foolish with my mouth hanging open.

"So you see," she added. "We've had enough to worry about without your problems as well."

I knew she was right and I couldn't think of anything to say, which was unusual for me.

"I want to help more," I said eventually. "I'm going to Alcoholics Anonymous every week. I'm on the Twelve Point Plan."

"I hope it works out for you," she said, twisting her mouth to one side. "But the children can't stay with you if they're going to be terrified of your friends."

"Rosanna didn't see any of my friends," I pleaded.

"Who was it soaking wet and dripping all over your stairs then?" she asked.

I wish I knew.

"It must've been a bad dream," I replied. "If she has nightmares here then it makes sense that she also has them at my place."

"It's true, it's true!" Jackson shouted, sprinting down the stairs. "Mum's house is haunted. Isn't it, Rosie?"

Rosanna stayed where she was.

"You see," Debbie said, one eyebrow raised. "You teach them all kinds of weird stuff and it frightens them to death."

I sighed. "The house has strange energy. We've all seen and heard things."

It sounded lame. She crossed her arms and shook her head.

Jackson rested his arm across my shoulder.

"Please don't stop us from seeing Mum," he cried.

"It's up to your father," she shrugged.

"He won't talk to me," I told her. "I've tried calling him."

"He was very annoyed about rescuing the children from your house in the middle of the night," she said.

"I'm so sorry," I apologised again.

"I know you want to see your children," she conceded. "But they need to be safe and happy."

"I agree," I said.

"So what's the answer?" she asked, taking me by surprise.

"Ummm," was all I could think of saying.

"Why don't we compromise?" she suggested. "You take the children out for the day, to the cinema or the park and drop them back in the evening."

"That would work," I said, clapping my hands and making her jump.

"I'll need to talk to Cliff, but we could try that for a while and see how it goes," she said as she got up and went to the bottom of the stairs.

"Rosie," she called as I gritted my teeth. "Would you like days out with your mum?"

There was no reply and Debbie returned to the room wringing her hands.

"Give her time," I said. "I hope she'll forgive me for being such a crap mum."

Debbie continued to wring her hands, staring at the blank TV screen. I sensed this as my cue to leave.

"I appreciate you taking the time to hear me out," I said, heading for the door.

"It's down to Charlie," she confessed. "She's got such huge faith in your recovery."

"I know," I said. "And I won't let her or the kids down. I promise."

She almost smiled. I kissed Jackson and left.

I returned home feeling optimistic. Mark was banging about in the kitchen and I called out to him before ascending the stairs to my study. We kept a pile of old towels at the ready to mop up the wet carpet. River water I called it, although Mark still insisted there must be a leak.

Dozens of my fan's emails popped up as the computer

sprung into life. One name jumped out at me: Ed Johns, Alfred's grandson. He'd sent some family snaps of his grandmother.

There was one of a woman sitting on a seawall wearing a large black hat that hid most of her face. That excited me as I remembered Lydia wearing a similar hat and letting Mavis try it on. Another showed a toddler with chubby legs reaching toward the camera. Arthur, Alfred Johns was typed underneath. The last photo was a portrait of a young woman with light-coloured hair. I tried to enlarge it, but it was out of focus. I looked at the face through a magnifying glass and nearly fell off my chair.

I raced down to the kitchen and found Mark pounding a large piece of dough.

"It's Mavis!" I cried.

"What's happened to her?" he said, hesitating mid-knead.

"Her hair went grey prematurely," I said triumphantly.

"That's a shame," he mumbled, resuming efforts with the dough.

"Don't you see?" I shook his arm. "The woman standing behind Alfred with the light hair is Mavis."

"Not Lydia?" he asked.

"Mavis and Alfred's grandson sent me some family pictures," I explained. "They didn't look very interesting until I magnified one of a woman with light hair. I was expecting to find Lydia, but it was Mavis. Her face was round and cheerful, whilst Lydia's face was more chiselled with high cheekbones."

"But Mavis had dark hair," he said, frowning.

"Until she went completely grey," I repeated.

"So you're sure now that it's Mavis who lived with Alfred in Cornwall?" he asked.

"Yes, I am," I replied, grinning.

"But that means that you still don't know what happened to Lydia," he said.

In my excitement, I'd overlooked the fact that if Mavis was in Cornwall then Lydia never made it.

"Oh, bugger!" I exclaimed.

CHAPTER FORTY-SIX

What Lies Beneath

As Mark seemed engrossed in his baking, I went for a walk by the river to clear my head. The day was grey and drizzly even though it was only late summer. The river was in full spate due to heavy downpours earlier in the week. It surged brown and foamy, bursting its banks and submerging trees and shrubs. I walked along the jetty that jutted out into the deeper water. Large branches and plastic rubbish swirled and tumbled in the water.

My phone vibrated, disturbing my peace.

"Hi Mark," I answered.

"Cliff was here looking for you," Mark said. "He's still pissed off. Something about you hassling his wife?"

"I didn't hassle her," I said. "I went to see her about the kids."

"Well, he's not happy," Mark sighed. "He barged his way in and when I told him you'd gone for a walk, he flew out of the door to find you."

"Thanks for letting me know," I said. "I'll look out for him."

Cliff was striding along the towpath towards me as I put my phone in my pocket. I leaned against the metal rail as he trod heavily on the metal gangway of the jetty.

"What the bloody hell did you think you were doing?" he shouted.

I shrugged.

"You dare to lecture my wife," he said.

EYES OF CHINA BLUE

"I went for a chat," I said. "I certainly didn't lecture her."

"You made her agree to days out with the children," he accused.

"It was her idea. We reached a compromise," I explained. "I don't understand what you're so angry about?"

His dark blue eyes blazed.

"Rosanna has slept with us every night since she stayed at your house," he shouted. "She's terrified."

"I'm sorry."

"Debbie wouldn't tell you all this," he continued, waving his arms around. "She's too decent to want to worry you."

"They are my kids," I said. "If anything's wrong I should know."

Bitter laughter emitted from his throat.

"You have no idea what those kids have been through the past few years," he said, standing so close that I could smell his familiar aftershave.

"Tears and sleepless nights," he continued. "Asking where Mummy is and why hasn't she turned up again this time."

I turned away, feeling decimated and small, knowing everything he said was true.

"I can't even begin…" I stammered.

"Save it!" he growled.

I spied Mark hurrying towards us, calling my name.

"Here he comes. Another in the series of Moira's drunken parasites," Cliff grinned sarcastically.

I stepped away from him, unable to take any more criticism.

I reached for the guard rail, but my hand grasped at thin air. I was standing by a gap where the boats moored and unloaded passengers.

Cliff looked alarmed and reached out, catching my raincoat belt.

The belt wasn't fastened and it slipped quickly through the loops.

A sting of cold water blasted against my head and back as I hit the surging current.

I spun over and over in the churning water, furiously paddling with my hands to stabilise myself. I held my breath, although my lungs felt like they might explode.

Then I saw her.

Her platinum hair streamed behind her in a fan shape and her china blue eyes lit up as she glided gracefully through the water. I stopped struggling and floated as her long, icy fingers reached out and held my hand. She brought her beautiful face close to mine as I began to lose consciousness.

Lydia's desperation to show me what happened in the last agonising moments of her life appeared as a movie-like vision in my mind. I had to fight to survive; I had to complete Lydia's story so that the world would know what happened.

She peered into my eyes, and a look of tranquillity flickered across her features as she let go of my hand. The long gown she wore billowed as the current carried her off.

I couldn't struggle or swim, I couldn't feel my limbs. I would understand later I was only in the water for a few minutes, but it felt like hours to me.

Two strong arms engulfed me and hauled me to the surface. I spat out filthy water and inhaled, filling my depleted lungs. Mark had me in a secure hold, gasping as he swam towards the bank.

Cliff was running at full pelt, along the riverside, barking orders into his phone. As we got closer to the bank, he waded into the foaming water and grabbed Mark's shirt. It was a major struggle to haul us out of the rushing, deadly current and onto the slippery, muddy bank. Both men strained every sinew to save me.

Eventually, Mark and I flopped on our bellies and crawled like some kind of prehistoric life up the embankment.

Cliff took off his coat and wrapped it around me.

"I'm so sorry," he cried, picking me up under my arms.

My mouth tasted of mud and my chest heaved, still unaccustomed to drawing a natural breath.

Cliff lowered me onto the grass and went back for Mark. He gently helped him to scurry up the rest of the bank. We heard shouting and saw a couple of people running our way.

Mark and I shivered uncontrollably, more with fear than cold. I drew him into Cliff's coat and put my arms around his waist, my head against his wet heaving chest.

Cliff seemed to tower over us. He cupped his face with the palms of his hands, his mouth wide open.

"It's all my fault," Cliff cried. "I can't believe I nearly killed you both."

"We're fine," Mark croaked. "Just bloody freezing."

Cliff knelt before us, patches of river mud on his face.

"I know I've been harsh," he sobbed, taking my cold hand. "I suppose the truth is – I wanted to punish you for leaving me."

I managed a weak smile and squeezed his hand.

"Please forgive me?" he said, pulling the coat tighter around me.

My face was already wet, but I felt additional warm tears.

"There's the ambulance," he said, standing and waving.

"I saw Lydia," I whispered to Mark.

"In the river?" he asked.

"She was so beautiful," I smiled.

"You know how it ends?" he gasped.

"She wanted me to know her true story," I added. "Because she never reached Alfred."

Heavy footsteps ran towards us down the bank.

Second Draft

Lydia watched from the attic until she was sure Hubert's men had followed Mavis, as planned. She pinned her hat to her thick blonde hair, picked up a large holdall and crept downstairs.

The last train to London was leaving in ten minutes and it took four minutes to walk to the station.

She crossed the main road, from one side of the bridge to the other, peering around cautiously in case the two burly men doubled back.

"There you are, my dear," Hubert said, climbing the embankment on the station side of the bridge. "I wondered when you'd put in an appearance."

Lydia dropped her bag, her mouth open.

"Did you think the little drama with your suffragette friend would convince me? I watched from the bank as my men corralled her along the jetty and she fell into the water. I could also see her climb out on the opposite bank from here. She's a striking woman, but she does not have your class or breeding and I knew immediately it wasn't you."

He grinned and strode towards her, grabbing her arm.

"It's you, my dear wife, whom was supposed to perish today, one way or another," he hissed, his face close, his breath reeking of brandy.

"Get your hands off me," Lydia cried, struggling.

"Come along," he said, pinning her arm under his.

She looked wildly around for help as he dragged her across the bridge. It was getting dark and raining hard. Most respectable people were at home in front of a blazing fire.

The river gushed over the wooden slats of the jetty, brown and swirling. It lapped over Lydia's buttoned-up boots, soaking her feet and she opened her mouth to scream.

Hubert clamped his hand over her mouth. "I clearly can't trust you to uphold your end of the bargain."

He held her fast around the waist with his other arm. "You'll try to go to Alfred, even if I keep you locked up."

He shook her, his teeth clenched.

"You will never see your son or Alfred again," he whispered close to her ear.

Lydia moaned and twisted, but his grip held her rigid against him.

She wrenched an arm free and swung it in a crescent shape, driving a clenched fist into his temple. He released his arm from around her waist and grabbed her chin in his hand, forcing his lips against hers. She snapped her head away and he grabbed her by the throat.

She balanced precariously on the heels of her sodden boots, only his tight grip on her throat prevented her from toppling over the jetty

"Goodbye, my Lydia." He smiled, flicking open his fingers with a flourish.

Her hands clutched desperately at thin air as she plunged back into the water with a small shriek. Her arms flailed for a moment before the strong current swept her away.

Her body would be imprisoned by tree roots reaching out into the river, like long brown fingers, but she had drowned by then. Her eyeballs later provided a gourmet meal for cormorants and small carnivorous fish. When the tree finally surrendered the battered corpse, it was decayed beyond recognition.

Her cadaver would wash up downstream on Richmond foreshore and be found by a child collecting stones. The child would grow into an adult, forever disturbed by a soaking woman, crawling toward him in his dreams. His dwellings would have permanently wet stairs and his neighbours would complain.

E W GRANT

He would eventually take his own life by jumping off Richmond Bridge and plunging into the brown water.

CHAPTER FORTY-SEVEN

Encounters

Second Draft

Alfred scraped open the ill-fitting door to his cottage, to see Mavis standing across the narrow street, wearing a big black hat and clutching a small holdall.

"Mavis, what a surprise!" he said, crossing the road.

"Thank goodness you ventured out," she said. "I had no idea which house you lived in, just the street."

"Why are you here?" he asked.

"Has Miss Lydia not explained the plan?" she asked.

Alfred shook his head.

"I was to meet you all here," Mavis smiled. "Once things had calmed down back at home."

"Calmed down?" Alfred asked.

"Only when I was sure no one was looking for Miss Lydia," Mavis replied.

"Why would anyone be looking for her?" Alfred asked, frowning.

"In case they weren't convinced," Mavis replied, peering around the empty street.

"You're talking in riddles," Alfred said, scratching his head. "What's Miss Lydia been up to?"

309

"Blimey Alfred, you're hard work sometimes," Mavis said. "We wanted to be sure that my little swim in the river convinced them that Miss Lydia had perished."

"Miss Lydia perished?" Alfred grabbed her shoulders.

Mavis shook him off, her eyes narrowed.

"Why are you questioning me so?" she asked.

"You know how I feel about her," Alfred backed away.

"She's here?" Mavis grabbed his wrist, her face close to his. "She's here somewhere – in the kitchen or still abed?"

"What do you mean?" Alfred cried. "Why would she be here? She decided to stay with the boy and her husband. She couldn't face sharing a life of poverty with me."

Alfred felt a lump in his throat and turned away.

"My God!" Mavis screamed. "Are you saying Miss Lydia is not here?"

Alfred rubbed his temples, staring at the distraught woman.

"Miss Lydia is with her child and her husband. I've long accepted it and let that be an end to it." He sighed.

"No, she ain't," Mavis cried. "We made a plan. I was to be pursued by the men her husband employed to keep an eye on her. I wore her clothes and hat and her husband's thugs were supposed to think it were her. I led them to the jetty, where I made a pretence of falling into the water. I saw them laugh as they imagined I was drowning."

"And where was Lydia while this performance was taking place?" Alfred asked.

"She was supposed to wait for the men to follow

me and then sneak out to the train station and make her way here," Mavis replied.

Alfred lifted his hands to his face and peered between his fingers.

"She's not here. I've not seen hide nor hair of her," he murmured.

"So what the bloody hell happened to her?" Mavis asked.

Alfred noticed the silver strands shining through Mavis's dark hair as she tore off the big black hat.

"Come inside," Alfred said. "Explain to me exactly what happened."

I peered up at the extraordinary dome and elaborate glass sculpture hanging beneath it. The Victoria and Albert Museum had been an inspired choice by Lucy.

I hung onto Mark's arm as three hundred people milled around the elegant room, all of them wanting to meet me.

"You look amazing." Mark smiled down at me.

He did too, in his new evening suit, his dark hair gleaming under the spotlights.

"Oh, this old thing?" I joked, smoothing the silver silk of my full-length evening dress.

"I'm so proud of you," he added.

I looked down at my ridiculously expensive metallic silver shoes, feeling a lump in my throat.

"Don't you two scrub up well?" Charlie grinned, holding out her arms.

"I'm so glad you could make it," I whispered in her ear as she embraced me. "It's nerve-wracking being stone cold sober at my book launch."

Bill shook hands with Mark and kissed me on the cheek.

"You look fantastic," he said.

A waiter approached and offered them champagne, whilst handing Mark and me long-stemmed glasses, which we accepted.

Charlie raised her eyebrows.

"It's fizzy water," I explained. "I asked specifically that Mark and I had champagne flutes filled with water. It makes us feel part of the event without singling us out."

"Great idea!" Bill agreed.

"You've got a good turnout," Charlie noticed.

"Yes, the great and the good," I said.

"Are the children staying with Cliff?" she asked.

"Just for tonight," I answered. "They'll come back home to us tomorrow. Cliff and Debbie are taking them to the cinema at the weekend."

"Sharing custody seems to be working well," Charlie said. "Cliff and Debbie love having them at the weekend."

"They've got the easy option," Mark said. "I spend ages helping Rosanna and Jackson with their homework after I get home from the radio show!"

"You're so good at it though," I complimented.

"No more sightings of World War One soldiers or soaking women?" Bill asked.

"None at all," I sighed. "We now have a very ordinary home. It's still in need of renovation here and there, but at least the stair carpet is never sopping wet."

I didn't add how much I missed those china blue eyes staring at me and the drama being played out behind me in the mirror.

The crowd of people parted as an immaculately dressed woman with thick dark hair headed my way.

"Marie Lamarr," I announced as she air-kissed. "How lovely to see you."

"And you, darling," she gushed, hanging onto my hand with her bejewelled fingers.

Her breath smelt of stale cigarette smoke, her lips glistened with a thick glossy substance and I realised the impressive hairdo was a wig.

"Are you here on your own?" I asked.

"I know what you're asking." She grinned. The lip gloss filled the small vertical lines around her mouth. "I dumped that useless parasite Freddie months ago. I mean, darling, he's lovely to look at and good in bed – but what an absolute tosser!"

I was relieved that Mark, Charlie and Bill were engrossed in another discussion out of earshot.

"I suppose he made fools of both of us," I said.

"He certainly did," she agreed. "But he'll pay the price. No one in publishing, here or in New York, will ever employ him again. I've seen to it."

Freddie had made a powerful enemy; Marie was the queen of publishing, on both sides of the Atlantic.

"Well, I appreciate you coming to the launch of my book," I said.

"Is he your new man?" she asked, pointing at Mark.

"Yes," I replied, my face suddenly hot.

"Well done, darling," she patted my arm. "I remember him from breakfast TV. He's handsome in a Sean Bean sort of way. And congratulations on the book. I can't wait to read *Eyes of China Blue*."

She air-kissed and turned with a flourish, the air floating around her smelling of Chanel No. 5.

"You okay?" Mark put his arm around my waist.

"I'm fine," I smiled. "Just putting more demons to rest."

He pulled me close, kissing the top of my head.

"There's something I need to ask you about the day I fell in the river," I said, my arms around his neck.

"What is it?" he asked, his dark eyes searching my face.

"You jumped in after me," I whispered.

He nodded.

"You might have drowned," I said.

"I knew that," he nodded, biting his bottom lip. "I wouldn't've cared."

"Huh?"

"My life is only worthwhile if it's with you."

CHAPTER FORTY-EIGHT

A True Husband

Second Draft
5th May 1929
Falmouth

"Do you want to meet your son?" Mavis asked as Alfred hovered by the door.

Alfred came to the bed and took the tiny bundle from her arms.

"He's beautiful," Alfred smiled, his crooked smile. "I was worried the birth would be long and difficult, but the woman said you managed well for a first child."

"He looks just like you," she said.

"I wouldn't wish that on him," Alfred sighed. "What shall we call him?"

"I would like to call him Arthur," she said, looking into the distance. "He was my most favourite brother. He's the one who taught me to swim."

"Then that's what we shall call him," Alfred agreed, stroking her grey hair.

"I wish Miss Lydia were here to see him," she said.

"She's not here," Alfred said, kissing the baby. "Like we've said many times – we can only hope she escaped and made a good life for herself somewhere."

"There we disagree," Mavis said, shaking her head. "Miss Lydia was determined to make it here and would have done so. Something happened."

Alfred handed the child back to Mavis and went to the window.

"We can't keep having this disagreement," he murmured. "You don't know what happened after your swim in the river. Lydia might not have been able to bear leaving her child and decided to stay."

"Then why has no one seen her for years?" she asked. "Your sister, for instance."

"They wouldn't see her if she went to live in London," he replied. "My family have never even been to London."

"I still say something happened to her. Those two thugs must have doubled back and caught her getting on the train." Mavis bit her lip. "She loved you so much."

"Let's not speak about the past," he said, his eyes downcast. "Let's speak once again about the future and getting wed."

"I'll not wed you," she said.

"Our son needs a proper father," Alfred said.

"I'll not be your shoddy second-best," she said, sticking out her bottom lip.

"How many times do I have to tell you?" he said, his arms open. "I have room in my heart for two women. I loved Lydia for years and I can't say I'll ever stop loving her."

"And what if she had shown up here, as planned?" she asked. "I'd have been tossed aside?"

"I don't know." Alfred held his head in his hands. "She probably would have hated living in this tiny cottage and bartering for fish at the market. This is no place for a lady and I am no husband for a lady."

The baby began to whimper and Mavis put him to her breast.

"We're happy as we are and folk 'round here don't care if we're wed or not," she whispered.

"But I care," Alfred cried. "Since we've been together, I've come to love you with all my heart and I want you to be my wife."

"You told me once that you lay with Miss Lydia before her husband ever did, so you was her true husband," she said, stroking the baby's fluffy head.

"I wish I'd never told you that. It was just something between Lydia and me when we were so desperate to be together. We knew she would have to marry Hubert," he said, sitting on the bed. "Lydia wanted me to be the first. That's how much she loved me."

"I can't in all honesty say that you were my first," she said, shrugging and taking his hand. "But I do think of you as my true husband."

"If you'll do me the honour of walking down the aisle, I will be your true husband," he said.

"Mary, Joseph and Jesus," she exclaimed. "You're wearing me out. I've just given birth to your son. For pity's sake give me a moment's rest."

"I'm sorry, my love," he said, kissing her forehead and the top of the baby's head. "I'll bother you no more. But please, promise that you'll think about getting wed?"

"I'll think about it," she promised.

The End

ACKNOWLEDGEMENT

My husband, Julian, was brilliant throughout the creation of this novel. His attention to detail is second to none and I appreciate his forthright opinions, even if it doesn't seem like I do at the time.

Also to my loyal band of early reviewers who willingly gave up their time to read and review my scribblings. They are my son Kyle, to whom this book is dedicated with much love; Annette a great friend and honest critic; Emma, thank you for reminding me that this novel is a love story as well as a ghost story and last but not least John for his thorough, candid appraisal.

ABOUT THE AUTHOR

E W Grant

Elaine W Grant was born in London on May 6, 1959. After many years of working in business communications, Elaine decided to turn her attention to creative writing. This coincided with the pandemic of 2020, when Elaine and her husband found themselves in lockdown on their boat in Marina Lagos in Portugal.

The result of being confined to a small space was her debut novel, Little White Bones, published in English and French on Amazon.

Eyes of China Blue, Elaine's second novel, was inspired by a large, rambling Victorian house near the River Thames at Hampton Court from which a solitary light high up in a hexagonal garret seemed to constantly be switched on despite no other signs of occupancy being visible.

Elaine and her husband have recently settled on The Silver Coast of Portugal.

BOOKS BY THIS AUTHOR

Little White Bones

On the surface, Kayleigh Marron has the perfect life. Great job. Rich City banker boyfriend. Lovely house in the suburbs. Singing on stage with her musician friend Jay at weekends.
But underneath, dark currents are stirring. Why is she seeing flashbacks of the past? Why is she dreaming about rows of little bony feet? And what does any of this have to do with the new priest at her mother's church?

Les Petits Os Blancs

En apparence, Kayleigh Marron mène la vie idéale. Un boulot génial, un riche banquier de la City en guise de petit ami et une ravissante maison de banlieue chic. Le week-end, elle se produit sur scène avec son ami musicien Jay. Mais derrière cette apparente perfection, de sombres courants s'agitent.
Pourquoi voit-elle des flashbacks du passé ?
Pourquoi rêve-t-elle de rangées de petits pieds décharnés?
Et qu'est-ce que le nouveau prêtre de l'église de sa mère a à voir avec tout ça ?

Made in the USA
Coppell, TX
16 March 2023